CONNER'S ODYSSEY
BOOK ONE - DISCOVERY

To Carrie Stelly –
a gift to the world
of academia.
– Ian Bristow

Ian C. Bristow

DEDICATION

To Imagination, an artist's greatest muse.
To Nicholas Bacon, who has invested a great many
hours into this story.
To everyone else who has been there to support me.

CONTENTS

CHAPTER 1

Resentment

His kitchen looked foreign as he entered it, barren and lifeless. All the knickknacks and appliances had already been packed away. Nothing felt familiar, almost as if he was in someone else's home. He left the kitchen and entered the living room. It was nearly empty as well.

"Conner, can you come help me with the entertainment system?" his mother called from the opposite side of the room.

"Yeah, sure," Conner replied, trying to suppress his feelings of resentment as he approached her. She turned to face him, her expression pained. He avoided eye contact with her and moved toward the entertainment system on the far wall. "I'll get this side," he said, dutifully. "It's heavier than that side," he added for clarification, gesturing to the left side of the large piece of furniture.

"Conner, I'm sorry that we're moving to Montana," Mrs. Mathews burst out, sounding desperate, as if she wanted nothing more than for her son to understand. "Your father *needs* this new job. It's not realistic for us to live here anymore. We just can't afford it…"

"What's wrong with the job dad has now?" Conner asked, fighting back an upsurge of confusion-fueled anger. "Why can't we afford to live here anymore? I don't understand."

"It's not… I don't…" Mrs. Mathews looked as though she was at war with herself. She lowered her voice. "Promise me you won't

1

say anything to your dad… I told him you would ask eventually," she went on, speaking more to herself than Conner. "It's only fair that you would want to know…"

Conner looked on curiously, waiting for his mom to get to the point.

"If I tell you, you have to promise me you won't say anything. Promise?"

Conner nodded. "Yeah, I promise."

"Dad was laid off from his job."

"What?"

"Shhh!"

"Sorry," Conner said, bringing his voice down. "Why did he get laid off?"

"That's not important." Mrs. Mathews said dismissively. "What's important is that we get through this as a family. Dad needs us to stand behind him and be understanding."

"Understanding?" Conner flared up. "What about me? Is ripping me away from my life understanding? All my friends and memories are here in Santa Ana. What about Chris? He's been my best friend since first grade! Now we're never going to see each other again!"

Mrs. Mathews' eyes narrowed. "You should be ashamed of yourself… The world doesn't revolve around you, Conner. Why don't you try looking on the bright side? At least you're not being forced to transfer in the middle of the school year. You'll be starting fresh with everyone else… And we're moving into Grandma Alice's old house. It's really nice. You'll have all kinds of room to run around and play."

"Mom, I'm fourteen," Conner replied harshly, "I don't care about having all kinds of room to run around and play by myself. I want to stay here, where I actually have friends."

"At least *try* and find something positive to focus on," Mrs. Mathews said, her eyes tearing up. "Someday you will have to make tough decisions as well. Life isn't always fair. But we have to do our best to make the right choices, even if that means upsetting or disappointing the ones we love."

Conner wanted to understand. He wanted to feel better about leaving everything he loved, but it wasn't that easy. "I'll try, Mom," he said, his tone sounding as dejected and lifeless as he felt.

Mrs. Mathews made a feeble attempt to reach out to her son, as if her body was attempting to reach him in the way she hoped her words had. She let her arm fall and settled for giving him an understanding nod.

Conner made a vague gesture of acknowledgment, somewhere between understanding and bitterness. Sensing that the moment had grown awkward, he helped his mom move the entertainment system to the garage and then headed back upstairs to finish packing.

He could hear the faint sound of his dad loading the last of their possessions into the moving van as he threw the remaining items around his room unceremoniously into a box. 'I'd better start on the closet,' he thought, feeling thoroughly unmotivated.

A timeline of his childhood poured out as he opened his closet door. Action figures, sports balls, assignments from school, birthday cards, a kite, old tennis shoes, and the remnants of a cops and robbers set, which he remembered being his favorite toy because his dad would pretend to be the bad guy, and he would always get to bring him to justice.

He was about to close the closet door when a small square of folded notebook paper caught his eye. He opened it up and remembered it instantly. Chris had written it to him in math class a few years ago, asking if he wanted to spend the night at his house and play video games in his dad's theater room. Conner remembered writing back "yes" happily, knowing it meant he would be in gaming heaven later that day. He smiled reminiscently as he read the note, but that faded quickly into a frown with the reality of his loss. There would never be another chance to pass notes in class with Chris, never another chance to sneak into Chris' dad's theater room for an all-nighter playing their favorite games.

He closed his eyes as the ache of loss crept through him. A vivid image of Chris' smiling face swam across his mind, causing burning tears to stream down his cheeks. He blinked his eyes open, and a gasp of shock escaped him. Imprinted upon the note was the same image he'd just seen in his mind's eye. He quickly wiped the remaining tears away from his eyes and refocused on the piece of paper he was holding. The image was gone. Had he been imagining things? Was his mind playing tricks on him? He reformed the picture of Chris in his mind, waited a moment, and looked back down at the paper.

Nothing was there.

Feeling disheartened, he crinkled up the note and threw it into a bag for trash. He didn't want to see it again.

* * *

'Almost Ten P.M. now. We'd better be out of here in the next hour,' thought Mr. Mathews, checking his watch for the umpteenth time. He had a twenty-hour straight drive ahead of him, and it was crucial that he made it to the new house in time to get a few hours of sleep. He couldn't afford to make a bad impression the first day at his new job — a job that would provide his wife Breanne, and son Conner, with the financial stability they deserved. He knew Conner was upset with him at the moment, but the boy would understand one day. If he didn't take this job, they would be homeless.

Mr. Mathews went into the house to grab the few things that remained. He saw his wife in the next room. "Hun?"

Breanne was peering miserably out the window at their soon-to-be old street, her expression revealing the sorrow clutching her heart. "Yes, Dear?"

"Are you about ready?" he asked gently as he walked over to put his arm around her. "We have to leave tonight, or I won't get any sleep. I want to make a good —"

"I know, Scott. It's okay. You don't have to explain yourself." Breanne's tone was of absolute understanding, but her expression remained stricken.

For a long moment, Scott gazed lovingly into his wife's soft, hazel eyes. Finally, he said, "I'll check and see if Conner is ready to go." He walked to the foot of the stairs and called, "Conner, you ready, Son?"

"Yeah, Dad, I just need to bring down a few more boxes," Conner called back.

By eleven that night, Scott had finished loading the moving van. Breanne opened the van door and gestured for Conner to climb in.

"Conner — Hey *Conner! Wait!*" A boy came hurtling down the street on his bike, skidding to a halt next to the open van door. "Hey, Conner," he said, breathing hard.

"Chris, what are you doing here?" Conner asked incredulously. "It's eleven o'clock. If your mom knew you were all the way over here at this time of night, you'd be grounded for weeks."

Chris shrugged indifferently and removed the backpack he was wearing. He set it down and began sifting through its contents.

Breanne crossed her arms and looked at Chris disapprovingly, but she refrained from saying anything.

"I just wanted to give this back before you left," said Chris, handing Conner a thin, rectangular case.

Conner took it and realized immediately that it was his favorite videogame. "I thought I grabbed all my games from your room," he said, not removing his gaze from the thin case.

"Yeah, so did I," Chris replied as he grabbed his backpack from the road and threw it over his shoulder.

"Thanks." Conner said, looking up from the game to glance at Chris, who looked away quickly, his eyes glistening.

"Well, I'd better get home," Chris said with a forced casual tone. Conner nodded, and Chris rode off in the direction he had come.

Scott and Breanne both gave their son a sympathetic look before prompting him into the van. Scott helped Breanne in, checked all the connections to the car hitched behind the van, and climbed into the driver's seat. He put the key in the ignition and turned. The engine roared to life. "Give it one last look," he said, turning his head to take in the view of their house.

Conner gave his house one miserable glance as they set off for their new life in Lockwood — a small town just outside Billings, Montana.

CHAPTER 2

A Pathway in the Trees

"Wake up. We're there."

Conner's mom was nudging him in the shoulder. He attempted to ignore her, but she continued to elbow him relentlessly. He didn't want to wake up. He didn't want to face the nightmare of his reality. At least when he was asleep he could dream about being back home.

He opened his eyes reluctantly as they pulled up the gravel drive to his new home. There wasn't even another neighbor in sight. 'Great,' he thought sarcastically. 'That's really going to make it easy to find new friends,' he added, feeling more disappointed with the location of his new home than he had thought possible.

"Conner, honey, why don't you just take the essentials to your room and go back to bed," Breanne suggested. "I know you're tired."

Conner grabbed his blanket and pillow and headed for the room that was likely to become the place where he would spend the majority of his dull existence from now on. As he made his way down the little hall that led to the living room he couldn't help but notice how nice the house was with all of its natural woodwork, even if the place did have the pungently remnant smell of mothballs. The far wall of the living room was home to a sizeable fireplace, which gave it a cozy feel. Large windows lined the walls, and had there been any daylight, he would have been able to see the stunning view out past the back deck.

"Dad, which one's my room?" Conner asked, completely unaware of the gorgeous landscape that existed just beyond the perimeter of his new home.

"Down the hall, last one on the left."

Conner reached the small, square room, dropped his bedding in the corner, and went back to the moving van for his TV, Gamestation, and games. "She did say essentials after all," he laughed as he grabbed the backpack containing his electronics and slung it over his shoulder. Then he found his TV and took everything to his room.

Ten minutes later, he had hooked up the gaming equipment and was flipping through his games to find one that sounded fun. But this quickly became a problem, as almost every one of them was multiplayer. Conner thought of the best friend he would never see again and found that he didn't want to play his games anymore. Instead, he went to the corner where his bedding was, laid down, and fell asleep.

* * *

The next morning was clear and bright. Blinding rays of sunlight beamed into Conner's face, demanding that he wake up. He put his hand over his eyes to block them out, crossed the room, and yanked down his window shade. It was a rude awakening to a rude new life.

The game Chris had given him was lying on the floor. Deciding to play for a while, he sat down and turned on his Gamestation... The light on the front didn't come on. He tried again, anger on the verge of spewing out of him…

Nothing.

He checked all the connections and tried a third time. The Gamestation failed to power on again and he officially lost his temper. *"Gah! Could my life be any worse!"* he yelled at the top of his lungs.

"Time for breakfast," his mother called from the kitchen, ignoring the furious yells that had just issued from her son's room.

Still fuming with anger, Conner went out to eat.

"Conner, it looks like we live on a really cool piece of land," Breanne told him encouragingly. "Why don't you go check it out after breakfast?"

"Sure mom," Conner replied, rolling his eyes.

"You know, Conner" — Breanne got up from the table and busied herself with the dishes, an unmistakable air of frustration about her — "I understand that you're unhappy about the move, and I'm not afraid to admit, it wasn't my first choice to move out here either… But it was really our only option. Your grandmother was kind enough to let us stay here rent-free until dad settles into his new job."

Conner jabbed his fork grumpily at the hash browns that remained on his plate.

"You could at least try to make the most of —"

"It's just not fair!" Conner burst out, cutting across his mother. "I get dragged to the middle of nowhere because dad got laid off from his job!"

Breanne turned to face her son, her expression livid. "If you had even the slightest idea how he feels… If you were able to step outside your own selfish world for even a second…" She turned her back on

Conner. Her shoulders began to tremble.

Conner sat, contemplating her words. Moments ago, he would have thought it was impossible to feel any worse than he already did, but now he had shame to add to the list of unwanted emotions stewing within.

Breanne wheeled around. "Why don't you do something useful?" she said, the grief in her tone turning to anger. "Like go and get the rest of the stuff from the moving van. Your father has to return it as soon as he gets home or they'll charge us a late fee."

Conner gave her a defeated glance and finished eating quickly. He went back to his room, threw on a pair of shoes, and headed out front. Daylight revealed the area around his house in further detail. There wasn't another building visible in any direction. Anger smoldered within him as he made his way to the back of the moving van and flung open the door.

'This is going to take hours,' he thought furiously as the extensive piles of boxes came into view. Wondering what he'd done to deserve this, he got to work, loading stacks of boxes on the dolly and taking them to the garage. It was dull work, but its lacking need for mental focus allowed his mind to wander. Soon he was scheming elaborate ways in which he could run away to California. He concluded that the best thing would be to hitchhike there, but he hadn't worked out where he would live. If Chris' mom knew he was there, she would surely call his mom.

There was, however, that secret way up to the rooftops of his school, and it was the beginning of summer vacation. He would have three months to figure something out. A depressingly reasonable voice in his head reminded him that he was only fourteen — he wouldn't be able to get a job for another two years. There would be no way of coming up with money for food.

The sound of crunching gravel pulled Conner from his thoughts. He looked up to find his dad coming down the drive. Bitterness filled him as he watched Scott put the car in park and get out with an enthusiastic air.

"Isn't it beautiful out here, Conner?" he asked happily when he saw his son loading a new stack of boxes on the dolly.

Conner met his eye with an incredulous expression.

"Oh, come on. Haven't you looked around? Have you seen the forest out behind the house? It must be hundreds of acres! All yours to roam whenever you want." Scott watched his son with hopeful expectance.

"Dad, I don't... You don't... You know what — forget it. You aren't going to understand."

"Understand what?" Scott asked, his tone becoming severe. "Understand what it's like to get dragged away from your friends? How do you know if I 'understand' what it's like? Have you ever taken the time to ask?"

Conner shifted uneasily. He was well aware of the answer and felt ashamed of it.

"No, you haven't," Scott went on, "because you're fourteen, and your world is all that matters. No one knows how you feel... Life is unfair..." He walked up and placed a hand on Conner's shoulder. "Let me give you the best piece of advice my father ever gave me: 'Life is what we make it...'" He searched Conner's eyes. "If you choose to sit around and sulk, I can promise — you *will* be miserable. But if you open your eyes to what's around you… If you find a new outlet… If you choose to make the most of what you have — well — your whole attitude will change."

"But, Dad, I've got no friends here" — Conner's eyes swept the landscape all around them — "and there isn't anyone around for miles."

Scott nodded gravely. "I'm not saying it will be easy for you to adjust. What I'm saying is that if all you plant are seeds of negativity, negativity is all you will harvest. You know what I mean?"

"Yeah, I get what you're saying." Conner replied, finding it hard to look his dad in the eye.

Scott smiled and gave Conner a one-armed hug around the shoulder. "Come on, I'll help you with the rest of this," he said, grabbing the dolly and rolling it to the nearest stack of boxes.

Conner watched him for a moment, unsure of how to feel. Settling for confused, he picked up a box and handed it to his dad to stack.

* * *

Conner and his dad finished unloading the moving van just before five that evening. Scott went into the house to let Breanne know he was ready to go into town and return it. She would need to follow him so he'd have a way of getting home.

"You want to ride with, Conner?" Scott asked as he climbed into the van.

"No, I think I'm just gonna stay here," Conner replied, trying not to sound too depressed.

Scott gave him a knowing look and let his eyes wander purposefully to the forest behind their house.

Conner watched as his parents pulled out of the driveway and disappeared from view. He decided he would try to fix his Gamestation as he made his way back up to the house. Maybe the connections just needed to be unplugged and plugged back in. Or maybe he had plugged it into an outlet that didn't work anymore. The house was extremely old after all.

It wasn't long before the harsh truth had crushed his spirit: his gaming system was officially broken. Nothing he did to fix it worked. He eventually gave up, wondering if things could be any worse. He had no friends, no games, no life.

He went out to the kitchen for a glass of water, and as he waited for his cup to fill, he gazed out the window. The view that met his eyes was nothing short of breathtaking. His yard descended into a forest of old growth trees, layering one another tirelessly into the faint horizon. His dad's words came back to him. 'All yours to roam whenever you want.' He felt a stab of excitement in spite of his own misery. There were no boundaries here. He could explore to his heart's content. It wasn't like the city, where 'no trespassing' signs mark the entrance to every remaining piece of undeveloped land.

He gulped down the glass of water and went back to his room to find some old jeans, a scrubby shirt, and the shoes he used to mow the lawn.

As he stepped out onto his front porch, he noticed for the first time how incredible the air was here: fresh and clean. He took a few breaths just to enjoy them and they eased his mind in a way he never would have expected. A breeze drifted past him as he rounded the corner that led to the back of the house, carrying with it the subtle smells of grass, pine, and flowers.

The moment Conner entered the old forest, so full of the life that thrives in places far from cities, his aggressions, his bitter feelings and his desire to be back in the Santa Ana began to melt away like a candle that had burned for far too long. So many different kinds of plants littered the forest floor that he didn't know which ones captured him the most. Endless ferns grew like stylized umbrellas, covering towns where delicate little flowers were people who would perish without their unceasing protection. Thorny bushes sprouted up around the ferns, warning all predators who sought to eat the lush and leafy stalks of the consequences their actions may hold. Trees encompassed the entire habitat, providing shade from the sun's penetrating rays, keeping all life beneath them from withering.

It was hard to decide which way to go at first, but he eventually elected to carry on in the direction he'd already been traveling because he thought he heard the sounds of trickling water.

Less than a minute passed before he came upon a small stream flowing happily along a shallow groove of rock, dirt, and moss. He crossed it and continued, his eyes wandering happily, lingering on the things he found most fascinating.

A bird perched on a branch above him sang a clever little melody; a second later, he heard the same notes from somewhere in the distance. The bird above him chirped its melody again. Conner smiled and sat down to listen as the two birds sang to one another.

A nearby bush rustled. He peeked over the tops of the ferns that surrounded him and saw a doe leading her fawn toward the stream he'd crossed earlier. The young deer looked as though it was no more than a few months old. Conner sat and watched them until they drank their fill and moved on. He decided to move on as well.

His foot stubbed up against something hard that hadn't been visible in the knee-high brushes and grass. After nursing his aggravated toes, he decided to investigate. He discovered a group of rocks in the shape of a circle, like a fire-pit. Thick, sponge-like moss draped from one stone to the next, making it difficult to decipher the size or shape of any one of them in particular — clearly the fire-pit had been there for a very long time. Conner concluded that a group of hunters must have built it at some point and left it behind to continue exploring.

He came upon a large fallen tree whose trunk had rotted out so badly that as he attempted to climb over it all he gained for his efforts were large handfuls of sodden bark dust. Eventually, after mounting a few other futile attempts, he found his way over the tree and continued his exploration of the forest.

Something up ahead had grabbed his attention like nothing he'd seen so far. There was a sort of natural pathway in a grouping of trees. How far the path went he neither knew nor cared. He felt a strong impulse to take it, but before he had a chance, his mother's voice reverberated through the trees.

"Conner — dinner..."

He stood there, his mind feeling torn in two. He knew it was in his best interest to heed his mother's call. He wasn't on her best side right now, and missing dinner would greatly worsen the situation — she had strict rules about sitting down for dinner as a family. However, this pathway in the trees was urging him to explore.

"Conner… Where are you? Time for dinner…"

His mother's voice rang out again, forcing him to concede to the fact that he would just have to continue exploring tomorrow morning. He studied the area around the path carefully to make sure he located a few distinct landmarks. Otherwise, it might be difficult to find his way back.

As he made his way up to the house, he was shocked to find that he had only gone a short way into the forest. He'd spent so much time enjoying every aspect of its beauty that his movements had been extremely slow. A true feeling of joy came over him for the first time in weeks. It wasn't the same as the joy that comes from friendship or games — it was the joy of inner peace. He had found something that drove him, moved him, took his focus away from things he had no control over. It wasn't a replacement for companionship, but in its own way, it was just as fulfilling.

* * *

"So you decided to explore the forest?" Scott asked, twirling up a new forkful of spaghetti.

Conner finished chewing before he answered, "Yeah, I figured I might as well go check it out, you know. I mean, it's our property… We should know what we've got."

Breanne smiled and looked on attentively as her husband responded.

"I couldn't agree more. Maybe this weekend we can go out there together and find a good place to build a tree fort. What do you think?"

Initially, Conner felt that a tree fort was a bit young for him. He was fourteen after all. But as he looked into his dad's expectant face, a thought occurred to him. There was no one here to impress. No one was going to make fun of him for having a tree fort. Plus, a project would be a good way to pass the time. "Okay, that sounds like fun," he said, smiling.

Scott gave his son an approving nod and took a healthy bite of garlic bread. "That's settled then," he said happily, making an animated hand gesture. "I'll pick up supplies after work tomorrow and Friday, and then Saturday morning we can get started."

"Here, I can take that," Breanne told Conner, extending a hand to take his plate.

"Thanks, Mom," Conner replied, handing her his dish and getting up from the table.

"Oh, by the way," Scott began, "I got you something. It's in your room," he finished, barely repressing a grin.

Conner grinned back and hurried to his room. Sitting next to his TV was a brand new Gamestation. He ran back out to the kitchen. "How did you know?" he asked, nearly laughing his words.

"Your mother heard you yelling about something this morning, so she went to check while you were unloading the moving van... She noticed your old one was plugged in, but she couldn't turn it on..."

"Mom — I — thank you so much!" Conner exclaimed. He crossed the kitchen and gave his mother a hug, fighting back tears of shame. He had been nothing but a sulking, complaining little brat for the last two weeks, yet she still cared enough to go out of her way for him. "Guys," he said, releasing his mom and focusing on both his parents, "I'm really sorry for the way I've been acting... I..."

"We're sorry we had to take you from your friends," Scott replied before his son could finish. "We know it isn't easy..."

Conner hugged his mom again before giving one to his dad.

"Alright, now go and have fun," Scott told him in a fake version of a strict tone.

It only took Conner a few minutes to hook up the new system. After playing a couple different games, his eyes grew too tired to continue. He turned everything off and climbed into bed.

* * *

Conner awoke the following morning feeling cheerful. It was still hard to accept the fact that he would never see Chris again, but his overall mood had improved considerably. He went to turn on his Gamestation but stopped himself just before his finger reached the on-switch. The image of the pathway in the trees had found the front of his mind.

He went to his window and lifted the shade. It was just past dawn, and the sky was crystal-clear. Excitement rose within him as he threw on his clothes. He crept silently to the kitchen, grabbed an apple, and left for the forest. His first objective was to find the stream. After that, he felt sure he knew how to find the fallen tree, which was no more than a few hundred yards from the pathway.

When ten minutes passed, and he still hadn't found what he was looking for, Conner began to wonder if he'd gone the wrong direction. It didn't seem likely, due to his feeling sure he remembered the way. He stopped and surveyed the area around him. A tree whose trunk bent oddly in its attempt to find the sun caught his eye. He distinctly remembered marking it in his mind.

As he moved through the foliage blocking his way, the fallen tree came into view. He smiled, quickened his pace, and clambered over the tree. It wasn't long before the path came into view. He felt its allure — just as he had before. An odd sensation came over him the instant he entered it. He couldn't find an explanation, but it felt like he was meant to be here. Up ahead, the dazzling light from the sun shone warmly upon a vast field.

CHAPTER 3

Rohwen

Wind whipped Conner's face as he stepped into an expansive valley. He turned on the spot to take in his surroundings, wondering how he hadn't noticed such a vast break in the trees from his kitchen window. Rolling hills stretched into the border of a forest to the west. A herd of bison grazed peacefully from the abundance of lush grass. To the north, a towering mountain range loomed in a thread of low clouds, the tip of the tallest peak poking through them. Clusters of trees integrated into the landscape to the east, where the vague hint of a massive river gleamed in the sunlight. Small tributaries branched off the main fork in all directions, making it look like a lightning bolt had carved itself into the valley floor. The land to the south was level and stretched endlessly into the horizon.

As Conner stood there, trying to decide which way to go, a faint noise drifting on the western breeze found his ears. He strained to hear it more clearly and discovered that it had a rhythmic flow — like a musical beat, but of a type he had never heard, almost as if all the instruments were wooden.

Feeling a rush of curiosity, he headed for the source. Warm rays of sun beat down upon his neck as he made his way across the valley between him and the forest. It was hard to believe the sun had already risen to the center of the sky. Dawn only felt like an hour ago, maybe even less. He thought about how often the hours slipped past like seconds when he was enjoying himself, as opposed to the seconds creeping by like hours when he wasn't. Shrugging, he admitted to himself that he would never understand the anomaly of time.

Three massive birds flew overhead. Their shadows bent over the rolling hills as they passed. Conner wondered what breed they were. 'Maybe they're eagles…?' he thought, watching the birds as they flew to the north. "Well, if they are eagles … they're definitely the biggest ones I've ever seen,' he concluded.

It seemed to take considerably longer than it should have to reach the forest, but the once faint music had grown louder with each passing minute, and his curiosity to know where it was coming from kept him from losing interest.

As Conner came upon the edge of the forest, he was delighted to find a sizable stretch of blackberry bushes that actually had ripe berries. It was baffling to think that he'd found ripe blackberries in the first week of July. He tried one; it was perfect. Smiling, he began eating enthusiastically.

Once he'd eaten his fill, he started to fight his way into the thick underbrush of the forest. His first thought was that this forest had been here for a very long time. It was abundant in plant life that was easily a hundred times older than he was. The amount of foliage was so dense that it was difficult to tell where one plant started and the next one ended. Countless branches covered in thick, yellow-green moss sprawled invasively into the space of their neighbors. Bushes and brambles of every type wrapped and knotted into a tangled mess, making it difficult to find a suitable path to take.

Conner navigated his way around the natural obstacles, avoiding areas that appeared impossible to move beyond. It seemed to take forever to make any headway, but time wasn't important. This place was like something out of a fantasy book. It was incredible. He half expected to see fairies fluttering playfully out from amongst the flowers at any moment, perhaps even dancing to the musical beat, which had grown considerably louder — the sounds were now so clear that he could appreciate every note.

A large clearing became visible through the trees. Conner gasped as he moved closer. Hundreds of huts enveloped its expanses, almost as if it were a housing development.

Some tribe of people were inhabiting this forest. Conner hid behind a tree and scanned the expanse of their village. Children were running around, playing some kind of game he'd never seen before and laughing the whole time. Groups of men and women stood around conversing while others tended to what must have been their daily duties. Sitting around a fire-pit was an assembly of tribesmen, playing an assortment of wooden instruments.

Fear and intrigue consumed Conner simultaneously. He knew nothing about this tribe's traditions, beliefs, or feelings toward outsiders. Deciding quickly it would be best to avoid them, he stayed hidden behind the tree and waited for the right moment to flee. A group of men who'd been facing his general direction turned their attention elsewhere. He seized his chance, spun around, and ran.

To his horror, he found that ropes were all around him before he could take more than two steps. Within seconds, his arms and legs had been bound, and he was being hauled forcefully toward a man who appeared to be chief. The man spoke.

"My name is Nayati: chief of the Satria tribe," he started, gesturing to the expansive village all around him. "What is your purpose here?"

Before Conner could so much as fathom the chief's first question, Nayati spoke again.

"Do you serve Vellix?" he interrogated, his voice severe and accusing.

Conner's mind abandoned him as he stood there, trembling with fear. He couldn't form a single rational thought. The chief pierced his eyes with a cold, condemning stare.

A man with skin so loose it looked in danger of falling off, shuffled slowly over and whispered in the chief's ear. "My thoughts exactly, Yorick," Nayati replied, still eyeing Conner disapprovingly. "Why have you been sent to spy on us?"

This accusation was so unjust that Conner's mind snapped back on in order to defend his integrity. "I wasn't sp-spying on you, s-sir," he said, trying to sound as respectful as possible while shaking with fear.

"Why should I believe you?" Nayati asked, crossing his arms, clearly unmoved. "Given the present climate, I'm finding it hard to believe that you just so happened to be hiding on the edge of my village, watching us for no reason. You were sent by Vellix to spy on us, weren't you?"

"No, I w-wasn't sent by anyone. I just followed the sounds of — of music that were coming from the f-forest. Please, sir. I'm telling the truth." Conner wished he would stop stuttering. He thought about his mother. In trying to persuade her to believe him, he knew stumbling over his words to be the first and biggest mistake.

"Your story seems unlikely to me," Nayati replied, but as he spoke, he surveyed Conner's appearance, properly, for the first time; it seemed to astonish him. His eyes broadened comprehensively.

Conner detected that the chief might have lost some conviction in his words as he said them. Seeing his opportunity to speak, he said, "I swear, I wouldn't have intruded on your space, but like I said, the music lured me." He pulled his face into an expression that he thought would look convincingly honest.

"What is your name, boy?"

"It's Conner, sir…"

The chief stared at him for a moment before he spoke again, a look of wonderment pulling at his features. "Do you know where you are?" he asked curiously.

Conner thought about his answer, feeling unsure. Naturally, he wanted to say Montana. What other answer could there be? But, as he thought about the facts, it felt less and less likely that he'd found a huge valley with an expansive mountain range, vast river, and this ancient forest, which some unknown tribe of people was inhabiting, out on his grandmother's property. At the very least, he would have seen the mountains from the view his kitchen window provided.

Nayati smiled at Conner, reading his silence as an obvious "no."

Conner shrugged and gave Nayati the only answer he had. Well, the only sane answer anyway. "Montana?"

The chief looked at him quizzically. "Montana?" he queried, making it more than apparent that he had no clue what Conner was talking about.

Conner felt a wave of anxiety crash over him. How could he not be in Montana? It was ridiculous to assume anything otherwise.

Nayati gestured toward one of his tribesmen and then toward Conner.

Fear took hold of Conner as the tribesman moved meaningfully toward him, pulling a knife from a holster at his waist. Conner closed his eyes and braced himself. The suspense of waiting to be stabbed was like torture. Where would it happen? Would it be as painful as he imagined, or would he go into shock and feel only the initial stab?

A cold blade was touching his skin. He tensed up, anticipating the pain he would endure, but it never came. The man cut his bindings loose and went back to whatever it was he'd been doing previously. An indescribable feeling of relief came over Conner, sending a tingling sensation throughout his whole body. For a moment, he had been sure his life was about to end. He stood rooted to the spot, still not exactly sure what was going on. It seemed that the chief no longer suspected him of being a spy, but assuming anything when you're in a vulnerable state can be a huge mistake.

Nayati surveyed Conner's unease, smiling broadly, "It is okay," he laughed. "You need not worry. I no longer believe you are a spy, and I do not wish to harm you in any way."

The chief's words allowed Conner to breathe easy. He gave Nayati a polite nod, wondering what would happen next.

"Now, to the matters at hand," said Nayati. "Medwin, come over here!" he boomed in a thunderous voice.

"Yes, father?" replied a young boy of about fifteen as he jogged to the spot where Nayati stood, his long, dark hair rippling behind him. His build was similar to that of the majority of his tribe: sleek and strong. He wore only a leather flap around his waist, leaving most of his tan skin exposed. There were two stripes of white marked around his upper arms and lower legs, and his face carried a look of knowledge beyond his years.

When the chief spoke next, Conner thought he seemed to choose his words carefully. "This boy" — he surveyed Conner before continuing — "knows not of this land. His name is, Conner. Do you remember what we talked about? About how you would be the one to take him?"

Medwin threw his father a shocked glance, nodded, and ran to a nearby hut, returning a minute later with a pack slung over his shoulder.

"Remember," Nayati said, giving his son a severe look, "you must find him yourself. I cannot tell you anything other than what I already have. However, I trust that you have the sense to make the correct deductions."

"Thank you," said Medwin, bowing to his father. "I won't fail you."

Nayati nodded. "Did you remember to grab some meat for the trip?"

"Yes, I have what I am able to carry in my pack."

"Good."

As Conner watched Medwin and his father converse, his feelings of anxiety shifted. He was no longer in danger of being killed for the crime of spying, but now that his initial fear had subsided, it seemed that a million other worries had been waiting to flood his mind. What was going on? What were they talking about? Was the boy taking him somewhere? If so, for what reason?

"Come on," said the boy named Medwin, gesturing for Conner to follow him.

Conner looked up from the patch of flowers he'd been staring at. "What's going on?" he asked, unable to suppress the concern he felt. "Where are you taking me?" he continued as he started after Medwin. "I've got to get home before too long... My mom doesn't like it when I miss dinner..." Conner waited for Medwin to respond, but he just walked silently away from the village. "Hey, did you hear me?" Conner asked as he quickened his pace to keep up. "Where are we going?" he asked again.

"I'll explain on the way," Medwin replied, stepping skillfully past the undergrowth that Conner was fighting his way through. Conner glanced around, contemplating the idea of trying to sneak off and head back for home, but a truly depressing reality crushed that plan — he had no idea which way home was any more. He was lost. Medwin was the only one who seemed to know where they were.

When they'd been walking for quite some time, and Medwin hadn't said another word, a true sense of panic began to consume Conner, but in spite of his own fear, intrigue spurred him to carry on.

Eventually, they exited the forest and headed south.

Even though Conner's mind was swirling with battling thoughts of fear and curiosity, he couldn't help but focus his attention on the beauty of the landscape around him. The sky was so perfectly blue that it almost looked fake. The grassy rolling hills were like an animated version of the most breathtaking painting he'd ever seen. Wind swept sporadically over their expanses, causing the sun to reflect off the infinite blades of grass as they bowed obediently. As a result, it appeared that a shimmering snake was slithering across the plains with great confusion as to which way it should go.

Medwin spoke, and the extended silence it broke caused Conner to flinch. "So, you're probably wondering where you are, huh?"

"That's exactly what I'm wondering," Conner replied, relieved that Medwin had finally said something to break the silence. "I'm also wondering what we're doing…" he added, hoping Medwin might shed some light on his situation.

"Let's just start with where you're at," Medwin said. "This is Rohwen."

Conner thought he must have misheard Medwin for a moment, but the look on his face told him he had not. "I've never heard of any place called Rohwen," he said, observing his surroundings instinctually.

Medwin gave him an odd sort of glance, almost as if he couldn't believe Conner would feel the need to voice something so obvious, but he didn't reply.

'This guy must be crazy!' Conner thought realistically. 'There's no such place as Rohwen… Who's ever heard of Rohwen?' he went on, trying to vindicate himself. But the longer he thought about it, the more he realized he had no explanation that would lead him to disbelieve Medwin. In fact, everything pointed to Medwin being correct. A new battle started in his mind. One part — the logical part — said, 'You must be dreaming. There just isn't any other valid explanation. You're going to wake up any moment and laugh about this.'

The other part — the speculative part — retorted, 'what if this is all real? What if you've actually discovered something truly amazing? What if this is like … some other world…?' In the end, he decided that all he could do was let things play out. The answers to his questions were bound to come in due time.

The sun started to nestle behind a distant tree line to the west. Pinks and reds of a violent variety illuminated the edges of the sparse clouds drifting idly across the sky. Conner looked north and saw the mountains from earlier. They shone with the same pinks and reds as the clouds, making them a beautiful sight to behold. Yet, for some reason, staring at the tallest mountain gave him an unusual feeling. Without thinking, he asked, "Who is Vellix?"

Medwin remained silent for a long moment before he finally said, "Vellix is an enemy to this land." When Conner gave him a look that clearly stated he'd been hoping for a better explanation, Medwin continued. "He is an evil man. I don't know many details, but I do know that he desires only power and control over Rohwen. And that he has destroyed countless lives in order to attain them. Father says his hatred for all that is pure, or decent, has made him bitter and resentful."

"What made him so evil?" Conner asked, unable to imagine anyone hating a place as beautiful as this. No sooner than he had asked his question, he found himself wondering why he was inquiring about the one thing that would cause this place to be any less than perfect. It wasn't affecting him in any way, so why bother with it?

"There is speculation about that question," said Medwin, bending down to look at something on the ground. "It is, indeed, a great question," he continued as he stood back up and carried on walking. "I wish I had a good answer for you."

Darkness was approaching quickly. A deep shade of blue, strewn with the faint twinkles of the heavens' brightest stars, now overshadowed all the vibrant hues of sunset. Medwin decided it was a prudent time for a fire and some food. "Since we're having a fire, we'll need to keep out of sight of the skies," he said knowledgably as he gathered an armful of wood.

Conner tilted his head inquisitively.

"There are winged creatures employed by Vellix to snatch up stragglers," Medwin explained, noticing Conner's gesture of curiosity. "Nobody knows where they are taken, because they never return." He stopped to investigate the ground again. "I suppose this spot is as good as any," he muttered to himself, finding a rock that was about the size of a door handle.

Conner was about to confirm his earlier theory, that Medwin was definitely quite crazy, when something astonishing happened. Medwin grabbed the rock and pulled. The ground lifted up in a four-foot-by-four-foot square, one side apparently on an invisible hinge. "Come on," he said, allowing himself a little smirk.

Completely blown away, Conner followed Medwin into a spacious underground room equipped with a fire-pit and two basic looking dirt beds. "What the...?" he started, but Medwin cut across him.

"I know! Neat, huh?" he said happily, making it quite apparent that he'd been eager to show off his ability to Conner. "It's a power my people have." He dropped his armful of wood into the pit, reached into his pack, and pulled out two different stones and some balled up dead grass.

Still not sure how what just happened could have actually happened, Conner asked, "How did you do that?"

"I am one of a select few in my tribe that are learned in a skill that allows us to bend and shape the land in beneficial ways. For example,

33

we needed a fire to cook dinner, but we mustn't be seen. We were way too far from natural shelter — this valley, as you will have noticed, is by no means small…"

"…Go on," Conner insisted, now completely engulfed by curiosity.

"So I created this room in my mind, focused on it, and — well, here we are…"

Conner gawked at Medwin, overwhelmed by fascination.

"My people have been working to unlock the secrets of the art for centuries," Medwin continued as he struck one stone against the other, sending a spark into the balled up grass. He picked up the grass, blew on it steadily until the spark turned to flame, set it down, and sprinkled a handful of kindling over the top.

"So," Conner said, trying to wrap his head around what Medwin was telling him, "you can just think of something and it will become real?"

"Not exactly… It requires great concentration. The user must have incredible mental strength, or nothing will happen," Medwin said as he carefully placed a few larger branches over his kindling. "If someone were to become mentally at one with this land, I believe they would be able to bend it to their will in amazing ways."

As Conner sat, staring into the fire and silently contemplating what Medwin had told him, he started to wonder why the small room wasn't becoming thick with smoke. He let his eyes wander from the flames to the plume of emanating smoke they created and watched as it funneled into a hole in an upper part of the room's back wall. Assuming this hole was acting as a chimney, Conner asked, "Won't all that smoke give us away if those winged creatures come around?"

Medwin chuckled. "The smoke isn't going up to the surface. It's filling up a much larger secondary room that I created to keep the air in this one clean."

"Ah, that makes sense," Conner said, watching as Medwin pulled two cuts of meat from his pack and skewered them with a strong-looking branch.

Before long, the aroma of fire-cooked meat started to fill the room. Tantalizing smells drifted from two sizzling venison steaks and found Conner's nose. His stomach lurched, forcing him to realize how hungry he was.

"So, how old are you, Medwin?" he asked, in order to distract his mind from thoughts of delicious food. "It is Medwin, right?" he added, realizing that he wasn't properly sure he remembered what the chief had called him.

"Yeah, it's Medwin … and I'm fifteen." Medwin gave the steaks a slight turn to see how the other side was coming along. After a moments glance he grinned and flipped them the rest of the way over.

"So you're a year older than me," Conner said. "I turned fourteen a couple weeks ago in June."

"June?" Medwin queried, as if he was trying to think of a time that he might have heard the term.

"It's a time of the year in my…" Conner was about to say "world," but he didn't seem to be able to bring himself to it. Even though he had plenty of convincing proof, saying it aloud would be a full admittance that he was, in fact, in another world.

"…In your world … right?" Medwin uttered slowly.

Conner gaped silently.

"I know you're not from here…" Medwin went on, fiddling with the steaks to keep himself occupied through this awkward moment.

"I knew it must be true," said Conner. "I was just having a hard time admitting it to myself. It's not exactly easy to believe…"

Medwin nodded reassuringly before handing him a chunk of meat, a handful of blackberries, and a pouch of water.

"This looks delicious," Conner said appreciatively.

"Thanks," Medwin replied with a grin. "Let's just hope it tastes as good as it looks." He grinned again and ripped off a piece of steak with his teeth.

Conner grinned back and did the same. As he bit into his steak, flavors unlike anything he had ever experienced overwhelmed his taste buds. He gave Medwin a wide-eyed look of approval, swallowed his first bite, and ripped off a second, eager for more.

The two boys didn't say a word as they devoured their food, but every so often they would exchange a satisfied glance, smile, and then re-devote themselves to their meal.

Conner took his last bite, savoring it as if he would never eat again. His stomach was full to a point of perfect contentment. He leaned against the wall and let out a long sigh.

"I think we should get some sleep," Medwin suggested, climbing onto his bed.

"Sounds like a plan," Conner replied. He got on his bed and found a comfortable position. His body was beyond ready for sleep, but his mind was full of the day's revelations. He had actually discovered another world. The longer he thought about it, the more it captivated him, filling his mind with wonder and intrigue.

But as he lay, pondering his discovery, a terrible thought struck him. Was he ever going to find his way home? Would he ever see his parents again? The thought was nearly unbearable. Tears began to trickle down his cheek. He rolled over quickly so Medwin wouldn't notice his grief and, telling himself repeatedly that everything would be all right, he drifted slowly to sleep.

CHAPTER 4

Vellix and the Mirthless

In the distant horizon, three bird-like creatures were flying toward the highest peak of a mountain. Vellix wondered if they finally had good news. They'd been searching for well over a week now, and his tolerance was at its breaking point. If they had failed again, he would have to punish them.

As the creatures drew closer, they spread their massive wings and landed at the mouth of a cavernous, torch-lit chamber. They drew themselves up to their full, towering height and waited for their master to approach.

"Well?" Vellix interrogated as he moved slowly toward them.

"There has been no sighting of Zelimir, Master," one of the creatures replied, cowering.

"Once again, Zarmena, you fail me!"

Before Zarmena could react, the stone floor had clasped firmly around her feet. She looked down instinctually before fixing Vellix with a fear-stricken gaze.

Vellix made a tight fist with his right hand; Zarmena immediately began to writhe, her screeches of pain echoing dissonantly off the cavern walls.

Vellix opened his hand, and her squirming body went limp.

Somewhere deep in shadow a chain began to rattle, followed by inarticulate moans.

"Silence!" Vellix spat furiously. He pointed a hand toward the shadows. A horrific shriek filled the chamber, and then all was silent. Vellix turned back to the bird-like creatures. "I would have thought those Idenites I so generously gave you would have upped your work rate! I will not continue to tolerate failure!" The floor released its grip from around Zarmena's feet.

The three creatures bowed deeply.

"Master," started the creature to Zarmena's right, glancing fearfully at the look of pain still imprinted upon her face.

"Spare me," Vellix responded with a lazy wave of his hand.

"Master," the creature said again, its voice shaking with fear.

"What is it Zedge?" Vellix flared up.

"Master — it's just that — we — well..."

"Spit it out, Zedge!"

"We spotted a boy during our search for Zelimir... He may have fit the descriptio —"

"*What! Are you sure?*" Vellix bellowed before Zedge could finish his last word.

"Well, not exactly," Zedge continued quickly. "We didn't dare investigate. He was on the edge of the Ancient Forest... But, from what I could see, he was definitely clad in strange garments..."

Vellix seemed to gather himself before he spoke again. "No ... no, it would not have been wise to show interest in the boy so close to the Satria."

After going virtually unnoticed, the creature on the left finally said, "Master?"

"Shut it, Saura!" Zarmena grumbled. "We ain't gettin' no meat tonight."

Vellix didn't reply. He turned away from the three creatures, apparently deep in thought.

Realizing their dismissal, the beasts took flight, their wings sending wind swirling around the chamber like a small tornado.

Vellix walked over to a throne that rose from the rocky floor as if molded from clay. He sat heavily and gazed across the room. A huge mirror reflected his face back at him in the flickering torchlight. Deep lines of age patterned his cheeks and brow, and in his sunken eyes, he saw something that hadn't been there for years: fear…

* * *

The sound of a crackling fire found Conner's ears. He stretched and yawned gratefully.

"Morning," Medwin said brightly.

Conner's heart jolted as he remembered where he was.

Medwin was already fixing a small breakfast and looked like he might have been up for hours.

"What time is it?" Conner asked through another huge yawn.

"About two hours past dawn," Medwin answered, reaching out to hand Conner what was left of last night's dinner.

"What about you?" Conner asked, reluctant to take the last chunk of venison.

"I already ate my share," Medwin reassured him, placing the steak in Conner's partially outstretched hand.

Conner smiled and started eating without further hesitation.

Medwin watched him for a moment. "I suppose it is time for me to tell you what we're doing," he said.

Conner looked up from his food. He had almost forgotten about the fact that he had no idea where Medwin was taking him — or why. A familiar feeling of anxiety churned in his stomach.

"We're headed for a city called Beach Bay."

Knowing he wasn't going to recognize names of places in a world he knew nothing about, Conner remained silent and allowed Medwin to speak without interruptions.

"Once we get there, we need to find my friend Lenny — well, actually, I don't know if I'd call him a friend, more of an acquaintance," Medwin mumbled, speaking to himself. "Anyway," he said, redirecting his attention to Conner, "with his help, we'll find a way to sail to Rhona. You should find answers to your questions there."

Conner followed Medwin up out of the underground room, his mind spinning with thoughts. 'What does he mean, find answers to my questions?' He pondered Medwin's words for a long while before coming to a simple conclusion: he was in a world he knew nothing about — of course he had questions. Medwin hadn't said anything about knowing what his questions were specifically. He had merely made it clear that he knew Conner must have questions.

* * *

Some hours later, the sound of rushing water broke the, otherwise, silent air.

"That'll be the Brio River," Medwin said, perking an ear to hear the sounds a bit better. "West fork, to be exact."

"Do we have to cross it?" Conner asked tentatively. He wasn't keen on getting wet, being as he only had one pair of clothes.

"Yeah, we do," Medwin replied casually, "But don't worry," he added as he noticed the look of displeasure on Conner's face.

"Oh — there's a bridge," said Conner, feeling instantly at ease.

"No, but there are plenty of trees along the bank," Medwin replied as he pulled a handsome-looking hatchet out of his pack. "I'll just cut one of the smaller ones down, and we'll use it to cross."

"Can't you just do that — that concentration thingy and make a bridge?"

Medwin smiled and said, "I'm not skilled enough for that. Plus, I try not to abuse the power. Like all things, you can overdo it. I was taught by the elders that power should be respected, not abused."

"Yeah, I guess that's probably true," Conner replied, still wishing Medwin could just make a bridge.

As they reached the river, Medwin found a suitable tree and began cutting it down. Conner sat on the bank and looked over the edge. It was a ten-foot drop to the river below. Large rocks poked their jagged faces through the surface, creating sporadic changes in the water's flow. He was watching the rushing water contently when something caught the corner of his eye. He turned quickly to look, but nothing was there. "Medwin, I think something just moved over there."

"Which direction?" Medwin asked, his eyes growing wide with fear.

"That way," Conner replied, pointing east.

Medwin ran over to the section of bushes and trees that Conner had pointed out and searched it. "I didn't see anything," he said as he walked back to the tree that he'd been cutting and set to work on it once more, "but let's take that as a good reminder to stay on our guard. Vellix has spies of all types. You can never be too careful. I imagine he has at least one from nearly every civilization in Rohwen… I know that sounds like a negative outlook, but it is realistic. He is extremely powerful, and the weak minded will always seek refuge in the powerful — even if it means succumbing to evil."

"How many different civilizations are there in Rohwen?" Conner asked, realizing for the first time that there must be more people than just the Satria living in this world.

"How many major civilizations?" Medwin asked.

Conner nodded, understanding that his question would have taken a great amount of effort to answer if Medwin had gone into trying to name every little settlement.

"Well, there are the people of Beach Bay," Medwin began, lifting his thumb, "the Idenites, the Edelish, the Botanicans, and the Ryvelians," he finished, all five of his fingers raised now.

"Is there something wrong with the Ryvelians?" Conner asked, noticing a dark overtone in Medwin's voice as he mentioned them.

Medwin nodded, but he didn't look away from the tree he was chopping down. "They're evil."

"Let me guess," Conner said sarcastically, "they serve Vellix?"

"They do," Medwin replied. "My people, joined by the Edelish, fought them and Vellix's creatures in this very valley. Our combined forces were too much for them. Eventually, they realized defeat and fled…

"Unfortunately," Medwin continued, "the Edelish were punished severely for their acts of bravery in that battle. When Vellix discovered that they had been involved, he destroyed the land upon which they had thrived for centuries, scorching its once beautiful luster into a barren wasteland. How many of the Edelish people survived … I don't know…" Medwin looked away from Conner mournfully. "Those who did survive are no doubt in hiding. Edelan, the land in which they once lived, is now known as the Forsaken Desert…" He broke off from his speech and went back to hacking at the tree.

Conner stared at Medwin for a moment, a look of disgust upon his face. "That might be one of the worst things I have ever heard… I mean, who could *do* that?"

"Someone who values themselves so far above others, that they see them as inferior, pathetic, unworthy to exist, unless it is to serve." Medwin tore his attention away from the tree to give Conner a revolted glance.

"What about the Satria? Why didn't Vellix do the same thing to your people?" Conner asked. "I'm glad he didn't, of course," he added hastily, realizing his question had sounded horrible.

"The Satria are a warrior tribe, with power that far exceeds that of the Edelish. With his armies depleted so badly from battle, Vellix was wise not to attempt a direct attack on my people." Medwin paused as the tree began to splinter and crack. "There we go," he said, watching it fall across the river and hit the opposite bank with a thud. He stepped up onto the trunk and walked foot-over-foot across it with apparent ease. "Come on!" he called from the other side.

Feeling nervous, Conner started to cross. Unlike Medwin, he lied down on the trunk and inched forward, using his arms to pull the rest of his body. He was about halfway across when a branch he was using for support broke, causing him to slip off. Acting quickly, he grabbed one of the many other branches, but it wasn't thick enough to support his weight. It broke, and he fell ten feet to the river below.

Ice-cold water constricted his muscles the instant he plunged into the river's depths. He felt like all the breath was sucked out of him as the strong current thrust him into rock after rock, bashing him senseless. He fought tirelessly against the raging current, but he was no match for its absurd power. Just when he thought he might die from lack of air, he surfaced. He was no longer moving with the mighty current of the river — he was on a large, flat rock that hadn't been there a moment ago.

"Conner!" Medwin called out from somewhere above. "Are you okay?"

"Yeah, I think I'm alright," Conner called back, checking to make sure all his joints were working. "How am I going to get back up?"

"Hold on," Medwin yelled. He ran over to one of the bigger trees and started to hack off a branch. After a few minutes, he returned, dragging it behind him. "Here, climb up," he told Conner as he lowered it down.

Conner grabbed the branch and gazed at it for a moment, searching to find nubs, notches, and anything else that would help make the climb easier. The task was difficult, but his determination to make it back to the bank was greater than the strain of the climb. With one last surge of energy, he was back up and working to regain his breath.

As he lay there panting, his thoughts were directed to the way that rock had appeared. "Medwin ... I think I ... did it!" he exclaimed, still attempting to catch his breath.

"Did what?" Medwin replied ignorantly, though Conner thought there was a look of smug satisfaction on his face.

"I — I think I made a rock appear ... and it ... it saved my life..."

To confirm Conner's suspicions, Medwin didn't look at all surprised as he said, "I figured you must have, considering the fact that there's no other way you would be standing here talking to me otherwise."

"Is it — well — normal for someone to be able —"

"Get down!" Medwin yelled urgently, cutting Conner off mid-sentence. "Out of sight!"

Hearing the stress in Medwin's voice, Conner obeyed without hesitation.

Three large birds flew overhead. Luckily, Medwin had said something quickly enough that they were both able to jump into a nearby bush and go unnoticed.

"*Mirthless!*" Medwin hissed.

"Are they bad?" Conner asked, watching as the three birds disappeared from the small view he had through the bush's leaves. "I saw three large birds just like those before I entered your forest."

"You *did?*" Medwin replied, sounding taken aback. "They must not have seen you."

"I don't know how they wouldn't have seen me," Conner said, shrugging. "I was out in the open..."

Medwin looked at Conner for a moment, his expression strained with impatience. "Conner, I don't think you understand. If they had seen you, we wouldn't be having this conversation. You're lucky to be alive."

"Are those the winged creatures that take people to Vellix?"

"The very same," Medwin replied, searching the skies. "I think they've gone now. Let's get a fire going before you freeze to death."

CHAPTER 5

The Cliffs of Elders

The fire felt so good that Conner thought he could sit by it forever, and it was much to his dismay when Medwin told him that they had better keep moving. He stood up to find that the effects of his river incident had caught up with him: his muscles had grown stiff, and bruises covered his forearms and shins. He stretched, grimacing with the pain it caused him.

"Are you going be okay to travel?" Medwin asked as he cleared the remains of their fire.

Conner took a minute to evaluate his pain. It would have been nice to sit for a while longer, but in all honesty, he knew his muscles would just end up stiffer than they already were if he didn't use them. "Yeah, I think I'll be alright," he finally said.

The rest of the day wasn't one Conner would choose to remember. His body was in so much pain that every step he took felt like it might be the last he could possibly manage. But between conversation with Medwin and enjoying the beauty of the land around him, he had enough distraction to keep from focusing wholly on it. He was, however, still incredibly grateful when the sky lit up with the colors of sunset, telling him he would soon be able to lie down and relax.

"We'll just go on for a bit longer, and then we can stop for the night," said Medwin, looking up at the sky.

Conner nodded stiffly.

"I doubt it'll be much more than an hour," Medwin added, clearly aware of the pain Conner was in and wanting to reassure him that he wouldn't have to endure it much longer.

* * *

Medwin stopped just before night fell completely. He scanned the area around him until his eyes came to rest on a particular spot. His face screwed up with concentration, and a moment later, he was heading down into his underground room, Conner limping pitifully just behind him.

They had a quick bite to eat and climbed into bed; Conner was asleep within moments.

His eyes opened to an underwater world. He took a breath and found that the cold water in his lungs was something he craved. He took a few more, breathing even deeper, and enjoyed it immensely. Looking down, he realized with a start that he no longer had hands, but fins instead. He wiggled each of one in turn to get a feel for them and started swimming languidly with the flow of the river.

Quite suddenly, he was human again. He needed air — he desperately needed air — his lungs were about to burst — he felt sharp teeth clamp tightly around his arm — something was dragging him out of the water... His eyes came into focus. It looked like a wolf...

Conner awoke with a jerk, sweat dripping from his face. 'What was that about?' he thought, still breathing hard, as if the dream had truly caused him to need oxygen. He lied back down and attempted to repress the anxious feeling in his stomach. It wasn't long before he realized that listening to Medwin's steady snores seemed to calm his mind. He tried to focus on his own breathing, hoping to repel thoughts of the dream, and eventually, after much effort, he fell back to sleep.

At dawn the next morning, he and Medwin set out to continue their journey toward Beach Bay. The night's sleep had helped rejuvenate Conner, but he was still sore all over. The pain was like an infuriatingly efficient reminder of how many moving parts a body has. He constantly had to remind himself that things could be worse in order to stay positive. 'You could've easily broken a bone,' he kept saying. 'At least you can walk.'

* * *

"We're in the Mesala Plains now," Medwin said a few hours into the day. "It's important to keep your eyes open for Mirthless while we cross. There is no shelter, and it would be easy for them to spot us out here."

Hearing the name, "Mirthless," triggered a question in Conner's mind that he had been trying to ask the day before. "So, Medwin, is it normal for someone that's not from Rohwen to be able to use that — whatever you call the power you have?"

Medwin glanced at him and smiled. "It's called cognition — and no, it is not even normal for people *from here* to be able to do it. In fact, as far as I know, my people are the only ones who can, and we keep the knowledge of it to ourselves. However, I do believe that Vellix has a similar power."

"What makes you think that?" Conner asked.

"It seems like he has done something unnatural to the land around Mt. Cirrus. I get an ominous feeling when I look toward it." Medwin pointed at the tallest peak of a great mountain range to the north.

"Yeah," Conner agreed, looking toward the towering mountain, "I felt weird when I looked at the mountains as we were leaving the forest." He paused for a moment, his eyes lingering on the clouds that spiraled around the mountain's sharp peak. "So, if the Satria are the only ones who can do cognition ... then why do you think I was able to?"

"You ask mindful questions, Conner... My father has always told me: 'the clear path to knowledge is in our questions...' Anyway, all I can say is that I'm not the one to tell you."

Conner gave him a confused look. "Well, if you're not the one to tell me — who is?"

"I am taking you to see Vivek. He is a man of great wisdom."

"So you already knew there was something ... special about me?" Conner mumbled, feeling like the jigsaw puzzle of thoughts in his mind was finally starting to form a vague picture. "And that's why you're taking me on this journey?"

"Yes," Medwin replied, "that is why."

"When your dad said my name, he made it sound like it was ... significant," said Conner, hoping that he didn't sound like an idiot for thinking this. "Why is that?"

Medwin let out a satisfied little laugh. "You are sharp, Conner. You'll have the answers to your questions soon enough. Vivek will answer them far better than I can."

The day seemed to be passing quickly. Both boys were thinking deeply. Conner was curious and a little nervous about meeting Vivek. Was he truly special? Or was the river incident just a freak occurrence? A memory flashed across his mind: the imprinted image of Chris' face on the note. Could it be that he had already done cognition before arriving in Rohwen? If so, what did it mean? Absorbed in thought, he barely noticed he was walking.

His mind snapped back to reality when Medwin took off running without any warning. "Hey, wait — where are you going?" he yelled as Medwin disappeared into a small knot of trees *"Medwin — wait!"* he yelled louder still, but Medwin didn't respond. Conner ran over to the cluster of trees Medwin had disappeared behind and searched frantically for any sign of him but saw nothing other than trees and bushes.

He sat down, feeling completely deflated. Had Medwin just abandoned him? Why would he? He had been so friendly, taught him so much about this place. Was this some kind of sick joke? Had following Medwin so willingly been a mistake? 'You didn't really have any other choice but to follow him,' Conner reminded himself. What would he do now? 'Keep heading the way you have been,' he told himself. 'At least then you're not going straight back where you came from —'

'No,' said another voice tersely. 'You need to go back. Home is somewhere that way.' He gave an automatic glance back in the direction that he and Medwin had come. Again, he found himself contemplating whether he would ever be able to find his way home. The thought was truly depressing. At the very least, by the time he did get home, he would have been gone for so long that he would be indefinitely grounded — in fact, his mom was probably already so worried that she had called the police. Images began to form in his mind: a team of police with dogs searching the forest behind his house, followed by a picture of his dad consoling his sobbing mother, followed by a picture of his face on missing child ads at all the local supermarkets. His stomach squirmed with sickness and guilt, and his eyes started to burn as tears filled his eyelids. Why hadn't he attempted to find his way home while he was still in the general vicinity of the porthole, or gateway, or whatever it was that had transported him to Rohwen.

Just when he started to wish he had never ended up in Rohwen at all, he saw the silhouette of someone in the darkening distance, walking toward him and holding something in one hand.

As the figure came closer, Conner realized it was Medwin. His mind sighed in relief.

Soon, Medwin was within earshot; Conner quickly wiped the tears from his eyes and called out, "What's that you've got?"

Medwin held it up and said, "Dinner."

Conner could barely make out what it was in the dim evening light: a pheasant. "Oh, that's why you went running off." He felt slightly ashamed that he was so quick to assume Medwin had abandoned him and decided to keep the thoughts he'd had to himself.

"Sorry for running off like that," Medwin admitted as he gathered firewood. "It's just that I couldn't pass up an opportunity for food. If I had stopped to tell you what I was doing, the pheasant would've gotten away.

Conner nodded. "Don't worry about it," he said, now feeling

thoroughly ashamed.

Medwin returned Conner's nod and continued. "Tomorrow we will reach the Cliffs of Elders. We're going to need the energy."

"…Can I ask you something?" Conner queried, sounding as unsure about the question he wanted to ask as he felt.

"Of course," Medwin replied in a tone that clearly stated he was aware of Conner's discomfort.

Conner made a gesture of thanks before asking his question. "Would you be willing to help me find my way home?" Medwin was about to respond, but Conner continued before he had the chance. "You see, I don't really know how I'm gonna find my way back, and my parents are probably worried sick by now."

Medwin looked as if he had been expecting this topic to arise sooner or later. "I can definitely try," he said, his tone of voice accurately portrayed his feelings on the matter. "Do you remember anything about the area where you arrived?" he continued, making it clear that he had absolutely no idea where to start looking.

"Well, at first I was in the forest behind my house… And then I was in a massive field, and I could see your forest in the distance. In fact, I was close enough to your forest to pick up the faint sound of music, which is why I ended up there in the first place."

Medwin's expression relaxed. "If that's the case, it shouldn't be too much trouble. I'm sure between the two of us we will find it."

Conner's expression relaxed as well. "Good, because as much as I'm curious about why I was able to do that cognation thing…"

"…Cognition…"

"Right. As much as I'm curious about why I was able to do

cognition, I would really like to go home before I end up being grounded for the rest of my life."

Medwin gave Conner a puzzled look before responding. "I understand that you want to go home to your mother and father, but I cannot help you find your way home until after I have taken you to Vivek."

"What? Why?" Conner felt his temper begin to rise as he glared at Medwin, who remained calm and collected.

"Because I made a promise to my father." Medwin responded tersely. "I will not let him down. You will understand in due time, but for now, you are going to have to trust me."

Conner looked Medwin in the eye. As upset as he was, he couldn't help but notice the conviction in Medwin's gaze. "How long will it take?"

"Give me a week."

"A week! My mom is going to kill me!"

"Please trust me. You will understand the importance of all this in due time."

Feeling defeated, Conner nodded.

* * *

The next morning Conner awoke feeling less than rested. He had endured a nearly sleepless night, due to the fact that every time he closed his eyes, all he could see were images his of mom crying on his dad's shoulder. Even though it had been a night of troubling thoughts and images, he was able to find positive elements in it. He had reached a point of realization and acceptance in his situation: he was lost in a world he knew nothing about… The best thing he could do was take things one step at a time. There was no way for him to change the facts or make the rules. If he ever wanted to see his parents again, he would have to follow Medwin's lead.

After eating the last of their pheasant dinner, the two boys put out the smoldering embers of their fire and continued heading south.

They'd only been traveling a few hours when the wind started to pick up, carrying with it the smell of fresh sea air. Gusts of thirty-plus miles-per-hour rattled through Conner's bones. "Are we near the Cliffs of Elders now?" he asked, nearly having to yell over the roaring wind.

"Noticed the wind picking up, did you?"

"Yeah," Conner replied. "And the smell of sea air."

"We are very close now," Medwin said, grinning.

"Why are they called the Cliffs of Elders anyway?" Conner inquired as he took note that Medwin seemed to be in good spirits considering the conversation they'd had the night before. After a moment's contemplation, he concluded that Medwin had probably been expecting to have that conversation eventually and was happy to have it behind him.

"The cliffs were made by the Satria Elders," Medwin said. "My people," he added with a hint of pride in his voice. "Using cognition, they created the deadly cliffs for the purpose of initiating boys into manhood.

Conner tilted his head quizzically.

Medwin smiled at his obvious curiosity. "They take you down to the bottom on the eve of your thirteenth birthday and leave you there with only a pack of essentials — like the one I've got right now — and until you climb back up, you're not considered a man by the rest of the tribe."

"So you've already done it," said Conner, sounding impressed.

"Yes," Medwin answered seriously. "It was grueling. It took every ounce of willpower I had. It was there, at the bottom of the cliffs, that I made Lenny's acquaintance."

Conner started to worry. If it was that difficult to climb up the cliffs, would he even be able to make it down them?

Medwin seemed to notice his worries and said, "My cognition is good enough to make a crude staircase down the cliff-side."

"Oh, good," Conner replied, barely covering his tone of relief.

As they carried on walking, the smell of sea air continued to grow stronger until the ocean came into view. A stunning shade of sapphire-blue, accented by sparkles of reflected light that glistened under the sun's watchful eye, made the water dazzling.

'Wow,' Conner thought as he gazed out upon the vast body of water that stretched much farther than he could see. In the distance, he saw the faded outlines of several islands, one of which he assumed must be Rhona.

From the height of the cliffs, Conner could see the shadows of a coral reef under the water. Massive ships were anchored along a harbor that belonged to an expansive coastal city. They looked as if they'd been built in the sixteenth or seventeenth century.

"This is amazing!" Conner exclaimed.

Medwin nodded in acknowledgment, his expression amused.

Conner looked back out to sea and took a huge gulp of fresh air with great appreciation. From the corner of his eye, he saw that Medwin looked deep in concentration. A moment later, crude, yet effective stairs started to carve their way into the side of the cliff, forcing thousands of chunks of rock to shower down into the ocean below. Medwin took the lead, stepping carefully down the stairs.

Conner followed close behind, and as the sounds of rocks splashing into the ocean met his ears, he made the mistake of looking straight down the cliff-face. It was with an unpleasant shock, which seemed to force his stomach right into his throat, that he realized there was only a short piece of sandy shore below them. The rest of the cliffs descended straight into an ocean scattered heavily with boulders. Waves pounded relentlessly through the huge rocks, crashing into their rugged surfaces in an endless effort to make them smooth.

Deciding it was in his best interest not to look down again, Conner tried to make conversation, hoping it would be enough to take his mind off thoughts of plummeting hundreds of feet to his death. *"Medwin."* He had to yell in order to project his voice over the combined sounds of wind and waves.

"Yeah?" Medwin called back.

"Won't these stairs ruin the initiation process for the next boys to become men?"

"No, once I stop focusing on them they will disappear."

"Oh, I see… Well does that mean the elders are constantly focused on the cliffs? You know — so they won't disappear?"

"Again with the great questions!" Medwin laughed. *"No, their cognition is so strong that they were able to make these cliffs*

permanent."

'Cool,' Conner thought, running his hand along the face of the cliff.

They were most of the way down the malformed staircase now. Medwin looked like he was getting ready to say something else when he stepped on a loose rock. He slipped and hit his head hard on the cliff-face, knocking himself out instantly. His concentration was broken and the stairs ceased to exist.

Conner had realized this would happen just in time to stick his feet under the strap of Medwin's pack and grab a large root that was protruding from the cliff. It was agony trying to hold up his and Medwin's combined weights. The strain it put on his already sore body was almost more than he could stand. 'I need the staircase back!' he thought, trying to picture what the stairs had looked like with all his might. 'Please! I need the staircase back! *I need the staircase! I need —*'

To his astonishment, and great relief, the stairs re-formed underneath them. He sat down and tried to catch his breath. "Medwin!" he yelled, slapping him hard across his face. He wasn't sure how long he'd be able to keep the stairs in existence. "*Medwin!*" He slapped him again. Still nothing. Feeling frantic, he began dragging Medwin's limp body down the steps.

After a few agonizingly long minutes, Medwin opened his eyes; they were glossy and unfocused. "What are you doing?" he asked, gazing at Conner curiously, completely unaware of the situation. "What happened?"

"You slipped and hit your head on the cliff."

Medwin moved his hand unthinkingly to the spot where his head had started bleeding as Conner told him about his injury.

"I couldn't get you to wake up, so I was dragging you down the stairs. Speaking of which, can you take over keeping the stairs in existence? I'm not sure how much longer I can do it."

Medwin almost jumped out of his skin as he realized they were still nearly one hundred feet up above the boulder-strewn ocean below. "Right," he answered quickly. His expression became serious. "Okay, you can stop. I've got it."

Conner sighed appreciatively as he allowed the stress of keeping the stairs in existence to leave his mind.

"Wow, Conner!" Medwin exclaimed as he made his way down the steps. "You were able to re-create my stairs! That's amazing!" His expression changed and became solemn. "You saved my life…"

"Well … yeah, I guess I did," Conner said, trying to sound as though it wasn't a big deal. He didn't really know Medwin's customs when it came to something like saving someone's life, but he knew he didn't want Medwin doing anything irrational in order to repay his debt. To Conner's relief, Medwin said thanks and seemed to put the moment behind him.

The two of them continued cautiously down the stairs, and, feeling like their bond of friendship had just become twice as strong, they reached the sandy shore bordering the cutthroat city known as Beach Bay.

CHAPTER 6

A Proposition

"Hey! Stop! Thief! Come back!"

"Nicked it fair an' square, didn' I?" Lenny gloated as he ran merrily away from the old shopkeeper who sold produce in Beach Bay.

"Lenny, you'll ge' wha's coming ter yeh one of these days!" yelled the shopkeeper, but by then Lenny was long out of earshot, eating his apple at a ravenous pace. 'Lot o' work fer a bite these days,' he thought with a small chuckle.

Lenny was a ruggedly handsome sixteen-year-old orphan who had spent his whole life fending for himself and doing as he pleased. He was tall, lanky, and had dark eyes, which held more truth of his past than he would've liked. His dirty blond hair poked out from his head like bits of straw, and there was a general look of lacking hygiene about him.

Sailing with Captain Bellamy and crew was his favorite pastime. 'They're not really pirates after all,' he would tell himself. 'More like — bounty hunters.' Captain Bellamy needed young muscle like him, and Lenny needed the money. The excitement of the high seas didn't hurt either. It was a month ago last time he'd been out to sea, and he could hardly wait for his next chance to set sail.

He finished his apple, threw the core and, as he set to work on a new one, he thought he saw… "Medwin!" he yelled with delight, but Medwin didn't seem to hear him. "Oi, Medwin!" he bellowed at the top of his lungs.

This time, Medwin looked over and noticed who was calling his name. "Lenny, how are you? Well, I hope."

"Wel' 'nuf," Lenny spluttered through a fresh bite of apple as he came to rest in front of Medwin. "An' oo's this?" he probed, gesturing toward Conner, his expression becoming increasingly amused the longer he took in the sight of him.

"Oh, right," Medwin said, "this is my friend Conner." He placed a hand on Conner's shoulder as he introduced him.

"Strange enough clothes then," Lenny laughed, surveying Conner again, baffled by his jeans, t-shirt, and tennis shoes. "No matter," he added quickly with a carefree wave of his hand, seeing that neither of them was laughing along with him. "Any friend o' Medwin's is a friend o' mine! Saved me life 'e did! Surrounded by three big blokes, wasn' I? Come runnin' at 'em with a hatchet 'e did, screamin' like a banshee!" Lenny burst back into laughter, spraying Medwin and Conner with small partly chewed chunks of apple. "So, what brings yeh ter Beach Bay?" He looked at Medwin curiously.

"I was actually going to try and find you," said Medwin as he wiped the chunks of apple from his face in disgust.

"Yeh came 'ere … ter find me?" Lenny seemed slightly bewildered, but he took no notice of Medwin's revulsion at being dowsed in pieces of his partially chewed food.

"I was hoping you would point us in the direction of a crew that could get us to Rhona and back," Medwin told him, his tone of voice carrying as much dignity as he felt he had left. "Maybe we could even sail with you — if you're currently on a crew that is…"

Lenny paused for a moment before saying, "'Course I'm 'currently' on a bleedin' crew! Now, as far as gettin' yeh ter Rhona 'n' back… Well, I'd 'ave ter ask Cap'n Bellamy, wouldn' I?"

"Captain Bellamy and his crew will be rewarded handsomely for safe passage there and back," Medwin said confidently.

Lenny glanced at him skeptically, then down at the ground, as if contemplating what he should do.

"The Satria are a wealthy tribe, and I am the chief's son," Medwin assured him. "You *will* be rewarded for safe passage to Rhona and back."

"Well come on then!" Lenny exclaimed, making it quite clear that no further persuasion was necessary. "We'll go an' see 'im righ' now."

They started down the dusty street, Lenny leading the way.

"I didn't think he would be able to pass up an easy opportunity for gold," Medwin whispered so that only Conner could hear him.

The putrid smells of souring food and rotting corpses invaded the once fresh sea air as they made their way deeper into the city. Loud cries of laughter mingled with those of pain and caused the hairs on the back of Conner's neck to stand on end. Occasional gunshots would rent the air, always followed by a chorus of women's high-pitched screams.

"Are you sure about this guy?" Conner whispered back, after yet another succession of gunshots filled his ears to bursting. "This place is" — he looked around — "these people are horrible… How do you know we can trust him?"

"We can trust him," Medwin said without hesitation. "He owes me his life. He might be a bit rough around the edges, but he still lives by a sailor's code."

"Well, if you trust him," Conner replied quietly, "then that's good enough for me." He continued to glance fearfully at his surroundings, pleading internally with the unknown inhabitants of this city to keep to themselves long enough for him to pass through.

They turned a corner and entered a street lined with small shops. Merchants waited eagerly to urge passersby to purchase their goods.

"You lad!" one of them hollered to Medwin. "You look as though you could do with some clothes… Yeh won' find no bet'er tailor in town!" He bustled over to Medwin, held a shirt up to his midsection to show him how good a fit it was, and raised his eyebrows hopefully.

"I'm fine, thanks," Medwin said, quickening his pace to escape the man.

A man selling an assortment of glistening necklaces and rings said, "Give 'er summat wha' shines an' I guarantee she'll be yours!" He gave them a sleazy little grin and winked.

Conner ignored the man and kept walking.

"Ah, come now!" he yelled as they passed. "Don' tell me yeh ain' go' a pret'y little thing yeh wan' ter impress! Me prices are fair mates, me prices are fair!"

A small grouping of tables laden with produce was up ahead. Lenny slowed his pace. "This way mates," he said, glancing cautiously at the shopkeeper before turning down a small alley.

Conner let Medwin enter the alley first, then entered himself. Within a minute, the smell of urine had become more than he could stand. He pulled his shirt over his mouth and nose to try concealing it. Conner figured Lenny must be used to the rancid smell, but he wondered how Medwin was able to stand it.

They came upon an apparent dead end. Lenny pulled a stack of boxes away from the wall to reveal a crawlspace. He entered the tunnel and crawled out of sight.

Medwin looked at Conner and shrugged before he, too, entered the crawlspace.

Conner watched as Medwin disappeared. He got down to follow, but before he could enter the tunnel, someone grabbed his leg and yanked him back. He turned to find two filthy boys standing over him.

"We'll be 'avin' yer clothes, mate," said the older of the two, punching at his own hand to warn Conner that he'd be beaten if he tried to resist.

"Medwin!" Conner cried out as the two boys advanced on him. "Help!"

"Wha's the mat'er?" goaded the younger boy. "Can'cha take care o' yerself?" He pulled a knife from his pocket. "Jus' give us yer clothes, an' we don' 'urt yeh. Easy as tha', mate."

"John! Gordon!" Lenny came bursting out of the crawl space, Medwin right behind him, "I'll beat yeh senseless!"

The two boys stepped away from Lenny, looking scared. "W-we didn' know 'e was with you, Lenny!" they said pleadingly.

"Wha' are yeh even doin' working this part of the town?" Lenny interrogated. "I wonder wha' Thatcher'd 'ave ter say if 'e knew the two o' yeh was trying ter leave 'im ou' o' the cut?"

The younger boy was frightened beyond words. He just gaped at

Lenny, waiting for what would happen next. But the older of the two found his voice. "We wasn' tryin' ter keep ol' Thatcher ou' o' the cut. We jus' wanted this bloke's clothes" — he tilted his head toward Conner — "an' tha's all."

Lenny didn't reply at first. Instead, he surveyed Conner's clothes, and for one awful moment, Conner thought he might actually be contemplating whether he should let these boys have them. Then he said, "Why the 'ell would yeh wan' this blokes clothes…? Now, get out o' 'ere!" he snarled. "Go on, get! An' 'urry up abou' it 'afore I change me mind an' thrash yeh instead!"

The two boys ran away as fast as they could, tripping over each other as they went.

"Bloody idiots," Lenny said as he watched them go.

"Thanks a lot!" said Conner.

"Don' mention it, mate," Lenny replied, smirking. "Le's go."

They exited the crawlspace into another section of alley. Lenny led them out to a larger street. "No' much farther now," he said as he turned a corner to his left.

It wasn't long before the harbor came into view. Conner couldn't help but smile. Anchored closest to them was a ship with the name 'Colossus' engraved in gold letters across the back. He stopped to study the ship in further detail. Medwin stopped as well.

"Beau'iful ain' she," Lenny said as he noticed that Conner and Medwin were both ogling the ship. "She's nearly one 'undred and fifty feet from bow-ta-stern" — he made an expansive gesture with his arms — "an' 'er main mast is at leas' seventy feet tall. She's the bigges' ship ter sail these waters." He scanned the upper deck for a moment.

Conner did the same, wondering what he was looking at, and noticed that there didn't appear to be anyone there. "It doesn't look like there's anyone aboard."

"All at Osman's, I'd wager," Lenny said, more to himself than as a response to Conner. He turned away from the ship and started down the harbor.

They came upon a run-down building close to the shore. The planks of wood that stretched the small building's perimeter were so faded that it looked as though someone had purposely stripped them of color. Dark rust streaked below each nail that held the boards in place. A weathered sign, swinging atop the door, which appeared to be closer to falling off of the building than hanging on, had the words 'Osman's Pub' scrawled across it.

Two burly men came bursting out of the front door like a hurricane, followed closely by another man, who appeared to be enjoying himself thoroughly. The two burly men exchanged heavy blow after heavy blow, beating each other senseless. Finally, one of them started to back off. The other man got right up in his opponent's battered face and spat, "Yeh'll pay Ammin what 'e's owed or I'll run yeh through! Yeh piece o' filth!"

"I'd like ter see yeh try, Bellamy! Ever since you been voted cap'n of *the Colossus* you been actin' like you can run this city an' all!"

It happened in a flash. Bellamy's sword was drawn. The other man fell to the ground, his body jerking convulsively. Then, with a final twitch, he lay still.

Bellamy sheathed his sword, reached into the man's pocket, and pulled out a bag that jingled. "'Ere, Ammin, catch."

The man who had watched the fight reached up and snatched the bag out of the air with great agility. "Fool," he said, looking down at the corpse.

"Cap'n!" Lenny yelled from the short distance he had kept during the fight.

Bellamy turned and saw Lenny. "Lenny m'boy!" he thundered, looking jolly. You never would have guessed that he had just killed a man without showing a single ounce of remorse. "Where you been, lad?" he asked, maintaining his jolly tones.

"'Ere an' there," Lenny replied with a casual shrug. "Go' a proposition fer yeh, Cap'n."

"Oh?" Bellamy roared as he strode toward the three boys.

Now that he was getting closer, Conner began to take in the captain's appearance. His hair and beard lived together in tangled harmony. There was a dirty hat perched upon his head. His old brown coat had a patch on one elbow and covered the majority of a dingy shirt, which seemed like it hadn't ever been washed. A musket-style pistol was stored in the large belt around his waist. He wore shoddy old boots, and his pants had holes in the knees. Overall, it looked as though a new set of clothes wouldn't hurt him.

"So, you got a proposition fer me, eh?" the captain queried. "Le's 'ear it then."

"Me mate, Medwin, 'ere says if we get 'im an' 'is mate, Conner, to Rhona an' back safely, we'll be rewarded handsome-like."

Bellamy eyed Conner and Medwin, scratching thoughtfully at his beard, an unquestionable air of doubt about him.

"Medwin's the son o' the Satria tribe's chief," Lenny said, as if hoping this information would remove some of his captain's visible uncertainty. "They're a very wealthy tribe," he went on, appearing pleased with himself for knowing such an important person.

"Is that so? An' 'ow long we gonna 'ave ter wait offshore fer yeh?" Bellamy asked, now staring down at Conner and Medwin with a raised eyebrow.

Conner found courage from somewhere and spoke up. "As long as it takes for me to ask Vivek some questions."

"Oh, an' 'e's a brave lad!" Bellamy roared enthusiastically, smacking Conner on the back. "Knows 'ow ter speak fer 'imself! An' 'oo's Vivek?"

Conner ignored this question. Still startled by his own confidence, but pleased with Bellamy's reaction, he said, "So are you in? I see that there are a few other ships in this harbor."

"Arrr! My type o' lad 'e is!" Bellamy laughed. "Ammin, round up the crew! We're settin' sail!"

Lenny couldn't have looked more pleased. The prospect of setting sail, knowing gold was a guaranteed bonus, had obviously upped his spirits tremendously.

Ammin ran into the pub. Soon the crew came clambering out. There was a general murmur of excitement among them, with things like, "Arrr! Settin' sail 'e says," becoming audible as they got closer.

Captain Bellamy addressed them all, his voice booming it's loudest yet. "We're settin' sail fer the Island of Rhona! These lads" — he waved a huge hand in the direction of Conner and Medwin — "are comin' with us."

A few of the sailors were about to speak out in protest, but Bellamy interrupted, "If yeh wan' yer cut o' the loot, an' yeh don' fancy yer neck meetin' the end o' a rope, you'll keep yer mouths shut!" After a short pause — within which he seemed to be waiting for anyone who was foolish enough to continue griping about the terms of their mission to speak up — he called over to the ship, "Grayson! Roland! Ahoy there!"

"Ahoy!" the two sailors called back.

"Apparently, there's at least a couple people aboard," Medwin said to Conner in a low voice.

"Probably to make sure no one gets idea of trying to steal the ship," Conner replied, keeping his voice low as well.

"Lower the gangplank!" Bellamy yelled.

"Or for that…" Medwin chortled.

"Or for that," Conner echoed, laughing as well.

Grayson and Roland lowered the gangplank. Bellamy and his crew boarded the ship, Conner and Medwin in their wake.

CHAPTER 7

Set Sail for Rhona

On board, Captain Bellamy seemed to be truly in his element, barking orders to the crew. "Weigh anchors! Get to the fo'c's'le, Skylar! Check 'n' see we ain't headin' fer a high spot in the reef, or this'll be a righ' short trip! Man the halyards and lower the sails, yeh swabs! Tigh'n the bowline!"

Conner could hardly believe the skill of the sailors as he watched them scramble to obey their captain's orders. The way they worked as a team was nearly perfect. Every man helped the next, making them unbelievably efficient. They treated each command with the same urgency as the last and appeared to be incapable of fatigue.

It quickly became obvious that Ammin was Bellamy's first mate. He was running around, leading the men as they performed their duties. Conner thought he must have been born on a ship. He couldn't imagine how else the man could have become such a proficient sailor.

Soon they were underway and gaining a considerable amount of speed. Medwin moved to the port side of the ship and leaned over the railing to look at the ocean below.

Conner went to join him, and as the spray of the sea flecked across his face, he realized how alive he felt: more so than ever before in his life. The way the ship moved with the ocean and the smell of salty air around him — it was indescribably exhilarating. For the first time in days, he wasn't worried about finding his way home; he wasn't concerned with why he was special in a world he hadn't even known existed. He was free.

A group of dolphins chased the ship out of the bay, as if they were kids trying to keep up with a relative who was leaving after a visit. They launched out of the water, and plunged back into its depths in perfectly timed motions.

"Look!" Conner suggested, pointing down at the dolphins with excitement.

Medwin nodded and smiled. He looked like he was having the time of his life. "Isn't this great?" he was saying happily when Lenny came over, wiping sweat off his brow.

"It's alrigh' fer you two!" he said, making a flippant gesture as he quirked his lips into a wry grin. "Enjoyin' the bloody view!"

"I can help," Conner said, not really sure if he could.

Lenny laughed menacingly. "Shouldn' 'ave said tha', mate!" He ran off to help a group of his shipmates with something, leaving Conner facing a man who was mopping the deck with unnecessary aggression.

The man thrust his mop into a bucket next to him and turned to Conner. "Yeh wan' ter help, boy?" he spat. "Then swab the deck! Go on then" — he extended the mop handle toward Conner — "take it! I shouldn' be bloody doin' it in the firs' place."

Conner took the mop and watched as the man stalked off, his eyes fixed on Ammin with a contemptuous glare.

"We can take turns if you want," Medwin said.

Conner nodded and got to work. It was a tedious and rather

disgusting job, but Conner didn't really mind. It made him feel like he was pulling his weight.

Eventually, Medwin gestured for Conner to give him the mop. "You've been at it for a while," he said. "You deserve a break."

"Thanks." Conner replied as he handed the mop over to Medwin. He went and leaned against the mainmast to take some of the weight off his feet. A few sailors speaking with concern in their voices grabbed his attention.

"Bloody 'ope she don' come after us…"

"Tha's just it though, in'it? Never know when she'll attack…"

"Ah, shut it, yeh superstitious prats!"

"Oh, an' I suppose you'd know all abou' it eh, Jonny? Been sailin' fer wha'? Three months now?"

"Dale, you know damn well it's been at least six," grumbled the man named Jonny.

"We ough' ter be more respectful like, Dale! Jonny 'ere's go' some *real experience!*"

"Aye, Landon! Yeh go' a poin'! 'E's a bleedin' veteran, tha' one!" Dale and Landon broke into exaggeratedly cruel laughter.

Jonny scowled at them furiously and stormed off.

Full of interest, Conner walked over to the two sailors and asked, "Sorry, sirs, but I can't help but wonder —"

"Oi, Dale, di'ja 'ere tha'?" Landon piped up, cutting Conner's question short. "Bleedin' 'sirs,' we are!" he exclaimed, looking over at Dale and trying to hold a wide-eyed expression of seriousness.

"Bloody 'ell, Landon!" said Dale in a tone to match Landon's expression. "An' on a ship wha's crewed by a bunch o' lowdown, good fer nothin', cutthroat sailors! We musta go' on the wrong boat! Bless me, I 'ope no one spo's us!"

"In our finest linens an' all," said Landon, whose voice broke and turned to fits of laughter as he pulled a few tattered folds of his filthy shirt away from his chest to survey them.

"Aye, mate!" Dale replied, roaring with laughter alongside him.

Conner was undeterred by Dale and Landon's jokes. In fact, it was quite the contrary. He had actually forgotten that they were making fun of the fact he had called them "sirs" and had started laughing with them.

Dale noticed that Conner was still standing there as he wiped the last of the tears from his eyes. "An' wha' was it yeh wanted ter know, mate?"

Conner tried to remember what it was he had wanted to ask. At first, the question seemed to elude him, but then the sailor named Jonny walked by, giving Dale and Landon disgusted looks, and the question re-surfaced. "When you say *'she'll attack,'* what is that supposed to mean? Who's *she*?"

Dale — the sailor closest to Conner — gave him a dark and meaningful look before saying, "The *'she'* tha' I'm referrin' to is Elandra."

"Sorry — but — who's Elandra?" Conner asked, still none the wiser.

"Elandra's a bloody sea dragon wha's been terrorizing these waters fer hundreds o' years! Sinkin' ships 'cause she don' think we got the righ' ter be out 'ere…" Dale told him. "Or maybe jus' fer fun. No one really knows fer sure."

Landon chimed in. "Bellamy was firs' mate on a war ship called *the Expeditious*, wha' got attacked by 'er 'afore 'e became cap'n o' *the Colossus*. Said she was bleedin' massive, 'e did!" Landon exclaimed dramatically. "Sank *the Expeditious* with no trouble at all. 'E told us 'ow she done it an' all. Reared up an' took out the masts first. Wanted ter disable the ship's movements I reckon. Af'er tha', she rammed the hull 'til the bloody *Expeditious* wen' down ter the depths! Most o' the crew with it! Bellamy survived o' course... 'E's bloomin' primeval 'e is."

"Hey, Conner — you think you could take over for a bit?" Medwin called out from somewhere behind him. "Yeah, sure," he called back. Dale and Landon gave him a nod and he left to relieve Medwin. But as soon as he grabbed the mop, Captain Bellamy hollered from up on the bridge.

"Oi! You lads!"

Conner and Medwin pointed at themselves, neither of them entirely sure if they were the ones the captain was addressing.

"Yeah, you lads! Take the mop and bucket down ter the hold an' come see me in me cabin."

Conner followed Medwin as he made his way down to the hold. The story about Elandra had shaken him, and fear now overshadowed his elated feelings of being out to sea.

Medwin approached a few sailors who were arguing over a glass bottle containing an amber liquid.

"You've 'ad yer three bumps already, Gavin!"

"Like 'ell I 'ave, James!"

"Oi, Quincy, yeh'll ge' yer pull in a sec, so shove off!"

"Where should we put these?" Medwin asked, holding up the bucket in his hand and tilting his head toward the mop Conner was holding.

The three men gestured to the corner of the room and went back to bickering over the bottle.

Medwin nodded his thanks to the men and went to set down the bucket. Conner followed, leaned the mop against the wall, and headed back for the stairs. Before he reached the top, he heard the unmistakable sound of breaking glass followed by the chorused moan of, "Bloody 'ell!"

Back up on the main deck, Conner saw Lenny scaling the mainmast with amazing speed in order to fasten a rope onto something. As Conner's eyes followed him up, the full size of the ship really sank in. The three towering masts and their many massive sails — full to the brim with wind — were truly a sight to see.

"You coming?" Medwin called from the foot of several steps leading to the ship's bridge.

"What? ...Oh, yeah," Conner replied distantly.

"It's amazing isn't it?" Medwin said, looking up at the same view Conner had been appreciating moments ago.

"It is."

* * *

"Come in," Bellamy yelled as a knock sounded from the heavy oak doors of his cabin.

Medwin pushed the door open just a crack at first, clearly feeling timid about entering the captain's quarters.

"Well?" Bellamy grumbled impatiently. "Yeh gonna come in or jus' stand ou' there an' peek in on me like a snoopin' prat?"

Medwin blushed with embarrassment and hastily pushed the door open the rest of the way, allowing a beam of sunlight to find its way into the dimly lit cabin. Conner trailed behind Medwin as he entered the room.

"Close the door and sit," Bellamy instructed them, gesturing the compass he was holding toward a few chairs on the opposite side of the well-polished mahogany desk he was sitting behind.

Conner's eyes wandered the room. Six thin windows, separated only by handsomely carved lengths of wooded trim, lined the back wall, providing enough natural light for Bellamy to see the charts and maps that littered his desk. Candles, burning in their elegantly wrought brass holders, lit the rest of the cabin just enough that Conner was able to see the few things the captain had hung on the walls: two sabers crossing over each other and a painting of a beautiful ship in the midst of a vicious storm.

"So," Bellamy said, setting his compass down upon a map that lay atop the many other sheets of parchment on the desk, "I'll start by sayin' this: I go' a lo' o' faith in every man in me crew; Lenny's no exception…"

Conner had no idea what to make of the captain's opening statement, but he got the feeling that something wasn't altogether friendly about it. He gave Medwin a quick glance and saw that he looked like he was straining to keep his expression indifferent.

"But," Bellamy went on, "I'll need ter see wha' kind o' payment yeh think be worthy o' me time before I go waitin' fer yeh off the coast o' Rhona. I go' a good plen'y o' other things I could be doin'.'"

Medwin nodded and began to dig through the contents of his pack.

"I didn' ask yeh in front o' the crew," the captain said, watching Medwin with a greedy eye, "'cause if they knew yeh had any kind o' loot — well — le's jus' say it would be a hazard to yer health," he finished, cackling with laughter.

"I understand," Medwin replied as he placed a sizable bar of gold on the desk in front of Bellamy.

The captain's eyes widened as he grabbed the gold and rotated it in his hands to inspect its quality. "This is pure, this is!" he exclaimed, holding the gold up to a window. "Probably weighs... Blimey, probably weighs at least five pounds! This is worth a bloody" — he rotated the bar again — "well I'm no' exactly sure wha' it's worth — bu' it's a bloody lot!"

Medwin nodded again, his lips hinting at a smirk. "I thought you might find the payment to be quite sufficient."

"Aye, lad." Bellamy placed the gold back on his desk. Conner watched as Medwin grabbed it and stuffed it back into the depths of his pack.

"Now," Bellamy said, "there's the mat'er o' 'ow long yeh wan' me ter wai' fer yeh off shore. I go' plen'y o' provisions aboard, so tha' ain' gonna be an issue."

"Well, we —"

"Importan' thing is," Bellamy went on, as if Medwin hadn't started to reply, "tha' I don' know wha' the 'ell yer up to on the island. Said summat abou' talkin' ter some guy. Far as I knew, the place was uninhabited — 'cept fer the animals. Don' know 'ow yeh go' ter thinkin' someone lives ou' there… Anyways" — he waved his hands, as if to discard what he was saying — "the poin' is, I go' no way o' knowin' if yer still alive ou' there."

"I see what you mean," Medwin said.

Conner felt fear crawling up inside his chest. 'Still alive,' he thought nervously.

"So 'eres what I'll do," Bellamy said. "I'll wait a week fer yeh. If yer no' back by then, I'll jus' assume yer dead an' leave. Tha' bein' said, I think it best if yeh leave the gold with me. 'Ell, if yeh die out there, you won' be needin' it." The captain started to cackle with laughter again.

Medwin didn't reply. He moved a hand reluctantly toward his pack.

"Don't worry, lad," Bellamy reassured him. "You got my word. I won' cheat yeh."

"I suppose it does make sense for me to leave it with you," Medwin agreed. "That way, in the event that something does happen to us, you and your crew will still get paid for your services."

"There's a good lad!" Bellamy thundered as Medwin handed him the bar of gold. The captain pulled a necklace from around his neck; dangling at the end was an iron key. He moved across the room to a small chest, slotted the key into its lock, and gave it a turn. Conner heard a metallic click as the mechanism within the chest broke free. Bellamy moved into a position that would restrict Conner and Medwin's view of the chest as he opened the lid and stowed the gold safely within. He quickly closed the lid and gave the key another turn. The mechanism locked with a satisfyingly loud clack.

Bellamy put the necklace back around his neck and stuffed the key under his shirt as he walked back to his chair. He sat down and picked his compass back up.

Conner's gaze fell instinctually to the place on the map where the compass had been lying. He saw a mass of land with smaller islands off its coast. In the surrounding ocean, there were dozens of arrows pointing in different directions — some were solid lines, while others consisted of many dots. He briefly wondered what the arrows represented before his eyes moved to the map's heading. It read: Rohwen — ocean currents and routes.

Conner quickly realized what the lines represented as he read the heading. He was curious to know which arrows where currents and which ones were routes, but he didn't want to bug the captain with silly questions, so he decided not to voice his curiosity.

"Is there summat you were wantin' ter say, lad?" Bellamy asked, looking up at Conner. Apparently, he had read Conner's expression of interest in the map.

"I was just wondering," Conner began, figuring he might as well ask his question now that he knew the captain had obviously noticed he had one, "which lines represent the currents and —"

"Which ones represen' the routes?" Bellamy said, finishing Conner's question.

Conner nodded. Bellamy grinned broadly, and Conner got the distinct impression that the captain was pleased to see someone show interest in the thing in which he was the most passionate.

"The solid lines are the currents," Bellamy said. "Nearly every current marked on this map I've discovered meself," he added proudly.

Conner felt the magnitude of how much time Bellamy must have spent sailing as he stared down at the many solid-lined arrows. "So the dotted lines are the routes then?"

"Aye, lad. Notice tha' some poin' ter the different mouths of rivers?"

Conner nodded again.

"Those are trade routes, those are. I ain' no merchan', an' *the Colossus* ain' no merchan' ship, but she can carry a righ' good amoun' o' cargo if I wan' 'er to. When I'm 'ard up, it can be worth making a trade voyage or two."

Conner continued to study the map until Bellamy told him and Medwin that he had a few things to tend to and wished to be left alone. As they were exiting the cabin, Bellamy said quickly, "'Old up, Medwin," as if he had remembered something he'd been meaning to say.

"Yeah," Medwin replied with a polite tone.

"Come 'ere a momen'."

"I'll catch up with you in a minute," Medwin told Conner as he re-entered the cabin.

Conner couldn't help but speculate over what Bellamy might be telling Medwin as he found a barrel to sit on. Was it something he didn't want Conner to know? Or was it just something Conner didn't need to know, which would give the captain no reason to call him back as well. Eventually, he concluded that Medwin would tell him whatever it was if it was important.

He turned his attention to the sailors, many of whom had taken to relaxing in various locations, due to there not having much to do. There were, however, a couple of men who still had jobs to do. There was someone in the crow's nest, his figure a silhouette against the bright afternoon sky, and a short, stocky man — one of the three that Conner had seen down in the hold, arguing over the bottle — was at the helm, steering the ship.

Medwin emerged from Bellamy's cabin after a few minutes. He quickly found Conner and told him they would be taking a rowboat to Rhona from almost a half-mile offshore.

"Half a mile is really far!" Conner groaned, thinking about the story of Elandra.

"I know, but Captain Bellamy has told me that it is not safe for a vessel of this size to approach the island any farther than that. Apparently, the water is too shallow over the coral reef, and there is no known gap large enough to sail through."

Conner looked out past the bow of the ship and saw that the outline of Rhona was no longer a faded haze on the horizon. He could see the island in full detail now; other than the small amount of sandy beach that made up its boundary, a thick jungle of trees, bushes, and other forms of foliage covered its expanse.

"Hoist the sails! Drop anchors! Look lively yeh scurvy dogs!" Captain Bellamy barked orders for slowing the ship as he strode from his cabin door to the ship's helm. "Quincy, I'll take over. Man the davit and prepare to lower the dinghy." He looked over at Conner and Medwin. "Oi, lads, hop'n the boat!"

Quincy ambled from the helm to the davit and ushered the boys into the dinghy.

CONNER'S ODYSSEY

Conner had never been in a rowboat in the ocean like this. He felt nervous and the water suddenly seemed to be twice as choppy. Looking over at Medwin, he could tell the feeling was mutual.

The two boys climbed into the boat, and Quincy started to lower them down immediately. As they approached the water's surface, Conner envisioned a huge sea dragon rising up from the depths.

"I'll row the boat," he told Medwin, feeling convinced that the only way to overcome his fear was to master his courage. It took immense effort to propel the little boat through such rough water, but finally, after what felt an eternity of rowing, and with muscles screaming out in objection, they reached the shores of Rhona.

CHAPTER 8

Into the Jungle

With a great amount of effort, Conner and Medwin managed to drag the dinghy far enough onto shore that it wouldn't be pulled right back out to sea with high tide. They turned to take in their surroundings. The sandy beach of Rhona sloped steadily up into a wall of flourishing plant life. Palm trees swayed happily in the wind. Huge foliage plants with almond shaped leafs and a wide variety of strikingly colorful flowers made the lower canopy of the jungle. From a distance, you couldn't even see a foot into it. Squawks of exotic birds were coming from all over — sometimes responded to by a cheerful group of monkeys.

Conner took one last look at *the Colossus* in the distance. "I hope this doesn't take too long. What if we get lost and can't find our way back before our week is up and Bellamy leaves?" he asked Medwin.

"We won't get lost," Medwin assured him. "Plus, a week is a long time. Far more than we'll need I'm sure. Come on, let's get going."

"Okay," Conner replied, feeding off Medwin's positivity. "Do you have any idea whereabouts we should start looking for Vivek?" he asked hopefully.

"Not really," Medwin said with a little shrug, "but I figure we should head for the center of the island first. It feels like a good place to start."

"Why is that?"

"Because, to be centered with one's self is very wise … and Vivek is probably the wisest man in all of Rohwen."

"So, you think he chose the center of the island to represent being centered as a person?" Conner inquired, feeling that this was a very intuitive guess on Medwin's part.

"Exactly. My father has been to see Vivek you know?" Medwin told Conner matter-of-factly. "Every successor to the chief of the Satria has to seek him out and speak with him before they can take their position as ruler of the tribe. Father never told me exactly how to find him on the island, though. I think he wanted me to figure it out for myself."

Conner realized for the first time that he was speaking with the future chief of the Satria. "Well, the whole center thing is a better theory than I'm going to come up with," he admitted, smiling broadly. Medwin laughed, and the two of them stepped into the thick jungle.

The air was heavy with oxygen and moisture. Conner noticed the difference immediately. It was unlike anything he'd ever experienced. He could actually feel the weight of it in his lungs with every breath he took. To his surprise, it energized him.

"Wait," said Medwin, putting his arm out to stop Conner from continuing. "Here, take this." He pulled a modest, yet nice-looking dagger out of his pack and handed it to Conner before reaching back in for his hatchet. "Bellamy asked me to bring that for you," he said as he looked up and saw the expression on Conner's face.

Conner was gazing at the dagger with great regard. "Bellamy said to give me this?"

"Yeah, I think he's taken a liking to you. He wanted you to have at least some kind of weapon going into the jungle."

Conner swung and jabbed the knife at the air to test its speed, as well as his own skill. "Cool!" he said after a few moments. A feeling of bravery began to creep into him as he clutched the knife tightly in his hand.

"Let's keep moving," said Medwin, who took the lead and started slashing a path into the thick foliage with his hatchet.

Their progress was slow going, and between the heat and humidity of the island, Conner was quickly drenched in sweat. But he didn't mind. It allowed the small amount of wind finding its way through the thick canopy of trees to cool him.

The deeper into the jungle the boys traveled, the more life began to appear around them. A group of monkeys swung playfully from tree to tree — possibly fighting over a banana, or who would get to eat the next pick of fleas. Birds of various color and size flew from branch to branch, squawking their songs. Lizards enjoyed a lazy afternoon, perched atop warm rocks.

Conner saw an antelope that looked young and lost. He hoped it would find its way back to the herd. In a way, he almost felt a connection to the animal. He, too, knew what it felt like to be unsure of how to find his way back home.

Medwin stopped and put his hand up. There was a large snake coiled idly around a tree branch, positioned so that as the sun's rays poked through the dense treetops, it would be bathed in their warmth. "Don't make any quick movements," he whispered. "Just stay here."

Conner nodded, wondering why Medwin was even worried about

the snake. It didn't seem to be interested in them at all, and what was more, it wasn't in their way.

Medwin crept silently toward the snake, his hatchet at the ready. The instant he was in range, he chopped the serpent's head off with one swift strike. He draped the length of its body over his shoulders and returned to where Conner was waiting.

"Why did you kill it?" Conner asked, taken aback by Medwin's behavior. He had assumed Medwin would have more respect for a living creature. "It wasn't in our way," he continued. "And it didn't seem to be a threat…"

"I killed it because I want to eat tonight."

"You eat snake?" Conner felt sickened by the very idea. The smell of snake alone was enough to ruin his appetite "That sounds disgusting!"

"I promise you, it isn't," Medwin told him. "And even if it was, I would still eat it. Snake meat is good for the body."

Medwin's assurances didn't convince Conner, but he knew his hunger would overcome him eventually, and he would try it anyway.

It became increasingly difficult to see as the day wore on. Conner could hardly imagine how dark it would get when the sun set completely. The jungle was already cloaked in deep, heavy shadows, and he knew it couldn't be much later than early evening. Medwin seemed to notice how fast they were losing light as well. He started to gather firewood. Conner joined him, and soon they both had healthy armfuls of the driest tinder they could find in such a moist climate.

Medwin's face screwed up with concentration. He grabbed a vine coiled on the floor in front of him and pulled — a square door in the ground lifted up. He headed down to the underground room, followed closely by Conner.

"Just drop your firewood here," Medwin said, discarding his own armful near a corner of the room opposite the two beds.

Conner dumped his bundle of wood and turned to Medwin. "Is there anything you need help with?"

Medwin pulled the snake off his neck and held it out for Conner to grab. "You can peel the skin off this while I get the fire started."

Conner took the snake with reluctance, privately wishing he hadn't offered to help. He sat down, clamped his knees onto the headless end of the serpent, and began attempting to peel its skin back. He soon realized that the task would be more difficult than he expected. He couldn't manage to get a good grip because his hands had become slippery with blood almost immediately.

"It would've been worse if I hadn't been letting the blood drain for the last two hours," Medwin said, sounding as though he was stifling a tone of amusement. "Why don't you use your dagger to make a light incision? The skin should peel much easier after that." Medwin gave Conner a small grin and went back to shaving flakes of wood from a branch with his hatchet.

"Why didn't I think of that?" Conner grumbled as he pulled the knife from his belt. He noticed that Medwin looked as though he had a few answers to his question, but he didn't say anything. Conner was grateful for his silence because he was pretty sure none of the answers would have been ones he wanted to hear.

He found himself wishing he'd spent more time camping and learning about survival as a child. It wasn't a good feeling to think that he'd probably die within a few days if left to his own devices. It suddenly seemed odd to him how unimportant it was to the average child in his world to know the things that were so obviously second nature to Medwin: things that had been vital knowledge in the history of Conner's world but had become unnecessary as people developed and became "civilized." There was no need for the average person to know how to hunt and prepare wild game; no need to know how to start a fire with nothing but a few stones.

Conner was so absorbed in his thoughts that he hardly noticed he'd already made an incision that ran the length of the snake's body and was in the process of peeling back the skin. "What should I do next?" he asked as he finished removing the skin with one final tug.

Medwin threw him one of the biggest branches they'd gathered. "Wrap it around that." He watched Conner for a moment. "Make sure you wrap it close to one end so my hand doesn't get burned while I cook it."

"Oh, right," Conner mumbled sheepishly. He uncoiled the snake from the branch and started again.

It wasn't long before the crackling sounds of fire filled the room. Medwin waited for his skillfully constructed stack of kindling to burn a minute before he added some substantial chunks of wood. Conner extended the branch he'd wrapped the snake around toward him.

"Hold on just a minute," Medwin said. "I want to add a few more pieces of wood first. That way I'll have some good embers to cook over."

"Okay," Conner replied, retracting his extended arm.

"So tell me," Medwin started conversationally, "what is your world like?"

Conner thought for a moment. What was his world like? In many ways it was very similar to Rohwen — or at least it had been many years ago, before the inventions of machines and technology. "In the past, it wasn't so different from Rohwen," he finally answered. "But the people of my world have created many things that changed it." Medwin looked at him quizzically. "Like computers, and cell phones, and cars..." Conner went on, feeling like his explanation was doing nothing but furthering Medwin's confusion. He didn't know how to describe the things from his world to someone who knew nothing about them. Where did he start?

"I have never heard these terms: computers, or cell phones, or cars," Medwin said as he gestured for Conner to hand him the snake-wrapped branch. "What are these things?"

"They're things the people of my world have created as conveniences — to make their lives easier," Conner said. "Like a car — it's a thing that travels across land much faster than we can walk, or even run. You steer it with a wheel — kind of like the helm of a ship — and it usually has enough room for five people to ride comfortably."

"Sounds very convenient," Medwin replied, rotating the snake over the fire.

"It is," Conner said. His mind began to form a picture of all the roads that cut through the landscape in his world. Then he thought of how beautiful Rohwen's countryside was, virtually unscathed by man. "But not everything about it is good..."

"What's not good about it?" Medwin asked curiously.

"Well, the cars require roads and the more roads that get put in, the more damage is inflicted upon the land…"

"I see," said Medwin, looking thoughtful. He ripped off a chunk of snake with his fingers and tasted it. "Just a couple more minutes," he said to himself as he stuck the meat back over the fire.

Conner watched Medwin, his mind stuck in a sort of trance. The conversation about his world had left him feeling strange. It was almost like trying to explain the future to someone who'd come from a long forgotten past. Not only that, but he hadn't ever taken the time to think about the negative impact of his world's luxuries.

"Perfect," Medwin announced, chewing a mouthful of snake. "You hungry enough to try it?" he asked, grinning broadly and offering Conner a handful of snake meat.

"Definitely," Conner said. "I don't care what it tastes like at this point. I'm starving."

Medwin laughed and handed Conner the handful of meat.

As he chewed his first bite, Conner was pleasantly surprised. The snake was actually quite good. It almost tasted like fish. There was a bit of a gamy flavor to it, but overall, he enjoyed it more than he ever would have thought possible.

"Good, isn't it?" Medwin gave him a knowing look.

"Yeah, you were right … snake meat is good," Conner said, laughing at Medwin's amusement.

They enjoyed the rest of their dinner with minimal conversation. Medwin headed for bed a few minutes after he finished eating, and Conner, whose body still ached from the effort of rowing the dinghy, was grateful that it was finally time to get some rest. It had been a long day, and he was sure the next would be no different.

* * *

The following morning was cool and refreshing. It made the first few hours of travel far more tolerable than it had been in the afternoon heat of the previous day. But by mid-morning, the inevitable jungle heat had returned.

"Do you think we're getting close to the center?" Conner asked, wiping the sweat from his brow.

"It's hard to say. There's no good way of getting your bearings out here." Medwin continued to slash away the thick foliage blocking his path as he answered.

"So how are we going to know when we get to the center then?" Conner asked, starting to feel a little worried. What if they couldn't actually determine when they'd reached the center of the island? What if, when they did reach the center, Medwin's assumptions had been wrong and Vivek wasn't there?

"All we can do is trust our instincts," Medwin replied.

'More like — trust *your* instincts,' Conner thought.

On they traveled, carving a path toward the heart of the jungle. The slashing noise of Medwin's hatchet that had become familiar ceased abruptly. "*Shhh,*" he hissed. "I think I saw..."

Conner's mind became instantly alert with fear. He scanned the surrounding area frantically in an attempt to locate whatever it was Medwin had seen.

"*Move!*" Medwin yelled as a jaguar pounced at them with incredible speed. Medwin dodged with rivaling speed, holding his hatchet ready to strike.

Conner jumped into a large-leafed plant for cover.

The jaguar pounced at Medwin again, and again Medwin dodged, this time grazing the beast's shoulder with his hatchet. The huge cat let out a growl of pain, but the attack didn't slow it down. Medwin's strike, however, had left the right side of his body vulnerable. With one quick swipe, the cunning beast connected, leaving four deep gashes just below his ribs. Blood was immediately spewing from the wounds. The jaguar was about to deliver a lethal strike —

"*No!*" Conner leapt from his cover, screaming with assorted fear, anger, and adrenaline.

Medwin made a gesture, telling Conner to save himself, but at that moment, the jaguar let out a yelping roar as it fell to the bottom of a deep pit that had appeared abruptly.

Full of rage, Conner ran over to the edge of the pit and threw his dagger at the beast. With a skill he never would have guessed he had, he hit it squarely between the eyes. The beast let out a low, winded groan and lay still.

Conner hurried over to Medwin, trying to stay calm as he asked, "How bad is it?"

"…It's bad," Medwin replied weakly, growing gaunter with every moment that passed.

Conner's mind was traveling a million miles per second, but not actually forming any practical thoughts. "Uh — just — er — stay calm," he said, looking around frantically. "Don't use your energy."

The faint sound of rustling leafs in the distance caught his attention. He jerked his head up to find the culprit, hoping beyond hope that it wasn't another jaguar, or some other predator. He saw a man wearing a long brown cloak watching him. From what he could tell, the man was extremely old. He knew who it was.

CHAPTER 9

Vivek the Wise

"Hang on, Medwin," Conner said, finally thinking clearly. He took off his shirt and tied it tightly around Medwin's waist. "Can you stand?"

Medwin didn't reply.

"Come on, Medwin, you've got to be strong! I'll help you!" Conner put Medwin's arm around his neck and lifted him up — he was weak. It was clear that he couldn't support himself. Conner allowed his full weight to lean upon him and began to struggle forward awkwardly. "Are you Vivek?" he called to the man, who was still watching silently from a short distance.

The man nodded, turned on the spot, and walked slowly away, as if silently saying, "Follow me."

Conner followed as fast as he could.

Medwin was chalk-white now. He seemed to realize what was going on and made his best efforts to increase their speed, but he was so weak that the attempt did little to make Conner's task any easier. He'd lost so much blood that his skin had grown cold; he fainted.

The minutes that followed — in which Conner had been forced to drag Medwin's, now, completely limp body — felt like hours.

Finally, Vivek stopped. He turned to face Conner and spoke. His voice was old and fragile. "Your friend is in need of assistance."

"Yes, sir, he's — he's dying!" Conner exclaimed desperately, unable to help but feel frustrated by the fact that Vivek was being nonchalant about their situation. His friend was bleeding to death, and all Vivek could do was point out the obvious. Of course he was in need of assistance!

A small fracture broke the jungle floor and started to form around them in the shape of a circle, issuing loud cracking noises as it went. It was like watching a miniature earthquake occur in perfect symmetry. The ground within the circle shuddered, and they were riding the chunk of land like an elevator into an underground room so large that it made Medwin's creation look miniscule. Scents of dirt and something bitter drifted idly across Conner's senses as they reached the bottom of the room.

"Show me the boy's wounds," Vivek demanded. He knelt down and propped Medwin's legs up on his lap.

"Yes, sir." Conner hurried to untie his blood-soaked shirt from around Medwin's waist. "Can you help him?" he asked anxiously. Not only was Medwin his only chance of ever finding his way home, he had also become a great friend. In fact, possibly one of the best he'd ever had. Conner couldn't stand the thought of losing him.

"Yes, I can help him," Vivek answered quickly, his voice sounding urgent. "But we must hurry. Use the shirt to keep pressure on his wounds."

Conner placed his shirt over Medwin's side and pushed down hard with both hands. He felt the heat of Medwin's blood against his palms. Every precious drop was like another second of Medwin's life slipping away.

Vivek closed his eyes. His expression became firm, as if he was focusing intently on something. After a moment, the color of Medwin's skin returned ever so slightly. Vivek hurried over to a jar-filled shelf, found what he was looking for, and came bustling back. "You can remove the shirt now," he said.

Conner nodded and pulled his shirt away. The sight that met his eyes made him gasp; not because the wounds looked grotesque; because they had closed, as if someone had stitched them crudely but without any stitches. "He's going to be okay, right?" Conner asked.

"Yes, Conner, he's going to be okay," Vivek replied as he started to dab a green, goopy substance on Medwin's gashes.

Conner looked up at Vivek, startled. *"How do you know my name?"*

"You used cognition to defeat the jaguar," Vivek said, his tone sounding as though the answer was obvious.

"So," Conner replied, feeling troubled about the fact that Vivek knew his name. Not only had they never met, they were from two different worlds. How could he possibly know?

"You," Vivek began, "are not of the Satria tribe, and they are the only ones — other than myself —who know how to use cognition."

"That still doesn't explain how you know my name — sir," Conner attempted to correct his tone, noticing the rudeness in the way he'd been speaking. Vivek had, after all, just saved Medwin's life.

"Your name means friend of wolf, or, wolf-lover," Vivek said, finally removing his gaze from Medwin's wounds and placing it firmly upon Conner.

Conner wished that Vivek would say something that made sense, but he chose not to speak.

Vivek continued. "It was written in an ancient document that a boy of strange origin would appear during a time of great evil."

Now Conner was listening intently.

"This boy would have the power of cognition without knowing it or asking for it. He would be able to use it in ways others have only dreamed of... How exactly, I admit, I do not know..."

"It is also said," Vivek continued, "that this boy would have the ability to befriend the lone wolf. The one wolf able to see the need for change, and therefore break free of the evil it was said would plague their kind for over one thousand years."

Conner's jaw dropped. He had dreamt about a wolf only a few nights ago. He tried to swallow, but there was a lump in his throat. "And — you think that boy is m — me?"

"Yes," Vivek replied simply.

"But I would be too scared to approach a wolf! They're carnivores! They'll eat humans if they're hungry enough!"

"Indeed, that is true. Tell me, Conner — since you arrived in Rohwen, how would you compare yourself to your former self?"

'What kind of question is that?' Conner thought, scratching the side of his head.

Vivek waited for Conner to answer with his fingers interlocked, a pleasantly expectant smile upon his face.

Conner felt stumped by the question. What did Vivek mean, how would he compare himself to his former self? He felt like the same person. 'Well I guess there are a few differences,' he supposed after a moment's contemplation, thinking about his newfound respect for nature and the ability to survive within it. But that didn't feel at all like the answer Vivek was waiting for.

He began playing back some of the moments from the last four days in his mind. As his thoughts came to the river incident, things started to make sense. He had used cognition to save his own life. At the time, it had felt like a freak occurrence. But then he had remembered the imprinted image of Chris' face on the note, and, because of that memory, when he used cognition on the Cliffs of Elders, a small part of him had believed he would be able to do it. Then, a short while ago, he had used it for a fourth time in order to defeat the jaguar, and on that occasion, he hadn't even questioned himself. He had known he could do it.

He was almost sure, now, that he knew what Vivek was getting at with his question, yet for some reason he couldn't find what he felt to be a suitable answer. He decided to skip the formalities and get straight to the point. "So what does it all mean?" he asked, trying to ignore his churning stomach. "Is there something I'm supposed to do?"

Vivek gave him an approving smile before he spoke. "Well, you see, I believe that you and the lone wolf are destined to meet... So, naturally, I think you should seek the wolf," he said, his face becoming serious.

Conner looked at him nervously. "But why, sir... It doesn't seem very wise to go looking for a wolf."

Vivek considered him for a moment. "Let me tell you a story. Maybe its relevance will help."

Conner remained politely silent as Vivek began.

"There was once a man named Evander, who lived in the shadow of fear, never taking risks that could jeopardize the comforts of life with which he had become accustom. He did not travel, for fear that his home might be intruded upon in his absence. He did not seek a partner, for fear that she would, one day, abandon him and seek the love of another. He had many acquaintances, but sought no close friendships, for fear that his companions might betray him.

"In his opinion, his view of life was very wise, because pain and misfortune only came to those who asked for them. Life was predictable when you sculpted your future with sensible decisions.

"And so, in this way he lived for many years, never realizing that the existence he chose was causing him to miss a great many of life's beauties.

"On a fall afternoon, as he collected wood for his evening fire, a haggard old woman crossed his path. He attempted to ignore the woman, but she seemed unable to notice his reluctance for conversation. She asked him for a warm meal and a place to lay her head that night. Disgusted by the idea of this woman in his house, and fearful that she might steal from him in his sleep, he refused her.

"She warned him that if he did not change, he would know pain and misery in ways most men could scarcely imagine. She told him to seek the misfortune he so desperately avoided, for with it came a great many wonders.

"Evander laughed at her. Told her she knew nothing of life and mocked her. He told her she was nothing but a raving old hag.

"She left, telling him again that if he did not change, he would regret it. He watched her go, laughing to himself. The woman was clearly out of her mind. What foolishness. Who in their right mind would seek misfortune?

"The years passed, and as Evander grew old, he began to feel a longing he had never known before. He longed for the love of a child. Someone he could pass the torch of life to; someone who would carry on his name. But he was much too old to become a father. He had wasted away the years of his prime, living in fear of loss. There had been women with whom he could have settled. Why hadn't he seen the folly of his decisions sooner?

"A feeling of misery began to clutch his heart. He felt a pain in which he could find no description. He remembered the words of warning the old woman had given him so long ago. They finally made sense. The misfortune he had so desperately avoided *was* the fortune he longed so greatly for now. Endless hours of regret finally drove Evander to madness.

"As his final days approached, he felt the full weight of his decisions crashing over him. Not one person cared that he was on the threshold of death. The material possessions he had valued more than friendship were all he had to keep him company.

"Late on a stormy night, there came a knock from his door. He ambled slowly to see who it could be. To his great surprise, it was the same woman from so long ago. She still looked exactly as she had. He invited her in out of the storm without hesitation. She no longer appalled him. In fact, he was overjoyed just to have someone to talk with. He offered her soup and bread and told her she was welcome to stay as long as she wished.

"The woman smiled and thanked him for his kindness, and before Evander had a chance to reply, something incredible happened. The woman's eyes began to glow a radiant white. Her old, gnarled skin shed away, leaving before him a vision of unrivaled beauty. Her body was young and flawless. Golden light wisped into the air all around her. She spoke, and her voice filled Evander with fear and awe.

"'I am Faylinn: one of the five who created all things.'

"Evander cowered before her, overcome by fear. The woman he had treated so disrespectfully was a goddess. He knew almost all of Edelan's stories and legends. He had heard them from his mother as a child. Faylinn was not just a goddess. She was the one who had created time. She had created the four other gods of whom she had employed to help her sculpt Rohwen.

"He begged for forgiveness for his foolish actions. He told her that the words she had spoken all those years ago had been truthful and that he had paid dearly for his ignorance.

"Faylinn smiled upon him. 'Rise' she said, and without the faintest effort, Evander found himself on his feet. He listened intently as Faylinn spoke. 'You, who knows pain more than any, who knows misery beyond words, shall set an example for the people of Rohwen. You will seek to bring love and friendship to all. You will have many descendants, and your name shall not be forgotten.'

"Evander looked down to find a bundle of wood in his arms. It was a fall afternoon. He was young again. He looked up and watched as a haggard old woman approached. When she arrived by his side, she asked for a warm meal and a place to lay her head for the night. He embraced the woman and told her she was more than welcome. From that day forth, Evander came to know the true meaning of life, and all who crossed his path were enlightened by his compassion."

Conner sat, watching Vivek as he finished. He wasn't quite sure what relevance the story had to his own situation. "Vivek, sir, what exactly does that have to do with me seeking a wolf?"

"Don't you remember what the old woman told Evander?" Vivek asked, sounding slightly exasperated. "She told him to seek the misfortune he so desperately avoided. Little did Evander know, what he considered to be misfortune was exactly the opposite... And so it may be with you. You obviously feel the idea that seeking a wolf is less than fortunate, but how can you know. What if seeking the wolf brings you great fortune?"

"But that was just a story," Conner said. "I mean, it's not like real life."

"Not all stories are fake, Conner. And nearly all of them hold elements of truth that only fools choose to ignore."

Conner nodded. He thought again of the fact that he had achieved cognition without even knowing what it was. He thought about the fact that Vivek had known his name.

"Will you seek the wolf?" Vivek probed, seeing the look on Conner's face and reading it well.

Conner nodded slowly.

Vivek clapped his hands together, looking joyful and relieved. "Be sure to remember that the wolf will be very alert to the presence of a spy. He will have abandoned his pack, and they will surely be hunting him. The pack will want him dead for his defiance. What I'm saying is: his guard will be up. Remember, he — like you until moments ago — will know nothing of your intertwined destinies."

"I understand," Conner uttered quietly. The magnitude of what he was, of what he had to do, began to set in. He felt truly sick to his stomach.

"Your friend's recovery is coming along quite well," said Vivek as he brushed his fingers lightly across Medwin's wounds.

Conner looked over at Medwin. His skin color had nearly returned to normal, and the gashes on his side now looked as if they'd been healing for at least a week. "What was it that you put on him?"

"It is a substance infused with advanced healing agents, of which I created by combining different types of plants — also of my own creation."

Conner stared speechlessly at Vivek for a moment before saying, "You mean, you actually created your own plants?"

"Yes, my cognition is very advanced, Conner." Vivek paused, as if to contemplate his next words, or perhaps his last. He continued. "It was I who taught the art of cognition to the Satria, in the early years of their known existence. Before teaching —"

"How old are you?" Conner blurted out, realizing he'd interrupted as soon as the question left his mouth. He wished he hadn't. "Sorry, sir, I didn't mean to interrupt..."

"It is quite alright. I am nearly two-thousand-years-old…"

Conner thought he must have misheard. It sounded as though Vivek had said nearly two-thousand-years old. "Sorry, but I think I misheard you," Conner said, trying to sound polite. "I thought you said nearly two-thousand-years…"

"I did," Vivek said, grinning at Conner's bewildered expression. "Cognition is a powerful tool, Conner. In time, you will learn just how powerful.

"As I was saying, though." He turned away from Conner and

placed his gaze back on Medwin's wounds. "Before my teaching the art of cognition to the Satria, to my knowledge, there were only two who had the ability to use it. We marveled at the wonders of its amazing power. The other that I speak of became obsessed with his abilities and began abusing the power… And, indeed, he became powerful … incredibly powerful…" Vivek's voice trailed off. He stared into space for a moment. A look of concern molded his features, as if his own words worried him.

"Eventually," he finally said, "we could no longer remain friends. He left and set out on his own path, which ended up becoming wicked and perverse. The name of the other that I speak of is, Vellix."

Conner listened intently as Vivek continued.

"I met a humble chief of the Satria tribe and decided to train him in the art of cognition, advising him to pass on the knowledge to those who were worthy in his tribe, and them on to the next generation, and so on. You see, by doing this, I was ensuring that there would always be someone to counter Vellix's power, in the event that something happened to me.

"After I had finished training the chief, I came here to Rhona to explore the uses of natural plant life when mixed with the plants of my own creation" — Vivek looked down at Medwin's almost completely healed wounds — "and as you can see, my results were quite good…

"Upon my exploration of the island, I stumbled upon a small cave entrance that was nearly unrecognizable, due to its being covered by a tangle of bushes and vines. I was curious, so I searched the cave. What I discovered made me realize that my original theory — that Vellix and I were the only ones to have had the power of cognition

— could not have been more wrong. There were documents hidden within the cave: The Scrolls of Hylan. They contained an abundance of information. Some of the techniques I learned in those scrolls were extremely advanced. I remembered from my childhood that I was able to perform many of the concepts of cognition, and as an adult, I became quite proficient with the art. But I had no idea of its true power.

"The more I read, the more obvious it became that Vellix and I must be descendants of the Hylanian people: the true race of cognition. This was the first moment in which I came to the hard realization that my entire ancestry is extinct, and my true family would never know me, or me them."

A look of absolute sadness and pain gleamed in Vivek's eyes that almost made Conner cry. He couldn't imagine what it would be like to discover something so tragic about his own past.

Vivek composed himself and continued. "It was within one of those scrolls that I discovered all of the things I have told you of your destiny.

"After that discovery, I chose to remain here on this island. I knew I must protect such profound pieces of information. My biggest fear is that Vellix found the scrolls before I did and, in having done so, knows the truths they hold. In which case, he will have been — and will still be — ever anticipating the arrival of a strange-looking boy…"

Conner's brow furrowed.

"When I say 'strange,' I mean to say that you don't look like a Rohwenite, dressed in those strange clothes," Vivek said, noticing the glare Conner had given him. "Well, you *didn't* look like one anyway. This should help you blend in a bit better." He walked over to the corner by his bed and grabbed a brown tunic-type garment. "Here," he said. "Put this on."

"Thanks," said Conner, happy to have something to wear. His shirt was, of course, completely ruined from all the blood that Medwin had stained it with. "Vivek, sir," Conner began curiously, "didn't you say earlier that you and the Satria are the only people that can do cognition?"

"I did."

"What about Vellix? He's still alive, isn't he?"

"He is."

"Well then, what about him?"

"What he does, I no longer call cognition!" Vivek flared up. "He is consumed by nothing but arrogance and hate. What he does is still technically cognition, but it is a disgrace!" Vivek sounded disgusted and bitter.

Conner didn't pursue the conversation. Unsure of what to say next, he began to glance around the room. It didn't hold any of the furnishings he would have normally expected to see in a comfortable living space. There were shelves on one of the walls, covered to the point of overflowing with jars that contained an assortment of things — most of which looked as though they came from the island or were at least organic. On the floor lay a magnificent throw rug, patterned by a mesmerizingly intricate design. Torches lined the walls, holding flames that danced cheerfully as they burned bright. A shabby old mat lay in the corner next to a large, rectangular wooden chest.

Across the room from the chest was a sizable workstation, littered with a variety of tools that reminded Conner of an elaborate chemistry set. Some kind of concoction was currently sitting over an open flame, letting off a low hissing noise and emitting a blue vapor into the air as it bubbled and spit its contents from the large beaker struggling to contain it.

Medwin began to stir. Conner abandoned his investigation of the room and gave him a tap on the shoulder. "Hey, how are you feeling?"

"Terrible…" Medwin replied weakly.

"Here, drink this," Vivek told Medwin, handing him a jar full of blue liquid. "It will help revive your energy."

Medwin drank it down in one great gulp.

"Now how do you feel?" Vivek asked, his expression almost becoming smug.

"Quite a bit better," said Medwin, astonished. He tried to move his arms and legs. "My muscles still feel a little weak, though. And I'm slightly nauseous…"

Vivek went to the shelf once more and came back with an armful of jars. "Here Medwin, put these in your pack. There are some revivers — like the one I just gave you — and one of the healing potions I put on your wounds. I am sure they will prove to be useful on your journey."

"Thanks, Vivek ... for everything," said Conner, reaching out a hand to shake the old man's.

"Yeah, I don't even want to think of where I'd be if you hadn't patched me up," Medwin added. "Thank you."

"You are quite welcome. It was my pleasure."

Conner looked over at Medwin. "We should probably get started on our journey back. I know we still have plenty of time, but I would rather not give Bellamy any reason to leave us."

"He does already have the gold," Medwin said, frowning in thought. "But there isn't really any reason for him to leave before our time is up. He said there were plenty of provisions aboard…"

Vivek looked perplexed. He shifted his gaze from Medwin to Conner. "You two aren't actually planning on traveling the jungle as night falls are you?"

Conner and Medwin glanced at each other. "Well, only 'til it gets dark," they replied. "Then we'll stop for the night."

"I honestly would have thought your natural instincts of self-preservation would be more alert," Vivek said, shaking his head with disbelief. "Particularly yours, Medwin, after what you've been through today." He ambled to the corner of the room, reached behind his trunk, pulled up a couple blankets, and walked back to the two boys. "Here," he said as he handed them each their own. "You will sleep here. I will wake you at dawn, and you can leave then, but I will not allow you to travel the jungle as night approaches."

* * *

"Conner … wake up…"

Conner heard a voice somewhere in the depths of his mind, but he wasn't sure what it was trying to say. He ignored it and fell back to sleep…

"Wake up…"

He heard the voice again, and this time whoever it belonged to was nudging him. He opened his eyes to find Vivek crouched next to him,

113

holding a burning candle. The light it cast upon his aged face sent hard shadows flickering and dancing randomly. The sight of the old man sent a chill down Conner's spine, but he brushed the sensation aside as he realized it was just Vivek. "Is it dawn already?" he asked, sitting up and rubbing his eyes. "I feel like I barely got any sleep."

"That's because you've only been asleep for a few hours," Vivek told him with a dismissive hand gesture.

Conner couldn't help but notice that Vivek seemed anxious. "Is everything okay Vivek, sir?"

Vivek motioned for Conner to follow him as he moved toward a corner of the room, far from where Medwin was sleeping. "I don't want to wake him," Vivek whispered, glancing over at Medwin's sleeping figure. "He needs all the sleep he can get after what he went through yesterday."

Conner nodded slowly. He felt like Vivek was acting strange. The old man didn't seem like the same person he'd met the previous day. His movements were sharper, his expression almost distressed.

"Is everything ... okay?" Conner asked again.

Vivek turned away from Conner. "Countless years waiting for the moment, rehearsing just how you'll say it, and when the time finally comes, you can't do it." He wheeled around quickly to face Conner and took a deep breath.

"Sir?" Conner was beginning to feel genuinely worried now.

"There is something I didn't tell you... Something else in the scrolls..."

Conner didn't know whether to be intrigued or scared. "What is it, sir? You can tell me."

Vivek stared at him dolefully.

"Sir? What is it?"

Vivek sighed, giving in to the miserable realism of his situation. It was essential that Conner heard the truth now. Any alternative would almost certainly result in catastrophe. He looked Conner in the eye. "You must face Vellix…"

"Me?" Conner pointed at himself incredulously. "Why?"

"Don't you remember what I said? The scroll spoke of one who would have the power of cognition without knowing it or asking for it, and he would be able to use it in ways others have only dreamed of. That is you."

Conner listened nervously as Vivek continued.

"The scroll said that the one to unknowingly have the power of cognition would be the one to face Vellix…" Vivek said seriously.

"But there's no way that can be right, sir," Conner replied, trying to remain polite as a feeling of fear-driven irritation rose within. The idea of him taking on a cognition master was completely ludicrous. "There's just no way that can be right," he said again.

"There is a way, Conner: that is what the scroll said."

"Who cares what the stupid scroll says!" Conner yelled heatedly, his frustration toward Vivek getting the better of his emotions.

"Shhh, you'll wake Medwin."

Conner lowered his voice. "Vivek, sir, I honestly don't care what the scroll says. I mean, I was already having a hard enough time with the idea of going out of my way to seek a wolf —"

"You must seek the wolf!" Vivek snapped desperately, almost sounding deranged. "You must!"

The sudden aggressiveness in Vivek's tone took Conner by surprise. He took an instinctual step back.

Vivek pursued him. "I'm sorry," he mumbled, making an apologetic gesture. "It's just that..." He looked away from Conner.

"It's just that what? Conner probed.

"I *need* you to understand the importance of all this." Vivek paused for a moment. Conner didn't reply. "And *I* need to understand how you must feel being told these things," Vivek went on, speaking to himself.

"How can you be sure these things are so important?" Conner asked, careful to keep his tone as skeptical as it was curious.

"I am sure, Conner. The fact that we are having this conversation proves the prophetic nature of the scrolls."

Conner contemplated Vivek's words. 'There's no other way he could have known your name unless the scroll was accurate,' said the voice of logic in his head that is often easier to ignore than accept. He thought again of the few times he had done cognition. These things were not just coincidence. He had to admit, Vivek had a point.

"Please, seek the wolf?" Vivek implored, breaking the silence.

"What if he kills me?" Conner asked, allowing his initial fears to regain control of his thoughts.

"He won't. I'm positive that he won't."

Looking into Vivek's pleading eyes, Conner couldn't help but feel that there was a significance to accepting this task that he couldn't even begin to understand. He made his mind up. "Okay... I'll seek the wolf."

Vivek looked as though he wanted to hug Conner. He didn't, however. He just nodded and said, "You don't know how grateful I am for your decision — how grateful all of Rohwen is..."

CHAPTER 10

A Plan

"Come on. Get up. I said I'd wake you at dawn... It's already nearly an hour passed." Vivek's voice rang loudly around the room. Conner heard Medwin stirring somewhere to his left. He wasn't ready to start the day. His body was reluctant to move, lethargic. All he wanted to do was get a few more hours of sleep.

"Conner, get up," Medwin pressed, noticing his lack of enthusiasm. Didn't you hear Vivek? We've already lost an hour."

"*Okay!*" Conner grumbled, unable to conceal his irritation. It was okay for Medwin. He hadn't been up over half the night, contemplating a foreboding future. He'd slept through the night, his mind at peace.

As he sat up, Conner felt an instant sense of guilt for his edgy reaction. Medwin was crouching down to grab his pack. The scars on his side still looked bad. The fact was, even with a full night's sleep, Medwin probably felt far worse than Conner did. He just wasn't allowing himself to succumb to weakness — his will was stronger.

"Sorry, Medwin," Conner mumbled. "I'm just tired..."

Medwin gave him a reassuring look and turned to Vivek. "We're ready."

Vivek nodded and took them back to the surface. "Wait just a moment before you go..." He closed his eyes, stuck out his hands, and raised them slowly toward the sky.

Conner looked on in astonishment as the small sprout of a tree pushed through the soil and continued to grow. Soon, a full-sized plum tree stood before him. It was as if he'd watched the tree's entire development in time-lapse.

Vivek reached up to one of the tree's lowest branches and plucked off a couple of the plums hanging there. "Here," he said, offering the perfectly ripened fruit to Conner and Medwin in turn before he went back to pick a few more.

As Conner bit into the plum, he could actually feel it hydrating him — his body felt rejuvenated, his mind less fogged. It was indescribably better than any plum he'd ever eaten, better than any fruit, period.

"Take these for later," Vivek told Medwin as he handed four more of the plums to him.

"Thank you," Medwin said with a small, appreciative nod. He took the fruit and placed it carefully in his pack. "Well, we'd better be off."

Vivek put a hand on Conner's shoulder. He smiled warmly and said, "You are going to be fine. I want you to know how much I respect you. You have shown great wisdom for such a young man — wisdom that many will never possess."

Conner smiled, blushing slightly.

Vivek grinned at his embarrassment and turned to Medwin. "And you, Medwin — your father is right to be as proud of you as he is."

Medwin beamed.

"Now, you'd better be off." Vivek made a dismissing gesture with his hands and watched as Conner and Medwin took off at a healthy pace. He waited until they were lost from view before heading back down to the underground room, his thoughts a raging battle between fear and hope.

* * *

Due to the speed at which they were traveling, it wasn't long before Conner and Medwin made it back to the place where they'd fought the jaguar.

Conner skidded to a sudden halt. "Hold up," he yelled when he noticed that Medwin wasn't stopping.

Medwin stopped and walked back toward Conner, looking puzzled. His expression shifted to surprise. "I can't believe your pit is still here," he said disbelievingly, pointing down at the large hole in the ground. "Incredible."

Conner had done cognition with confidence, and as a result, it was incredibly strong. Even though he'd stopped focusing on the pit sometime in the afternoon of the previous day, it had remained in existence, becoming a permanently missing part of the land. He jumped into the hole, narrowly avoiding the large jaguar's outstretched legs. His dagger was still deeply embedded between the cat's eyes. He grabbed the knife by its smooth handle, ripped it out, and used it to climb back to the surface.

"You saved me again... " Medwin said somberly, avoiding eye contact with Conner.

"Yeah..." Conner replied as unconcernedly as possible, aware of the fact that Medwin felt ashamed, that his pride had taken a blow.

"Thanks."

Conner gave Medwin a reassuring glance, similar to the one Medwin had given him earlier that morning. Medwin responded with a quick, thankful grin and pushed the conversation in a different direction.

"You should probably fill the hole."

"Good point," Conner replied. He focused on a picture in his mind. Dirt started spewing from both sides of the pit with intensity. It was astonishing to watch, knowing that *he* was doing it. This was the first time that he used cognition without there being some kind of life-threatening issue at hand.

'It's much easier to appreciate this power when you aren't about to die,' he thought, laughing to himself as the dirt filling the hole reached surface level. Satisfied with his work he asked, "You ready then?"

Medwin nodded, and they started toward the beach.

* * *

"So, how did the conversation with Vivek go?" Medwin asked after a while.

Conner's mind fell instantly to the one thing he hadn't been willing to accept. He still didn't feel ready to consent to the idea that he would have to face Vellix. He redirected his thoughts to his and Vivek's first conversation. "He told me that my existence was written about a really long time ago."

Medwin's expression appeared to be genuinely curious as he listened.

"He said that I'm the one to have the power of cognition without knowing it or asking for it … and that" — Conner couldn't help but feel stupid as the next words left his mouth — "I would be able to use it in ways others have only dreamed of…"

As Conner continued to fill Medwin in on the things he'd missed during their visit with Vivek, he noticed that Medwin seemed to be less than surprised by any of it. He made no gasping sounds, no gestures of shock. Conner started to wonder if the curious expression Medwin had given him at the beginning of his explanation had just been for show, if Medwin already knew everything he was telling him. The memory of a conversation they had a few days ago came to him. He had asked Medwin if he already knew he was special, and Medwin had said yes. Did Medwin already know everything?

Conner stopped walking. Medwin turned to see what the problem was. "You already know all of this, don't you?"

"Well, not quite," Medwin replied with a shrug. "I was never aware that Vivek had taught my people cognition. In fact, I didn't even know he could do it himself… Each chief must keep it a secret in order to protect Vivek's continued existence from reaching Vellix…"

"But you knew everything else," Conner said. He couldn't help but feel a little annoyed. What was the big deal about coming all the way out to the middle of the jungle when Medwin could have told him everything Vivek had?

"Yes, I knew everything else."

"So what exactly was the point of coming all the way out here?" Conner asked, his tone sounding exasperated. "I mean, seriously, what was the point? You had to give Bellamy all that gold, and you were nearly killed by a jaguar, just so you could avoid telling me what Vivek told me… How does that make any sense?"

"If I had been the one to tell you what he did, do you think you would have taken me seriously?" Medwin asked realistically.

"Probably…"

"…Not. The answer is probably not, Conner," Medwin said, putting a bit of severity in his tone. "Because you would have been hearing it from a fifteen-year-old; not an ancient man with wisdom far beyond mine."

Conner had no rebuttal. Medwin was right. There was definitely something about Vivek that had convinced him, made him believe.

"Now do you understand?" Medwin probed when Conner didn't reply.

"Yeah … but it just raises a new question."

"What's that?"

"Why Vivek even told the Satria anything in the first place. Wouldn't that just add to the risk of Vellix finding out?"

Medwin stared thoughtful into space. "I see what —"

"If Vellix doesn't already know that is," Conner muttered darkly, interrupting Medwin. "Sorry," he said, seeing the impatient look he was getting.

"As I was saying," Medwin continued. "I see what you mean, but you have to understand that only a few members of the tribe actually know: my father, his three most trusted elders, and me.

"Vivek made a special trip to our village to hold counsel with them less than a year ago. He said that the time of great evil — written about two thousand years ago — had approached. He told my father to be watchful for your arrival."

Conner was speechless. The idea of men in a world he hadn't even realized existed until mere days ago speaking of his future was completely absurd — absurd, but true. "So that's why your dad said my name in that strange way? 'Cause he knew it meant friend of wolf?"

"Yes," Medwin answered.

"Crazy…" Conner said, shaking his head.

Medwin waited a moment before continuing, as if to allow Conner's mind time to digest. "We had already predetermined what we would do if you ever arrived in our village. In fact, that's the reason I even know any of this. My father chose me as the one who would take you to Vivek. Naturally, he informed me of your importance so that I would make absolutely sure nothing happened to you…

"I believe that the reason father wanted me, specifically, to take you on this journey was because he knew it would be the perfect learning experience for me. I am his only son, and the tribe will become my inheritance. Life trials are important to prepare me for what it will take to become a good leader." Medwin paused briefly, as if contemplating his next words. "I am glad now that it *was* me he chose to take you. You have become a good friend."

"You too, Medwin," said Conner, allowing himself a smile in spite of his bleak mood. The fact was — Medwin would accompany him back to Beach Bay, wish him luck, and return home. His job would be done. It wasn't up to Medwin to seek the lone wolf.

* * *

As the hours passed, Conner's thoughts did nothing to improve his mood. If anything, the longer he dwelled on them, the worse he felt. It wasn't fair. Why was it up to him to do these things for a world that wasn't even his? Why wasn't Vivek the one to face Vellix? He was clearly far more advanced in cognition than Conner could even hope to be. Why did it have to be him? As that question continued to replay, a memory came to his mind: the feeling he'd gotten when he entered the pathway in the trees. It had felt like he was meant to be there, like some inexplicable force was drawing him in. Now he knew why — he *was* meant to be there. But that still didn't really explain anything. The question remained — why him?

"I think it's about time to stop for the night," Medwin announced as the amount of light they had to travel by began to fade.

Conner nodded lamely but didn't reply.

"You know, things aren't as bad as you're making them out to be," Medwin said sharply. "You've been sulking for hours."

"It's easy for you to say things aren't that bad …you don't have to seek a wolf!" Conner yelled, unable to contain his emotions any longer. "Not to mention, face some crazy evil guy whose probably gonna kill you before you even know what happened!"

Medwin gave him a confused look and said, "What do you mean, I don't have to seek a wolf? Did you think I was going to leave you on your own after going out of my way to make sure you were safe up until now?"

Conner wondered why he hadn't thought of that. "I — I guess I didn't really think about it that way…"

"Clearly," Medwin replied with a disbelieving shake of his head. "Might I suggest that you don't let your thoughts overwhelm you? Just focus on one thing at a time. Right now, the only thing you should be worried about is getting safely out of the jungle." Medwin stopped walking, lifted a square door in the ground, and headed down to his underground room.

"You're right," Conner said as he crossed the room and sat on his bed. "It's easier said than done, though."

"True" — Medwin tossed Conner two of the plums Vivek had given him earlier — "but the act of trying will require some of your attention, and that alone will be better than nothing."

Conner nodded and began eating the first of his two plums, wondering how his life could have become so unbelievably complex. Less than a week ago, he had been worried about moving away from his friends, as if it was the most challenging issue he would ever face. Now, in light of his situation, moving to Montana felt like a problem of such little significance that it was laughable. He was faced with a life-threatening task and had no way of letting his parents know what was going on; no way of saying goodbye if he never found his way home. The thought was beyond depressing. He closed his eyes and focused intently on his parents, as if to enter their minds with his thoughts, and said, 'Mom, Dad, if I never see you again, I love you and miss you…'

"I cannot predict the future," said Medwin, who had been watching Conner intently. "and neither can you. Try not to dwell on it too much." Medwin gazed at Conner with a knowing expression. "We will get through this one day at a time. For now, try to relax your mind and get some sleep."

"Thanks, Medwin," Conner replied as he settled into a comfortable position. "I'll do my best…"

* * *

Travel the next day was, for the most part, uneventful. Medwin had attempted to catch an armadillo around mid-day, but with no success. The armadillo had jumped into a marshy pond and they never saw it resurface. Medwin settled for finding some edible fruit, saying he didn't want to waste any more time hunting. It hadn't really bothered Conner settling for fruit. It was a type he'd never eaten, and he thought it was delicious — a perfect blend of sweet and sour.

By early evening, the two boys reached the edge of the jungle. They stepped out onto the beach, shielding their eyes from the sun because their pupils had adjusted to the dim jungle.

Fuzzy silhouettes began to regain their shape as Conner's dilated eyes contracted. He was immensely relieved to find that the dinghy was still where they had left it. He looked out to sea. The sun was getting low in the western horizon. Its bright radiance reflected off the water, making it look like thousands of gleaming diamonds were sparkling on the surface.

The Colossus was a small shadow in the distance — it might have been a toy boat for all the size it looked.

Both boys grabbed a side of the dinghy, dragged it back to the ocean, and pushed it in. Waves crashed heavily on them as they fought the boat back out past the first breaker; then the second; the third. Finally, with one last great heave, they were out past all four breakers and able to pull themselves in.

Medwin caught his breath and said, "I'll row this time. It's only fair." His voice carried an unwavering tone of finality. "You did it on the way here."

Conner noticed that the wind was blowing substantially harder today than it had been on the day he rowed to Rhona. As a result, the water had become increasingly choppy. He knew this would make Medwin's task much harder than his had been. He didn't bring it up, though. He was sure Medwin would be offended if it was implied that he might need help.

As the boys headed steadily back to *the Colossus*, they started working on a plan for finding the wolf.

"So," Medwin started, grunting with the effort of rowing, "I think we should head for the main fork of the Brio River… It seems like a good place to start," he continued with another grunt, "because there's plenty of life along it. The wolf will need easy hunting grounds. I mean, he's in hiding right? So he'll need a place where he can hunt" — Medwin paused for a moment to concentrate as he withdrew the oars, thrust them back into the water, and gave them another violent tug — "without exposing himself for long periods of time."

"Yeah, that makes sense," Conner agreed, trying not to pull his face into an expression that would expose him as feeling sorry for Medwin, who was now sweating profusely. A thought struck him. What if the thing he'd seen out of the corner of his eye back at the river was the wolf? "Hey, Medwin," he began.

"Yeah," Medwin replied, grunting as he plunged the oars back into the choppy ocean for what seemed like the thousandth time and pulled with all his might to force them through the resisting water.

"Remember when I said I'd seen something back at the river?" Conner asked hopefully.

Medwin glanced up at him skeptically. "You don't think?"

"Actually, for some reason, I do."

Medwin didn't look convinced. It seemed he thought the odds of such a thing happening were slim-to-none. "Conner, there are hundreds — thousands of animals that live along the river," he said with an impatient groan. "There wasn't really enough cover for a wolf to have just disappeared."

"We did," said Conner, who also remembered how they'd narrowly escaped being seen by the Mirthless.

Medwin looked slightly exhausted, but in this case, Conner didn't think it was at all from rowing the dinghy. "The Mirthless were hundreds of feet in the air," he said, taking a short break from rowing to catch his breath. "I'm sure that, had they been on the ground, we would've been spotted immediately."

"Maybe you're right," said Conner, starting to feel like his theory had been stupid. He changed the subject. "So, when we get back to Beach Bay, we're going to follow the Brio River?"

"That was my plan … if you agree, of course."

"Yeah, I think it's a good place to start," Conner replied. His feeling of gratefulness toward Medwin was almost indescribable. He was starting to find that he no longer felt daunted by the idea of searching for the wolf. In fact, he almost felt excited about continuing his adventure. As long as Medwin was with him, he felt that things would be okay.

CHAPTER 11

Elandra

Conner and Medwin were nearly upon the Colossus now. Its shadow, which was several times the size of the ship due to the position of the sun, cast itself over them. As they approached, Conner called up in the loudest voice he could muster. "Ahoy there!"

"*Ahoy!*" called back a voice that Conner recognized as Ammin's.

Medwin rowed them the rest of the way to the ship. He looked completely exhausted now and Conner knew that, this time, the look of exhaustion was not because of his farfetched theories.

Ammin lowered ropes down for them to attach to the dinghy. After tying them taut to the hooks on the front and back of the small boat, Conner called back up to the ship, "Okay, bring us up."

"I think the word you're looking for is *hoist* Conner," said Medwin, grinning.

Conner shot him a quick look of indignation as they began to rise steadily toward the main deck.

Back on board, the general atmosphere was of a lively party. Everyone was moving with a slight stagger. A few of the sailors had instruments. They were playing merry-sounding songs about lost loves, gold, and rum.

A group of sailors danced around the ship's mainmast. Conner noticed Dale and Landon amongst them. They had one arm interlocked, while the other rested pompously upon their hips. There was a mocking quality to the way they moved, as if they were making fun of anyone who thought it suitable to dance with elegance.

Captain Bellamy stumbled over to Conner and Medwin and said, in his loud and jolly voice, "An' 'ere's the lads!" He was holding a gallon jug that was almost empty. "Did yeh find wha' yeh was lookin' fer?" he asked, swaying on the spot he stood and giving them a bleary-eyed stare.

"Yeah," Conner answered. "By the way, thanks for the dagger! I already put it to good use."

"Think nothin' o' it!" Bellamy roared with a wave of the hand that was clutching the gallon jug. "Glad ter 'ere yeh got some use out o' it! Saw some action on the island then, did yeh?"

"We were attacked by a jaguar," Medwin told him seriously.

Bellamy gave them a surprised look that suggested he thought they should be dead.

"I hit it between the eyes with the dagger!" Conner exclaimed.

"Bit o' a natural then, eh?" said Bellamy as he stumbled, coming dangerously close to falling over face first.

"Yeah, I guess so."

"Named the knife then, I'll bet. Af'er a kill like tha'!"

"No, I didn't really think to name it," Conner replied.

"*No?* Well, go on then!"

Conner thought hard. What did he want to name the dagger? He didn't normally name his possessions. He wracked his brain for a name he felt was worthy. It couldn't be something stupid, but everything that popped in his head sounded stupid. "I don't know if I really want to name it," he finally said, hoping to escape the task.

"Ah, go on!" Bellamy pressed. "If yeh don' name it, it'll never truly be yers..."

"Alright, alright," Conner mumbled, delving back into thought for another minute. Then, as if a light had switched on in his head, it hit him.

"Scarlet," he pronounced, his head still lowered in concentration. "I think I will name it Scarlet," he confirmed, glancing up and beaming at the approving look on Bellamy's face. "To represent the color of blood, which it has already spilled in my ownership and defense," he added to illustrate the reason why he had chosen the name.

"*Arrr!* Tha's a great name, tha' is!"

"Thanks," Conner replied happily. He was impressed with the name he'd chosen as well. It had a nice ring to it.

"Well, no use lollygaggin'!" Bellamy started barking the usual orders for getting underway. "Raise anchors! Lower the sails! Look lively or I'll keel hull yeh!"

Conner thought better of asking, but his curiosity overcame him. "Captain ... what does keel hull mean?"

Bellamy grinned menacingly. "It means ter take a man, throw 'em off the bow, and let em' get dragged under the ship 'til they pop up astern. If they're still alive, yeh bring 'em back aboard." Bellamy roared with laughter — apparently, he thought this to be on the same level as a good joke.

Conner thought keel hulling sounded morbid. It was insane to him how little these men valued life. 'Well I guess when you put your life on the line for a living, its value declines a bit,' he thought, looking over at Medwin to see what his reaction to the definition of keel hulling was. But it appeared that Medwin hadn't been listening. His attention was on the busy crew.

Lenny went running by. "Oi mates!" he hollered as he arrived at a row of bitts: short posts that sailors tied rope around in order to keep the sails raised. He untied the ropes in a flash, crossed the ship, and did the same to the opposite side — one of the middle sails dropped into an open position.

'He's a really good sailor for his age,' Conner thought, still eyeing Lenny admirably as other men in the crew ran past him in all directions.

Before Conner knew it, *the Colossus* was underway once again. He leaned against the ship's railing and enjoyed the sea's cool, misty spray as it mixed with the warm summer wind. Medwin stood beside him, doing the same.

"You think we ought to try and help the crew?" Conner asked, feeling a little guilty about being lazy while the sailors scrambled around the deck, tending to their captain's orders.

"No," Medwin replied plainly. "I think we would get in the way."

"Yeah, you're probably right," Conner admitted. "It's just that I kinda feel useless standing here, doing nothing."

"I know what you mean," Medwin said. "At least I'm paying them, though. It makes me feel a little less guilty." He glanced at Conner out of the corner of his eye with a smirk. They both started to laugh.

"Let's go up to the front of the ship and see what the view is like from there," Medwin suggested.

"I think the word you're looking for is the *bow* of the ship, Medwin!" Conner laughed, enjoying his chance to prove that he knew a nautical term Medwin did not.

Medwin stared at him and said, "Okay, fine, you got me back." He was barely able to contain a grin as they arrived at the bow. Other than the spar of the ship, there were no obstructions standing in the way of their view as they gazed out to sea. The ocean was striking. Countless choppy peaks of water picked up the translucent colors of the setting sun, making it look as though they were sailing on a giant mosaic. *The Colossus* turned slightly to the left. Now the ship was heading northwest, on a direct course for Beach Bay.

Conner's heart gave an almighty jolt as he saw something moving in the water — a long shadow under the surface, surging towards them at an alarming speed. Whatever it was, it went right under the ship and disappeared from sight. "What was that?" Conner yelled, even though he was almost positive he already knew.

Medwin had seen it, too; he looked horrified. "I don't know, but we'd better tell the captain straight away!"

They headed for the bridge, running as fast as they could and ignoring the looks of bewilderment from the crew as they passed.

"Wha' are you on abou'?" said the blurred form of Lenny as they flew by.

"Captain — *Captain!*"

Bellamy was holding the helm with one hand. With his other, he was tilting back his gallon jug, draining the last few drops from it.

Both boys started speaking at the same time, their voices urgent. "Captain, we saw something in the wat —"

"'Old it lads!" Bellamy thundered. "One at a time!" He didn't appear to appreciate his moment of peace interrupted by two squawking boys.

Medwin gave Conner a glance that said, "You tell him."

Conner tried to remain calm as he spoke. "Captain, we saw the shadow of something really long moving towards us under the water."

Bellamy, who had gone back to humming one of the merry tunes that had been played earlier, obviously not thinking anything these two boys had to say would be very important, stopped his humming instantly.

"It swam right below the ship," Conner continued, sounding as helpless as he felt. "We couldn't really tell where it went after that…"

The captain's brow creased, and his usual jolly expression became sinister. He seemed to be instantly sober. "Elandra!"

From somewhere behind them came the sound of water breaking.

"There's somethin' astern o' the ship, Cap'n!" bellowed the sailor in the crow's nest.

Conner ran over to the taffrail and looked out past the back of the ship.

Something at least one hundred feet long was moving quickly toward them. Its spiky dorsal fin cut easily through the water, leaving a substantial wake behind. A massive, prehistoric head broke the surface.

"She'll not be takin' Colossus from me!" Bellamy cried at the top of his lungs.

As Elandra gained on the ship, she let out a nerve-shattering roar; cascades of white foamy water poured through the crevices of her long, sharp teeth, crashing ominously back into the ocean.

Her sleek body rose and fell in perfectly timed motions, exposing only short sections at a time. In her wet sheen, Conner could see incredibly strong muscles working furiously with every movement of her gigantic body.

Bellamy started barking orders. *"James! Gavin!* Round up yer gun crew an' get down ter the gun decks! The cannons ain' gonna man themselves!"

"We need powder monkeys!" James and Gavin screamed at anyone who would listen.

Lenny ran to the bridge, grabbed Medwin, and steered him toward the stairs that led to the lower decks.

Conner tried to follow, but Dale grabbed him by the arm, handed him a musket-style pistol, lit the slow burning fuse, and said, "Ge' up tha' ra' line! If you see the beast, shoot it!"

"What's the ratline?" Conner yelled in an attempt to throw his voice over the commotion all around him.

"The rope ladder, yeh bloody novice!" Dale roared.

"Oh, right," Conner said to himself as he ran over to the ladder and started to climb it.

A deafening sound filled the air as Elandra rammed *the Colossus'* hull. The great ship shuddered violently with the force of her first attack, and Conner struggled to keep a grip on the ladder he was halfway up.

After waiting a moment for the rope ladder to stop swaying, Conner overcame his nausea, kept climbing, and finally reached the top. His view of what was going on was much better from up here. The crew down below looked similar to the little action figures he played with when he was a kid. His brief sentiments of being a child dissolved in a flash as the murky, brown-colored body of Elandra surfaced again.

She reared up into the air threateningly and let out another earsplitting roar.

Conner shook with fear as he pulled the pistol from his belt. His hand trembling, he took a shot. It missed — the bullet splashed into the water somewhere out in front of her.

Elandra was about to strike the boat again.

B-BOOM! — BOOM!-BOOM! — BOOM!

Multiple shots fired from the cannons below. None hit their target, but they did enough to spook the beast temporarily. She dove back under the water and out of sight.

In Conner's opinion, her lack of visibility was almost more threatening than when he'd been able to see her.

The ship creaked and moaned as Bellamy steered it heavily to the right.

Conner noticed that this directional change was now taking them away from Beach Bay, but that was hardly important at the moment.

* * *

In the upper level of the ship's two gun decks, Medwin was trying to help reload the cannons as quickly as possible, while other sailors shot him dirty looks for his lacking ability.

James was screaming orders. "Gavin, ge' tha' piss poor excuse fer a powder monkey movin' or we'll be meetin' 'r'ends 'afore I'm good an' ready!"

"You 'eard 'im!" Gavin spat, trying to inspire a quicker work rate from Medwin. "Get tha' cannon loaded so Jonny can pack it! Elandra ain' waitin' fer —" *the Colossus* quaked as Elandra rammed her again. Gavin didn't finish his sentence. Apparently, he saw no reason to further his point.

Lenny was — as he had been at everything else Medwin had seen him do — very talented. He ran down the line of cannon's, pouring powder in each one with efficiency. He barely spilled a granule. "Medwin, get cannonballs in these so I can pack 'em!" he yelled with a sense of encouragement in his tone.

Medwin did his best to keep up with the intense pace set by Lenny and the other sailors, but the cannonballs were heavy, and the rate that he was expected to do something he'd never done before was unfair. But there was no such thing as fair right now. He knew he had to push himself. The speed in which he worked could mean life or death for the whole crew.

There was a thunderous crash from the upper deck, followed closely by heart wrenching cries.

Medwin thought of Conner, of how he'd saved his life twice now. It was almost like a drug. He seemed stronger somehow. Full of determination, he doubled his efforts.

* * *

Back on the main deck, it was complete and utter mayhem. Elandra had knocked over the mizzenmast, killing a good number of the crew. Their bodies lay in various places, broken from the weight of the huge piece of timber. A group of sailors hurried to try to erect the jury mast in its place, but with everything that was going on, they weren't having much luck.

"Ammin, I can' turn the bleedin' ship!" Bellamy shrieked hysterically. "I think there's somethin' jammed in the rudder!"

Without a word in response, Ammin ran to the bow of the ship. He grabbed two thick coils of rope, tied them together, tied one end to a rail post, the other to his leg, and dove off with perfect form, leaving almost no splash as he plunged into the ocean.

* * *

Ammin was under the water and facing the underbelly of *the Colossus*. After quickly finding the keel, he used it to guide himself down the length of the ship. Water rushed past him with such force that it was all he could do to resist it ripping him away. Sharp-edged barnacles scraped his skin, and by the time he reached the skeg, his cuts burned infuriatingly. A quick investigation of the skeg told him it was still intact. He moved on to the rudder itself — there was a large splintered chunk of mast wedged there. Ammin ripped, pushed, and kicked on it aggressively. Finally, after much effort, the piece of mast broke free.

He was on his last reserves of air. He needed to reach the surface quickly. The thought, 'just keep kicking,' echoed in his head repeatedly. Dots consumed his vision, and he became dizzy. Then, with lungs about to burst, his face broke the plane of water, and he was able to take huge, revitalizing breaths of glorious air.

Before he had a chance to do anything else, Ammin saw Elandra headed straight at him. In his struggle to reach the surface, he hadn't noticed her approaching. With a great amount of effort, he thrust his body out of her way. The sharp dorsal fin on her back cut the rope that was keeping him at pace with *the Colossus*. He watched as Elandra and the ship gained more and more distance from the place where he was now stuck, wading...

* * *

Conner had noticed something about the way Elandra was attacking. He needed to tell the captain. It might be their only chance to come out of this alive. He climbed down the ratline and headed for the bridge at top speed. On his way, he passed some sailors that were badly injured and moaning in agony. He grimaced as he noticed one of them had a large splinter of wood through his torso. Trying not to let these visions slow him down, Conner forced the idea to the front of his mind that, if his plan worked, it would prevent anyone else form getting hurt.

B-BOOM! — BOOM! — BOOM! — B-BOOM!-BOOM!

Cannons from the port side fired again but, like before, none hit their target. It seemed impossible to aim an accurate shot at the dragon. She was far too quick.

"Captain, I think I've realized something!" Conner yelled from a distance, still running toward Bellamy as fast as his legs would carry him.

"Out with it then, lad!" Bellamy snapped as Conner screeched to a halt in front of him.

"Every time Elandra attacks it's from the opposite side as the time before." Conner waited to see if Bellamy had comprehended what this could mean, but when the captain didn't respond, he plunged on. "I think she's doing it because she *thinks* it will keep us guessing where she'll come up next, but I figured —"

"Bu' yer bloody brilliant! We'll on'y get one shot a' this, Lad. Gawd I'm glad Ammin fixed tha' rudder! Oi, Skylar! Ge' over 'ere!"

Skylar came running over as quickly as possible. "Yer orders, Cap'n!" he said, sounding determined.

"I need yeh ter ge' up ter the starboard anchor. When I raise me 'and — drop the bleedin' thing withou' 'esitation! Go' it!"

"Aye, Cap'n!" Skylar ran off to the bow without a single question of his orders.

Conner hurried to the starboard railing and peered over it. The water was unnervingly calm. For a moment, he questioned himself. What if he was wrong? Just when his anxiety and doubts had reached their peak, Elandra's dorsal fin surfaced as she approached the ship for another attack.

"Now!" Conner screamed.

Bellamy raised his arm high.

Skylar dropped the anchor.

Bellamy cranked the ships wheel with amazing speed and power, showcasing his incredible strength. The result of this insane maneuver: *the Colossus* turned sharply to its right at the same moment that Elandra was rearing up out of the water. The long spar that extended from the ship's bow pierced through her thick, muscular neck.

The sea dragon writhed and thrashed in pain. Water splashed high into the air and crashed down onto the deck with thunderous force.

Eventually, her movements became slow. Her powerful muscles flexed one last time, snapping the end of the ship's spar. Elandra's massive body collapsed into the dark depths of the ocean and out of sight.

Captain Bellamy turned to applaud Conner on his brilliance, but he was lying on the deck. The sharp turn and impact of stabbing into the sea dragon had thrown him down. His head hit the wooded planks with such an immense force that it knocked him unconscious.

CHAPTER 12

Doubt

"Conner..." Someone was calling his name from far away. "Yeh alrigh', lad?"

"Oi, yeh gonna make it?"

Everything was black. Conner's head was throbbing with pain. Then, as if someone had turned his brain back on, memories of what had happened started to come back to him: the plan had worked, Elandra was dead, he had fallen to the deck, and everything after that was blank.

Conner opened his eyes to find Medwin, Captain Bellamy, and Lenny standing over him. "We did it, guys," he said quietly, massaging his temples.

"From what the captain tells me, it sounds like if it wasn't for you, we would all probably be dead," Medwin said, looking shaken but grinning.

"Yeh go' a righ' good 'ead on them shoulders, mate!" said Lenny as he reached out a hand to help Conner to his feet.

"Thanks," Conner replied, wishing internally that the others wouldn't give him too much credit. Any one of them would have noticed Elandra's attack pattern — had they been up that ladder with a perfect view of everything.

"Aye, the lad was brilliant 'e was," Bellamy said, giving Conner a hardy smack on the shoulder.

Conner was starting to feel frustrated now. Didn't they realize that all he'd done was climb a ladder, fire a shot that missed, and notice that Elandra was attacking from opposite sides of the ship? What about Medwin? What kind of determination must he have shown down on the gun deck to keep those cannons reloaded? What about Captain Bellamy? If it hadn't been for his knowledge of sailing and incredible strength, they never would have been able to put the plan into action. What about Ammin? He had keel hulled himself to fix the rudder! Were these not acts more deserving of praise than his own?

Conner scanned the deck in an attempt to locate Ammin, but he didn't see the captain's first mate anywhere. "Captain," he began with one last glance around the ship. "Where's Ammin?"

Bellamy's head went down and Conner knew what it meant. "Ammin … never made it back to the ship, lad," Bellamy answered with an uncharacteristically gloomy voice.

'We should be praising him,' Conner thought angrily. If he hadn't fixed the rudder, the maneuver never would've worked! He wanted to say something, but Bellamy seemed to be taking the loss of his first mate quite hard. Deciding that it would be a bit tactless just now, he settled for saying, "I'm sorry…"

* * *

The moon had long since replaced the sun as the primary orb in the sky. Broken fragments of yellow blended with the reflections of its gleaming white light, revealing the ship's sidelights to be lit.

There were no longer any dead bodies on the main deck. Conner assumed they had been given a sailor's burial, which is to be thrown overboard. He also figured the wounded were being treated somewhere down below.

The rest of the crew were celebrating their victory over Elandra with joyful music, the lyrics all of slaying sea dragons. Bellamy went over to sing and dance with his men. Years of life had given him enough wisdom to realize that sometimes the best way to mourn is to celebrate.

Conner was watching the captain, feeling badly about his loss, when a thought struck him. Who was steering the ship? He looked over at the helm to find that no one was there. He called over to Medwin, who was standing a short distance away. "Hey, Medwin, how come there isn't anybody steering the ship?"

"Oh yeah! You don't know yet, do you? When Captain Bellamy cranked the helm so violently the skeg snapped!"

"What's the skeg?" Conner asked, completely oblivious to the term.

"Yeah, that's what I said when they told me. It's the part of the ship that connects the rudder to the keel."

"So what you're saying is … the ship's completely disabled?"

"That's what I'm saying…"

Conner looked around to try getting his bearings, but it was too dark to see anything. "Where do you think we are?"

Lenny chimed in. Conner hadn't even noticed that he was standing within earshot. "Righ' near Misty Cove I'd fig'r," he said knowingly. "Cap'n says there's nothin' fer it, bu' ter ride the tide, an', where ol'

Colossus lands — well — tha'll 'ave ter do, won' it?"

"*Misty cove? We're that far east?*" Medwin yelled, sounding completely furious.

"'Ave summat o' a problem with tha', do yeh? Still alive, ain' yeh?" Lenny was eyeing Medwin like a riddle he couldn't quite figure out.

"Medwin looked suddenly embarrassed, as though he couldn't believe he had overlooked this important aspect of the situation. "No, you're right … I should be thankful that I'm alive," he admitted somberly.

"Tha's more like it," Lenny said, removing his puzzled stare from Medwin and replacing it with the usual buoyant one he so often wore. "I'm righ' proud of yeh fer keepin' up with me down on the gun deck, mate! Doin' as much as a grown man an' all!"

Medwin didn't reply, but as he turned away from Lenny, there was a bashful glow on his face.

Conner knew nothing of the lay of the land and was therefore completely in the dark as to where Misty Cove was. He was starting to wish he had a map as he asked, "Where *is* Misty Cove anyway?"

"It's right on the boarder of Iden," Medwin informed him. "This land is home to the Idenite's, and it's about as far from the Brio River as we could possibly be!"

Now Conner understood why Medwin seemed so upset about their current position. Their plan had been to follow the Brio River in hopes that the lone wolf would be using the area's abundance of life as an easy hunting ground. Conner had no idea how long it would take them to reach the river at this point, but he figured it would be days, at the very least.

Miniscule, dark shadows became visible in the distance. Conner knew it was land, but he didn't really care. Right now, all he wanted to do was sleep. He wondered what time it was. 'It must be the early hours of the morning,' he thought realistically. Either way, he was dead-tired. "Hey, Lenny, is there anywhere to sleep" — he made a hand gesture in the direction of the group of celebrating sailors — "away from all this racket?" The music was going strong, and it didn't seem like the crew would let up any time soon.

"Bit tired then, are yeh?" said Lenny, smirking. "I'd need a lie down too, af'er wha' you been through today. Come on then, I'll take yeh down ter the cabins."

Conner followed him gratefully, Medwin right on his heels.

Lenny showed them a couple of cots that were available and headed back for the celebration up top. On his way up, the boys heard him say, "Blimey, an' they're bloody younger 'n' me!"

Conner was exhausted beyond measure; sleep was more welcome than ever in his living memory.

* * *

There was an earthquake in the dream he was having, but as Conner woke up, it became obvious that this earthquake was actually *the Colossus* hitting land, resulting in its unavoidable beaching. He sat up and looked over at Medwin, who had woken up suddenly as well. Conner wasn't shocked that he'd woken, of course. Who could sleep through a jarring experience like that?

"We must have hit land," Medwin mumbled through a yawn. "Let's go up and check it out. Maybe we'll get lucky, and Lenny will have been wrong about where we would end up."

Full of the hope that only a good night's sleep can provide, the boys left the cabins and headed for the main deck.

The first thing that came into view as they stepped up out of the hatch was the majority of the crew, passed out in positions that hardly looked comfortable. The musicians were still holding their instruments, but they had slipped from playable positions now. Lenny was sleeping on a pile of rope, his mouth gaping so wide that it looked like an open invitation for spiders or any other insects that may be looking for a warm place to live. Captain Bellamy was leaned up against a pile of barrels — most of which had been tapped. He was still holding his tankard, which had tilted so far that the contents were on the verge of spilling. Dale and Landon were heaped up in a pile by the mainmast, both of them drooling. James had his head pressed against one of the untapped barrels; some kind of playing cards were scattered all across the top. There was a boot just visible behind the barrel, and Conner assumed it belonged to the other gunner, Gavin.

It seemed that the boys *were* the only ones the ship's beaching had woken up. They moved over toward the portside railing, stepping over sailors as they went.

Medwin made it to the railing first. He looked over the side and called back to Conner. "The damage looks pretty bad. From what I can tell, it looks like the bow's been punctured."

Conner, finally finished playing a sort of hopscotch where sailors were the lines and free sections of the deck were the squares, arrived next to Medwin. "Yeah, that doesn't look good. I'm not really surprised though. Not considering what it felt like when we hit."

Medwin nodded as he surveyed the area around them. "Well, it looks like Lenny was right," he said, with a disheartened tone. "This is definitely Misty Cove," he went on, some of his initial hope now dashed upon the rocks along with *the Colossus*.

Conner didn't reply. He merely stared out at nothing in particular, thinking about the, now much longer, journey ahead.

"What should we do?" Medwin asked. "You think we should just leave without saying anything?" he continued, not waiting for an answer.

"I don't know… It doesn't seem like that would be right." Conner glanced back at the sailors, still passed out in precarious positions. As he did, he felt Scarlet pressed between his hip and his belt. "I've really grown to like Captain Bellamy."

"Yeah, and if it wasn't for Lenny, we'd probably still be trying to figure out how to get to Rhona," Medwin admitted with a guilty shuffle of his feet.

The boys had convinced themselves that to leave unannounced would be nothing short of rude.

"Well, if crashing into shore didn't wake them, I don't know what will," Medwin laughed, looking thoroughly amused.

"Yeah, me either," Conner chuckled.

Medwin took in the sight of the deck again. "I'd say they need a few more hours."

"They probably had too much to drink."

"Probably?" Medwin asked, eyeing Conner expectantly.

Conner laughed, "Okay, they *definitely* had too much to drink!"

Medwin gave him a satisfied nod and said, "Maybe we should go and explore the area and get a general idea of what we're going to do when we leave?"

"Sounds good to me…" Conner replied.

Medwin grabbed a couple coils of rope. He crouched down, tied the two lengths firmly to the ship's railing, and began climbing down one of them. He was quite good at it. He did a kind of loop thing around his arm and leg; it worked well for him. He made it to the shore in no time at all.

Conner was a bit slower going. He tried not to look down for fear the view would cause his body to seize up. With the entirety of the ship's massive bow out of the water, it was like being on top of a large building. He wasn't completely afraid of heights, but the fact that there were dangerous rocks down below made the idea of a fall much more threatening. Remembering to stay focused on planting his feet firmly on solid ground, he finally reached the rocky shore.

Thick, low fog swathed Misty Cove, giving the place an ominous feel. Conner and Medwin stepped from rock to rock with extra care, due to poor visibility, and headed for a fairly thick belt of trees to the north.

Conner looked back at *the Colossus* once they had made enough ground to take in the full picture. He could see where the portside of the bow had hit the rocks. Splintered lengths of wood surrounded a gaping hole, the majority of which was consumed by the large boulder that had inflicted most of the damage upon the ship. For a moment, he wondered how long it might take to repair such damage, but he set the thoughts aside, realizing it was a topic of little concern for him. He needed to focus on his own situation.

"We're going to have to travel a really long way before we reach the Brio River..." Medwin said, sounding bleak. "And, on top of the distance, I'm not even the least bit familiar with the land out here. What if I get us lost? Or worse..." He was allowing himself to become overwhelmed by the severity of their situation again.

"I'm sure it will be okay," said Conner, using a tone of encouragement, even though he secretly felt just as concerned as Medwin did. "Maybe it won't be as bad as you're thinking it will," he added, hoping that if he told Medwin it might not be so bad, he would believe it as well.

"Thank you," Medwin replied, sounding suddenly dignified.

"For what?" Conner asked curiously.

"For having such a good outlook... For not getting discouraged... For keeping me from feeling sorry for myself in a situation that I have already realized I have no control over... It's not like there's any way I could've changed the fact that the ship would end up where the tide took it."

Conner looked up at Medwin and saw how sincere his expression was. "You're welcome," he replied simply. It felt strange to be the one speaking words of wisdom, as opposed to Medwin, who seemed to appropriately deal with every challenge that arose.

After a short silence, Medwin suggested, "Let's keep moving. The other side of these trees isn't too far now."

"Okay — yeah — good idea," Conner agreed, noticing that Medwin was trying to shrug off the somewhat uncomfortable moment they just had.

Wetland unlike anything they'd ever seen came into view as they reached the edge of the trees. To the east was a huge town, built completely on stilts and riddled with boardwalks that ran in all directions. Thousands of bamboo-made huts with thick layers of foliage for roofs lined the boardwalks. Rows of lanterns stood close enough to one another to keep the town well lit at night — they were still burning feebly, lighting up the thick lingering fog with an eerie glow.

"What a crazy town!" Conner whispered to avoid being heard in the dead-quiet."

"Yes, a very interesting location." Medwin whispered back. "I knew the Idenites dwelled in the southlands, but I had no idea that Iden was built on top of a marsh…"

Just then, a man came into sight from around the backside of one of the huts.

Conner and Medwin hid behind the nearest tree, fully aware that they couldn't take any chances. Who knew if the Idenites would be friendly if they caught two boys at what would appear to be spying?

The man approached the lantern nearest to him, blew it out, and began to stroll lazily toward the next one, stifling a yawn. Something huge and black swooped in on him from out of nowhere: a creature with an enormous wingspan. The unsuspecting man yelled with fright as he tried to draw his weapon, but it was no use. The Mirthless snatched him up at the shoulders with its hook-like claws and began to rise steadily toward the sky, beating its massive wings with such force that the heavy layer of fog drifting over the marsh blew away in a hazy swirl.

Two more of the beasts took flight from a few hundred feet down the same line of trees that Conner and Medwin were hiding amongst. The huge birds quickly caught up with the third as it lifted the screaming man high into the air.

The boys watched in absolute horror as the man was carried away, flailing like mad in a futile attempt at escaping the beast's grasp. It wasn't long before the three mirthless had turned into small dots, eventually disappearing into the distant horizon.

"Did you see that? That Mirthless just grabbed —"

"Shhh!" Medwin hissed, fixing Conner with an agitated stare. "Who knows what else is around…?"

"Sorry!" Conner whispered back, looking foolish. "It's just that … I didn't realize they were *that big!* I mean, that Mirthless just grabbed a fully grown man!"

"The Mirthless are capable of carrying the weight of one man with ease," Medwin whispered darkly. "I wouldn't be surprised if they could carry a man in each foot…"

There was a short pause, in which Conner and Medwin both continued to stare at the place in the sky the Mirthless had last been visible.

"Well," Medwin continued, "I am now completely convinced that Vellix lives in the north. Did you see which way they flew? Right in the direction of Mt. Cirrus…" Medwin looked like he might puke with the disgust of what he had just seen.

Conner had to admit, the whole thing was severely revolting. To think, a family in that town would wake up to find that they were missing a member: for the kids — a father, for the wife — a husband. Hatred for the Mirthless, for Vellix and any other creature that served him, boiled in Conner like molten lava. An intense desire to destroy, to maim, to punish them began to fill him uncontrollably. "Okay, let's focus on our mission," he finally said, when he could no longer stand the morbid thoughts and images that had crept into his mind like an infectious disease.

"Right," said Medwin, who seemed as though he was coming back from a dark corner of his mind as well. "As you can see, there are only small patches of travel-worthy land here," he said, now pointing toward an elaborate maze of waterways that carved through miniscule chunks of land to the north and west. "No matter which way we go about this, we're going to get wet." Medwin paused in apparent contemplation of the future discomfort he would have to endure. "I figure if we load my pack with as much dry kindling as possible, we won't have to take the time to gather some before making a fire once we've reached some consistently dry land. I'll just have to make absolutely sure I keep my pack dry."

Conner was only half listening. He was wondering if his cognition was good enough to get them through the marsh warm and dry. Sure, it would mean he would have to perform cognition that was vastly more advanced than anything he'd done so far, but why not give it a shot? He hadn't even tried to use his newfound power when Elandra had attacked *the Colossus*, due to his being sure there was no way his cognition would have worked on something as vast and powerful as the ocean... But this was different. This was land. He had some experience working with land. He decided to see what Medwin thought of the idea.

"Hey, Medwin?" he started timidly, suddenly feeling the pressure of bringing up the idea that he would have the skill necessary to perform cognition on such an advanced level.

"Yeah?" Medwin replied without an upward glance as he dug through his pack, looking for things he could do without in order to make room for kindling.

"What if I was able to use cognition to get us through this, you know? I could try to form a kind of path using all those bits of land," he said, aiming a pointed finger at a few of the areas he was referring to. "We wouldn't even get wet," he added quickly before awaiting Medwin's response.

Medwin didn't reply. He continued to gather firewood as if Conner hadn't addressed him with a question.

"Well? What do you think?" Conner probed after allowing another awkward moment of silence to pass.

"You could try..." Medwin finally said, his tone riddled with doubt. He looked up in time to watch as the glimmer of hope fell from Conner's face. "I mean, that would be really, *really* advanced stuff, Conner," he went on quickly in an attempt to recover himself from what he knew was a very skeptical answer.

"I know, I know ... but I'm supposed to be the one with power others have only dreamed of ... or whatever..." Conner felt more and more ridiculous the farther he got into his statement. Thoughts of doubt began to inundate his mind. Was he really this special person? It just didn't really make any sense. Out of all the people in Rohwen — all the people in his world for that matter — why would he be the one to have this incredible power of cognition? Again, he found himself wondering — why him?

'Why it's you isn't what matters,' he told himself. 'What matters is that there is no denying the truth: Vivek knew your name, you dreamt about the wolf, and you can do cognition — a power you didn't even know existed until a week ago.' He let these thoughts ring through his mind until they consumed him with validation. He still didn't understand any of it, but he was learning to accept it.

CHAPTER 13

A Destiny Decided

"Conner, I didn't mean to sound like I don't have any faith in you." Medwin said, his voice revealing how bad he was feeling for blatantly doubting Conner. "It's just that I — well, I think you should work up to cognition of that magnitude."

Conner, who was still staring off into space, lost in thought, found that Medwin's words seemed to bring him back to reality. His moment of acceptance had changed him. He felt different. He didn't feel doubtful anymore. He was ready to start training his mind, determined to do his best, no matter what. Medwin was right: he did need to work up to cognition of that magnitude.

He looked down at the ground, picturing it growing up and taking on the shape of a tiger — his favorite animal. A section of the moss-covered dirt at his feet sprang to life. Conner heard Medwin gasp as the dirt began to take form; it broke his concentration, and the dirt fell inanimately to the floor.

'Concentrate,' he told himself as he reset the picture in his mind. Once again, the ground came to life, and this time, Conner had plunged so deep into the picture he'd created that he wasn't even aware of what was happening around him. All that mattered was that the dirt obey his mental command.

He opened his eyes to find the real version of his mental image standing before him: a three-foot tall dirt sculpture of a leaping tiger with spongy green moss for fur.

Somewhere to his right, Conner heard Medwin whisper something inaudible, but he didn't need to hear the words to understand their meaning. Medwin had spoken them with an unmistakable tone of awe.

Conner turned to Medwin. "I'm going to try and form the path," he announced confidently, speaking with a resolute tone that matched the way he was feeling. "If it works, cool; if not ... we won't be any worse off, will we?"

This time, when Medwin replied, he took a different approach. It was full of encouragement instead of misgiving. "It would be *great* if we could cross the marsh without getting wet. I mean, for starters, we wouldn't need to have a fire until it was necessary for cooking. Not to mention, I would prefer to be dry for hours of travel, rather than the alternative."

Although Conner knew Medwin's doubts were most likely just as strong as they had been before, he was thankful that, this time, Medwin had chosen not to express them so willingly.

"We should probably head back to the ship. It's getting late," Medwin said with a glance up at the sun, reading it as easily as if it were a wrist watch.

"Yeah," Conner agreed. "It's probably been a couple of hours by now."

On their way back, Conner noticed that Medwin was picking up any kindling he could find. 'Probably a good idea,' he thought sensibly. What if he wasn't able to make the cognition path? They would need to be able to start a fire as quickly as possible once reaching dry land. He picked up a small armful of branches and took them over to Medwin. As he handed him the wood the boys exchanged looks of understanding — Conner understanding that Medwin didn't want to pass up the opportunity to gather kindling when it was right in front of them, and Medwin understanding that Conner was ready to accept the fact that maybe his cognition wasn't good enough to form the path.

The Colossus came into view as they exited the belt of trees and started to step carefully back across the rocks, from which the dense layer of fog had not yet lifted.

The crew was awake and moving groggily around the deck.

Captain Bellamy was on the shore, assessing the damage to his beloved ship. "I need me carpenters down 'ere, straigh' away!" he roared with both hands cupped around his mouth in order to project his already prominent voice even farther.

A sailor standing next to the captain asked a question, but his voice didn't have the same booming power as Bellamy's — Conner couldn't hear a word he said.

Bellamy's reply, however, was loud and clear. "Aye, Tom, we'll be able to fix 'er. 'S'long as I get me *carpenters!*" He yelled again for the men in his crew who were proficient in the art of woodwork. "Go' lucky we did," he went on, looking over the damage inflicted upon the front of his ship. "Any farther onter shore, an' we might not 'ave been able to get 'er back out ter sea, high tide er no'."

"Morning Captain," Conner said as he and Medwin reached the place where Bellamy and Tom were standing.

"An' wha' 'ave you lads been doin'?" Bellamy asked, turning to face them.

"Just scouting the area," Conner replied casually.

"Yeah, we were trying to get a feel for the land. Or should I say — the lack of land…" Medwin added.

"Oh? So does tha' mean you two are headin' ou' on foot then?"

Conner was quickest to answer. "Yeah, we need to get moving. We were kind of hoping to see Lenny before we left, though. Is he up yet?"

"Oh aye, the lad's up! Takin' a swim, 'e is. I fig'r 'e's tryin' to shake off the cobwebs o' las' nigh's excessive celebratin'." Bellamy laughed loudly at his own statement, smacking his upper leg a few times.

A splashing noise in the water caught Conner's attention. Lenny was swimming to shore. He reached the rocky coastline and stepped up onto one of the knee-high rocks. Conner thought the picture of him standing next to the massive, beached ship with the wind blowing his hair and clothes looked like something out of a movie.

"Cap'n, I checked the skeg while I was out there," Lenny said as he strode over toward Bellamy and the others. "Definitely gonna need the carpenters fer it," he added as he arrived at the captain's right-hand side.

"Aye," said Bellamy with a quick nod of his head. "Had a feeling it would. Good o' yeh ter check though, lad. Righ' then — *Carpenters! I need me bloody carpenters down 'ere, now!*"

Three sailors came running to the ship's railing and looked down. One of them called to the captain. "Jus' got ter grab our tools, Cap'n!"

"*Make it bloody quick then, could yeh?*"

Lenny moved over to Conner and Medwin. "Oi, mates! We'll

'ave yeh back ter Beach Bay soon as we can. Shouldn' take too long ter patch up the old hag." He jabbed his thumb toward *the Colossus*. Bellamy gave Lenny a reproachful look that he didn't notice; Conner was sure that the captain didn't take kindly to anyone calling his ship "old hag."

"Actually, we're not going to wait for *the Colossus* to be repaired," Medwin told Lenny bluntly.

"Yeah, we're going to continue our journey on foot from here," Conner said to further Medwin's statement.

Lenny's features shifted into an expression of bewilderment, as if he was having trouble processing what they were telling him. "Wha' are you two on abou' anyway? Yeh on some kind o' mission? Been wonderin' — wha' with yeh wantin' ter go ter Rhona an' everythin'. Jus' kind o' weird, in'it?" He continued to eye them inquisitively, clearly hoping for a decent answer to his question.

Neither Conner nor Medwin were sure what to say.

There was a short, awkward silence that Lenny ended saying, "None o' my business though, is it?"

Conner traded a look of relief with Medwin. He didn't want to think of how Lenny might react if he told him he was destined to befriend a wolf. The thought was still weird, even for him. "We just wanted to say thanks for helping us get to Rhona before we took off," he said, realizing that was the only thing left to say.

"Yer thankin' me? *Yer* thankin' me?" Lenny chuckled, looking thoroughly amused. "Should be thankin' *you*, shouldn' I? 'Afore yeh came along, I was dyin' ter put ter sea, wasn' I?" he laughed again.

"Well, it seems that everyone got what they were looking for, doesn't it?" Medwin interjected, sounding almost businesslike.

"Hey, Captain," Conner hollered to get Bellamy's attention. "Thanks again for the dagger!" He patted Scarlet with his hand as he thanked him.

"Oh, it was my pleasure, lad! No need ter thank me," Bellamy replied with a wave of his hand, as if swiping away the need for any thanks.

"You ready then?" Medwin asked.

"Yeah, I'm ready," Conner replied with a nod, and the two boys started toward the belt of trees that divided Misty Cove from the marshes of Iden.

* * *

"I'm really going to miss those guys," Conner admitted sincerely, giving one last backwards glance to *the Colossus*, before stepping into the forest of trees that he knew would permanently obscure his view of the great warship.

Medwin nodded. "Me too…"

"Let's get a little bit more kindling," Conner said, not just because he thought it was a good idea, but also because he wanted to change the subject to something other than that of Bellamy and the others — thinking about them would just make him miss them more.

"Good idea."

Conner's search for kindling took him to the edge of the woods. He decided to poke his head out and check to see if all was clear. Everything looked quiet and still, just as it had the first time they had been there. "Hey, it looks like we're clear to go if you're ready."

"Did you check the treetops?" Medwin asked, his tone severe.

Conner looked up along the tree line. "I don't see anything. I think it's safe for us to go."

Medwin walked over and did a quick visual sweep of his own. "Alright, let's go," he said, stepping out into the open, Conner not far behind.

Something whistled past their heads and stuck into the ground a few feet in front of them. Conner's stomach turned with horror as he realized it was an arrow. More were whining past them, coming incredibly close to finding their marks.

With a quick look back at Iden, Conner saw that there was a group of men on the edge of the boardwalk with bows — a few of them taking aim, others stringing arrows.

Medwin was already running tiptoe across the extremely wet ground, trying not to sink. He'd be forced to jump in the marsh water within his next few strides. "*Come on!*" he cried urgently.

Conner had briefly frozen in place. Medwin's yells snapped his mind back into focus. He needed to form a path — now more than ever — or he and Medwin wouldn't stand a chance of escaping the Idenite's arrows.

"Conner, hurry!" Medwin cried again as he prepared to plunge into the depths of the marsh.

Conner closed his eyes and formed a distinct image of what he needed so desperately, focusing on it with more intent than he'd put into anything in his life.

The ground around them started to tremble. It seemed to be drawing a huge, rumbling breath. Land came together from all the sparse areas that it existed out in the marsh, collecting in the form of a path out in front of them.

"Come on!" Conner yelled as he started to sprint down his cognition-made path, which was forming a split second ahead of him as he went.

Medwin's eyes bulged with shock as he ran down the path at top speed.

They ran without looking back, and before long, Conner was finding it hard to breathe. He started to develop a splitting side ache. The pain of it quickly became unbearable. He had to stop. "Medwin — Medwin, stop!" He fell to his knees, clutching his side in pain.

Medwin was forced to stop as the path ceased to continue forming where Conner had fallen to his knees.

"I can't ... I can't run anymore!" Conner spluttered, gasping for breath.

"I'm sure we're well out of range now," Medwin panted, looking back in the direction of Iden. "The Idenite's must be really agitated to have fired on us like that!" he exclaimed, still breathing hard.

"They don't know it was the Mirthless that took that man." Conner reminded him, grasping his side as he got to his feet. "They'll just be going off of the fact that one of their men has gone missing. Unfortunately for us, we were the first people they've seen since," he finished, wincing with pain as he attempted a deep breath. He focused on regaining his breath as Medwin replied.

"Yeah, that's a valid point. Good thing you were able to get us out of there. It's unbelievable how advanced your cognition has already become." He glanced down at the path that Conner had skillfully created. "I don't know that I will ever be able to achieve cognition this advanced," he admitted. He looked not only awed but discouraged as well.

Conner, who was busy being impressed with his abilities, didn't notice Medwin's obvious longing to be more efficient with his own skill. He suddenly felt like it had been foolish to have doubted himself. 'I mean, how much confirmation do you need?' said a cocky little voice in his head. 'Vivek told you who you are.'

Now full of confidence, Conner took a satisfyingly deep breath, exhaled steadily, and looked to the west. The path that extended only a few feet past where he and Medwin stood continued to form in front of them as far as they could see.

Medwin gaped as he watched the sparse chunks of land zip smoothly toward the end of the path, where they would shape and mold into the physical version of Conner's vivid mental image.

Conner set off at a leisurely pace, Medwin in stride behind him. With the prospect of getting wet while crossing the marsh long gone from their minds, the mood became bright. After a few minutes, in which they had been content to walk along in silence, they started to exchange stories of what had happened to them during the fight with Elandra in more detail.

"I figured you must have been going like crazy to keep those cannons loaded," Conner laughed as he did an exaggerated impression of Medwin running around grabbing cannon balls.

Medwin laughed so hard tears began to streak down his cheeks. It took him a minute to compose himself before he said, "I still can't believe you noticed Elandra had an attack pattern," his voice full of disbelief. He stared thoughtfully at the ground for a moment. "I wonder how many ships she sank."

"Who knows?" Conner said, shrugging. "A bunch, I'm sure."

Medwin nodded.

"Oh yeah, that reminds me," Conner went on quickly, "I forgot to tell you. I heard a story about Elandra on the trip to Rhona." He dove into the story of how Captain Bellamy had been first mate on a ship called *the Expeditious* and of how Elandra had attacked and sunk that ship, most of the crew along with it.

"So Bellamy survived an attack from her prior to the one she mounted on *the Colossus*?" Medwin asked, sounding impressed.

"Yep. Crazy huh? He's a — *ahhh!*"

Both boys sank abruptly into the marsh. The path had evaporated from existence as fast as Conner had formed it.

Medwin struggled frantically to get his pack off. If he could salvage any of the kindling, it would be better than nothing. "What happened?" he asked angrily, pulling his now soaking wet pack out of the water and trying not to look as upset as he was.

At first, Conner couldn't think of an answer. He was confused as to what had gone wrong. It wasn't until he stopped trying to find an explanation that the answer came to him. It was clear now. He had become complacent about his abilities: arrogant and unfocused. He looked over at Medwin, who was holding his pack above the water, which was now dripping wet.

Conner clenched his teeth in frustration toward himself for being so foolish. He closed his eyes and focused on the path re-forming;

nothing happened. The splashing sounds of Medwin fighting to keep his pack out of the water echoed like words of disappointment in his ears. Overwhelmed by shame, he wasn't able to focus properly.

"Are you going to be able to make the path again?" Medwin asked hopefully.

Conner didn't reply. Instead, he took a few calming breaths and dedicated his mind to the image of the path. Every speck of solid ground worked its way back to the place where the path had once existed as it reconstructed at Conner's will. 'This time you will not lose focus!' he demanded of himself, clambering back onto solid ground.

Medwin climbed up after him and started to walk cautiously. Evidently, he was expecting to step back into the water at any second. Conner followed like a puppy looking for approval or forgiveness from its master.

"It's okay," he said, hoping Medwin would forgive him for his mistake. "I'm not going to lose focus again," he added firmly. "I'm — really sorry that I let you down, Medwin ... I *really* am..."

"That's alright, Conner," Medwin said with an attempt at a cheery grin. "I was expecting to get wet anyway, remember?"

"Yeah, but if I hadn't lost my focus, we would still be dry."

"Lesson learned, Conner... Lesson learned."

Conner appreciated Medwin's ability to shrug off the fact that he had cost them, not only time, but also their comfort and dry kindling. He wouldn't have blamed Medwin for losing his temper.

"So, could you tell me more about the Satria?" Conner figured if he made conversation it would lighten the mood as well as help keep his mind off the fact that he was soaked and extremely uncomfortable.

"What would you like to know?" Medwin asked in response.

"I don't really know," Conner began, realizing he hadn't been ready to have his question answered with a question. "You said you're a warrior tribe, so I assume you must train a lot..."

Medwin replied with a glance that told Conner he had assumed correctly before saying, "Yeah, we do. The Satria use many techniques to achieve becoming great warriors. Fathers start training their sons when they reach the age of five — basically, as soon as we're stable on our feet. We're taught grappling, how to handle a sword, hatchet, or spear — archery, hunting, fishing, survival skills, and, for those of us the elders deem worthy, cognition."

"How do the elders determine who's worthy?"

"Well," Medwin started, his brow furrowed in thought, "I've never actually known how to be honest. It's not really something they tell us. But, if I had to guess, I would say they must keep a close watch over us as our skills develop. Those of us who show signs of wisdom and a strong hunger for knowledge are taken on a special hunting trip so we can learn the art of cognition in a real-life setting. If you are chosen to take this special trip, it is a great honor to your family. My father was very proud when I was chosen. It was on that hunting trip that I first learned how —"

"To make your underground room," Conner blurted out, finishing his sentence.

"Indeed," Medwin continued with a small grin. "Anyway, as I was saying, I was thirteen at the time that I took my trip. I went with an elder by the name of Yorick — my father's head advisor. He was extremely impressed with me. Of course, now that I've seen what you're capable of … my skills seem a bit obsolete." Medwin gave Conner a weak smile that didn't really make him look happy about having skills that were obsolete at all.

Conner's face briefly turned pink. "Your skills aren't obsolete, Medwin," he said confidently. "You're able to make that awesome underground room, and those stairs you carved into the Cliffs of Elders were pretty amazing … and…" He had run out of examples before he was ready.

"I appreciate you saying that, Conner," Medwin said calmly, "but you and I both know that my cognition pales in comparison to yours — which is fine," he added quickly. "You are the one that's supposed to have special power, so it really is a good thing that you're better at it than I am."

Conner wondered who Medwin was really attempting to convince — Conner, or himself.

Medwin stopped abruptly and looked down at something in the dirt.

"What's up?" Conner asked, unable to see anything on the ground that was worth stopping for.

Instead of answering, Medwin bent down and tried to pull up a branch that was poking a few inches out from the path. It wouldn't budge. Conner wondered why Medwin would go to this kind of effort to retrieve a stick, but he decided not to ask, for fear that his answer might make him feel like an idiot.

Medwin's shoulders rose and fell as he took a deep, steadying breath. He attempted to remove the branch again; this time, the path shifted itself from around the branch and he was able to pull it out with ease. He examined the stick for a moment, rotating it in his hands so he could view it from all angles. It seemed that he must be pleased with his find, as his face held a look of satisfaction.

"That looks like it'll make a nice walking stick," said Conner, who was wondering whether Medwin had done something that required the use of cognition just to remind himself that, even though he might not be the one with special power, he was still quite good at it. "Is that what you're going to use it for, a walking stick?"

"I will until we reach the end of the marsh," Medwin replied, still eyeing the branch with a pleased expression.

"What will you do with it after that?" Conner asked, curious as to what else this stick would be good for.

"I am going to use it to make a hunting spear, for the specific use of catching bull frogs." Medwin saw the puzzled look on Conner's face and decided to explain in further detail. "First, you sharpen one end of the stick into a point." He showed Conner the end that he was obviously intending to use. "Next, you make two crossing incisions in the point. They need to be around a finger's length in depth." He rested his finger against the branch to better illustrate his meaning. "Then, you shove twigs down into the incisions until you've spread the point, forming four separate prongs." He separated his index, middle, ring, and pinky fingers as an example of the prongs. "Finally, you take strong vines to use as twine, and tie everything securely together. The end result is that you get a four-prong spear, which is great because it quadruples your chances of a catch. Actually it improves your chances even more, due to the fact that the frog will often get wedged between the prongs."

"Sounds like — maybe — you know what you're doing!" Conner laughed. He was once again extremely impressed with Medwin's advanced knowledge.

"I sure hope so," Medwin said seriously. "I'm really hungry."

Conner's stomach growled. "Me too."

The sun was hanging low in the sky, and due to their western heading, Conner and Medwin were walking straight at it. A vivid reflection of the few fluffy white clouds gliding across the sky bounced off the motionless water, making it look as though, if the boys were to step off the path, they would fall into the sky.

As Conner soaked in the view, he noticed something faint in the distance. A feeling of elation caressed him as he realized it was trees. Trees meant wood, wood meant fire, and fire meant he and Medwin would soon be cozy and dry. "Hey, I think I see trees up ahead. That means we must be at the end of the marsh!" His voice was full of the joy a warm fire and food will always bring.

"Yeah, you're right! Those are definitely trees!" Medwin sounded excited as well.

It wasn't long after they had seen the trees that the bank of the marsh came into view.

"When we get to the woods up ahead, you should start searching for kindling immediately," Medwin ordered Conner, who didn't really mind being told what to do. In fact, he felt it was only fair that he be the one to collect the firewood, being as it was his fault they had none.

"Okay, no problem," he said enthusiastically.

"We're running out of daylight, so we need to hurry," Medwin said with urgency in order to bring to reality the severity of their situation.

"I'll get to work on my hunting spear."

"Sounds good," said Conner as he started jogging toward the bank. Before long, he reached the forest of trees beyond the marsh. As Medwin had said, he started searching for kindling immediately.

Medwin arrived after a few minutes. He found a decent clearing, sat down, and got to work on his four-prong spear.

Most of the wood Conner was finding was moist. Being that the trees kept that area in constant shade and that they were right next to a marsh, it wasn't all that surprising that he couldn't find anything dry enough to pass as decent kindling.

"Get some sap from a tree," Medwin advised him. "It will help us get that damp wood to burn."

"Good idea," said Conner. "I wish I knew more stuff about nature," he admitted, feeling like he should have already known to get some sap.

"It seems you won't be waiting long to get what you wish for. You are learning 'stuff' about nature as we speak."

Conner couldn't help but notice some sarcasm in Medwin's voice. "I wasn't trying to bug you," he mumbled.

Medwin looked away from his project and up at Conner. "You didn't bug me," he said unconcernedly.

"Oh... Well, it kinda seemed like it, with the way you responded just now..." Conner didn't know why he was still pursuing the subject at this point. The only result was that he was starting to feel more idiotic than before.

"Sorry about that," Medwin replied with a shrug. "I'm extremely hungry, cold, and wet. I guess maybe I'm a bit irritable at the moment."

"That's okay. Honestly, I wouldn't blame you for being mad at me. If it wasn't for me, we wouldn't even need a fire."

"We would if you want a hot meal," Medwin said, eyeing Conner wisely. "Not to mention, if it wasn't for you, we would've gotten wet the whole way across the marsh. Come to think of it," he continued, looking thoughtful, "if it wasn't for you, we might be dead... I'm not sure we would've been able to get out of range of the Idenite's arrows without the path you made."

Conner smiled. "Thanks, Medwin. I guess you're right."

"Of course I am! Now hurry up and get some sap! I'm freezing!"

Conner laughed and said, "Okay," as he went to collect the tree sap.

He returned a short while later, laden with wood. As Conner dropped the firewood in a pile and pulled the sap out of his pocket, Medwin said, "I'll get this fire going if you want to go and remove the path you made. I was just thinking — it's not very wise to leave something so unnatural in the landscape, lingering for unwanted eyes to see."

"That's true." Conner said with a nod. He strode over to the bank and focused on the marsh returning to its original state. He watched as all the patches of land that had come together to form the path were sucked back to their former locations. It was like watching a movie in rewind.

The sound of fire reached Conner's ears. He shivered involuntarily as he went over to sit beside it — not a cold shiver, but the shiver of warmth spreading throughout his whole body, as if he had just sank slowly into a hot bath. Conner sat gratefully next to the fire and took off his sponge-like socks and shoes.

"I think I'm done," Medwin announced, holding up his spear creation. It was well crafted, especially considering how little time he'd spent on it. "I'll be back with some bullfrogs ... I hope," he said with a wide-eyed, slightly deranged grin, which was telling of how maddening it would be if he returned from his hunt empty handed.

Conner tried to lighten the mood. "I'm sure you'll catch plenty." He glanced at Medwin's four-prong spear. "I mean, look at the spear you made... How could you not catch something with that?" His encouragement seemed to work a little because Medwin gave him a normal smile before he grabbed his pack and set off into the night.

Conner stared at the last spot he'd been able to see Medwin for a moment before turning his attention to the fire. The flames were hypnotic. He drifted euphorically into a slideshow of memories...

He was five; his dad had just been apprehended by the new sheriff in town, and he was riding off into the sunset on a dust-broom horse... He was eight; a boy named Chris was asking him to come over and play video games... He was twelve; a group of giggling girls were pointing at him and whispering... He was fourteen; his dad was telling him they were moving to Montana —

A rustling sound pulled him back from his memories. He glanced in the direction of the noise curiously. Fear struck his heart as a pair of glowing eyes met him in an unblinking stare. Their owner lunged at him. Sharp teeth guided by a powerful jaw sank easily into his arm. Hot blood began gushing freely from the point of impact.

Conner had to do something fast, but the shock of being attacked so suddenly was making it hard to focus. He thought of trying to reach Scarlet, but teeth had the natural arm for the job clamped firmly. Squinting his eyes, he was just able to make out the shape his attacker as he was dragged deeper into the woods. Before he even knew he was saying them, words seemed to spew out of his mouth. "You're the lone wolf!"

The beast released its grip on Conner's arm and tilted its head curiously.

With such a good first response, Conner went on. "My name is Conner."

The wolf's eyes widened quickly. Then, to Conner's disbelief, it replied. "And mine is Zelimir." His voice was surprisingly gentle.

"You … can talk…" Conner whispered, gaping at the wolf.

"*Conner, where are you?*" Medwin's voice echoed through the trees. He sounded stressed and afraid.

"Over here, Medwin," Conner called back, hoping his weakening voice was loud enough to direct Medwin to the place where he sat on the ground, losing liberal amounts of blood.

Medwin followed Conner's voice, and as he rounded the last bush blocking Conner from the view, the scene that met his eyes made him gasp. In the minimal amount of firelight finding its way over to them, he saw Conner sitting there, clutching at a badly mangled arm, with a wolf sitting next to him. Medwin dropped his pack to the ground and ran over to Conner, ignoring the beast entirely. "Let me see your arm!"

Conner moved his hand off the wound. The pain was excruciating, unlike anything he'd experienced. It was nearly incomprehensible.

"That doesn't look good," Medwin mumbled under his breath, grimacing. "What are we going —" Medwin stopped abruptly, a look of dawning comprehension emerging in his expression. He ran back over to his pack. The sound of glass jars clinking together filled the silent air. He returned to Conner, carrying a jar full of a goopy-looking substance.

Conner recognized the substance as Medwin dabbed it over his wound: the healing agent that Vivek had given them on Rhona. "Good thinking, Medwin," he said, sounding weak. He had started to feel lightheaded. The idea of passing out was becoming a good one.

Medwin, noticing that Conner was starting to drift off, smacked him hard across the face and told him to stay alert. He turned to face Zelimir. "You must be the lone wolf," he said, unable to think of any other reason the wolf would just be sitting there, not furthering its attack. "...But, I — I thought you were supposed to be different from the other wolves! Why did you attack Conner?" he yelled, his voice shaking from a combination of confusion and anger.

Zelimir sat, silent and unmoving for a moment, as if he hadn't heard a word Medwin said. Finally, he responded. "It is true — I am the lone wolf."

Medwin gasped with shock. He had spoken to the wolf because it was habit for him to express what he was thinking or feeling with words — especially when he was angry or upset about something. He hadn't actually expected the wolf to respond.

Zelimir spoke again, "My name, as I have already told your friend, Conner, is Zelimir. It is not normally my practice to attack humans, but I am desperate for nourishment. I haven't eaten anything for a very long time."

Conner, whose wounds had already started to heal from the effects of Vivek's potion, looked more closely at the wolf. He noticed upon further observation that an indent was clearly visible between every one of the beast's ribs.

"I heard two voices coming from just the other side of these trees." Zelimir jerked his head to the spot he was describing. "I investigated and saw two boys. One of them left for some reason, leaving the other sitting alone ... helpless. In my moment of weakness, I attacked..." Zelimir paused, allowing his words time for impact. "I am not proud of that moment of weakness. However, in the end, fate led me to this part of the woods with conscience-blinding hunger, for the one I seek now sits before me."

Conner and Medwin exchanged meaningful looks. Conner was completely taken aback. Vivek had said the lone wolf would know nothing of their intertwined destinies. "Wait a minute ... you're, seeking me? But, I'm — I'm seeking *you!* I was told that it was my destiny to befriend the lone wolf — you!"

"Well, your destiny was decided then, for I was sent to find you."

"You were sent to find me? By who?"

"Vellix."

CHAPTER 14

Zelimir's Tale

Medwin darted in the direction of his pack to retrieve his hatchet. Conner reached instinctually for his dagger, Scarlet: a useless move, due to the fact that he could barely even flex his right arm.

"*Wait!*" Zelimir shouted, his voice exuding power and authority.

Conner and Medwin jumped in alarm.

Zelimir continued. "If I wished to kill you, do you really think you would still be alive?" he asked significantly, shifting his stare from Medwin to Conner and back to Medwin, where he left it and went on speaking. "It is not my intention to harm you. Believe me, if you were so foolish as to attack me, you would be no match. Please allow me to explain myself. Shall we head back to the comfort of the fire?"

The boys nodded in agreement, looking as foolish as they felt.

Medwin strayed off from the path that Conner and Zelimir were taking back to the fire. He returned shortly after with a couple thin branches. The three of them gathered around the fire, and Medwin pulled the frogs from his pack. "I was able to catch a good number of bull frogs," he announced. "You're more than welcome to some legs, Zelimir."

"You are very kind — Medwin is it?"

"Yes, sir."

Zelimir chuckled. "Please, there is no need to call me 'sir'... You look like you are of the Satria tribe. Is that correct?"

"Yes, s — I mean, yeah, that is correct," Medwin replied as he started preparations for cooking the frog legs.

"There is no need to cook mine," Zelimir said. "I will take what you offer me raw."

Medwin looked up at Zelimir. "I guess you are a wolf, huh?"

"Yes, I am," he replied with another light chuckle.

"There you go." Medwin offered Zelimir his share of legs. The wolf ate them at a startling pace. Conner watched him, wondering if he had even chewed. 'I suppose he was hungry enough to eat me,' Conner thought, feeling revolted by the idea.

Medwin stabbed four frog legs onto a stick and handed it to Conner. The fact that he was finally going to eat cheered him up greatly. He had already been very hungry before losing substantial amounts of blood; now he was beyond any level of hunger he had ever known. He tried to lift the legs toward the fire, but sharp pain ran through his arm like an electric shock. It seemed that Vivek's healing agent hadn't done enough to give him free mobility yet. This was no problem. He switched arms and started cooking the legs with his left.

Zelimir initiated conversation. "I wish to tell you my tale, if you are ready to hear it?"

Conner and Medwin both looked at Zelimir with great attentiveness — Conner was incredibly curious to know how it came to be that the wolf he had been seeking, who was clearly non-hostile, was sent to seek him by Vellix. It didn't add up.

"Very well," Zelimir started, reading Conner and Medwin's looks of attention. "My tale begins when I abandoned my pack for their continued service to Vellix. However, I will not be entering it upon that day. I will, instead, begin on the day I was captured by the Mirthless…

"It was seven days ago. I had been taking cover in a dense group of trees and shrubbery along the western fork of the Brio River — this was for the simple fact that I am a carnivore, and life is abundant there. It wasn't an overall wise place to be, of course. Rais, and the rest of my former pack, would be sure to hunt for me there. This knowledge worried me greatly, but, in the end, I let hunger take control of my better judgment. I stayed, telling myself I would move on after I had found one good sustainable meal. After all, the river is hundreds of miles long. I had its extensive length on my side.

"I had taken to staying hidden during the day. The sound of footsteps met my ears. I knew immediately that it was not the wolves. The steps were of two-legged creatures — most likely humans. I peered out of the bushes to get a decent look. It was two boys, whom I daresay sit before me now."

Conner looked over at Medwin, trying his hardest not exhibit an "I told you so" expression.

"You two didn't look like you were of any threat to me. I would have remained still, but I could swear you saw me, Conner — right as I was ducking back down into my cover."

"I did see you!" Conner exclaimed. "At the time, I didn't know if I'd seen anything or not. I thought maybe my eyes were playing tricks on me…"

"It seems that they were not… Anyway, assuming I had been spotted, I got spooked and decided it was a sign to move on, before I was seen by unwelcome eyes. This proved to be a fateful mistake. Not long after abandoning my hiding place, I was attacked and captured by the Mirthless. I did not struggle, as it would have resulted in my unavoidable death. I employed something much stronger than physical strength: my intellect.

"The Mirthless were taking me straight in the direction of Mt. Cirrus. It could only mean one thing. Vellix sought an audience with me. But why? He knew I was a traitor to his cause. There had to be something he wanted, otherwise he would have had his Mirthless kill me on the spot.

"I knew it wouldn't be a short journey from the place I was captured to the mountain. I had time to formulate a plan: I would go along with Vellix's demands, act weak and regretful for my disobedience to him. He is already so prepared to believe that this is how any creature should behave in his presence that I knew my acting wouldn't even have to be that good to fool him. Of course, I still sought to do my best. If he would have seen through me," Zelimir said, shuddering involuntarily, "let's just say I might be alive but wishing I was dead…"

Conner wondered what exactly Zelimir meant by that, but he was far too enthralled in the wolf's story to interrupt.

"After what proved to be the most uncomfortable trip of my life, I arrived at the topmost peak of the mountain. There is a vast cave upon the peak — that is where Vellix dwells."

Medwin nodded, staring deeply into the entrancing flames of their fire.

"The first thing I heard was the crackling of fire coming from torches that kept the chamber dimly lit. The color of the flames was unnatural and foreboding. Then Vellix spoke. His voice was icy, menacing. He sounded pleased as he told Zarmena — the leader of the Mirthless — to bring me before him. It was time to put my plan into action. I cowered before him and pled for his forgiveness. 'Please my lord!' I said, sounding as pitiful as possible. 'I was a fool! Allow me to rectify my deeds of ignorance...'

"Vellix responded with the arrogance I had been counting on. 'What use would a pathetic excuse for a wolf like you be to me?' he asked, staring down on me as if I were something so ugly that he could hardly bear to look. I countered with quick-wit. I became as pathetic as he had already deemed me to be. 'It is for you to decide ... my liege.' " Zelimir bowed to Conner and Medwin for emphasis. "'I wish only to serve...' Vellix contemplated me for quite some time. It seemed he was still unsure if I was to be trusted. Finally, he said, 'Vega, take him to the holding chamber.'

"I heard the rattling of a chain as something came out of the shadows. As the torchlight cascaded over its face, I saw that the creature was contorted and grotesque. It almost appeared to have once been human — like either of you. Now it was deformed in ways that gave it the sickening look of an experiment gone horribly wrong. The chain I had heard was attached to an iron shackle around its neck. Vellix unlatched the chain from its clasp.

"As the creature came to collect me, I could see that there was pain of the type no being should ever endure in his eyes. At that moment, I realized what horrific deeds Vellix was capable of. The creature had once been human."

Conner clenched his hands into fists. He felt a fierce anger stir within the depths of his core. He attempted to repress it as Zelimir continued.

"I was taken down a stairway unlike any I have ever seen. It was as if it had always been a part of the mountain — like nobody had constructed it, it had always just existed.

"Deeper and deeper into the heart of the mountain we went.

"After what felt like many hours, a terrifying sound became audible. It sounded like the mingled cries of thousands of creatures.

"We reached an enormous hollow. Due to how dark it was, I have no idea the actual size. There was a small lake in the middle. Hundreds of rock-made shelves, which protruded varied distances, covered the walls. Each one harbored more horrendous-looking creatures: all of them products of Vellix's demented experiments. Some had the basic structures of humans, others of animals. Their mourning cries echoed off the chamber walls, sounding more demented as they bounced back than they had initially.

"As I lay there, awaiting my fate, I wondered if it was a fate similar to these poor creatures: a fate in which I would become one of Vellix's experiments. With nothing but disturbing cries and my own horrendous thoughts to focus on, my stay in the chamber felt timeless. Fortunately, my internal clock served me well. I knew only six days had passed.

"Fear that I had been mistaken about Vellix's intentions threatened to overwhelm me as something grabbed the scruff of my neck and yanked me to my feet. I focused my eyes and realized it was Vega — the creature that led me to the underground hollow. How he was able to come upon me without my hearing him, I still cannot say. I can only guess that it was owed to my being so consumed by fearful thoughts.

"The trip back up the nearly eternal stairway took every bit of intestinal fortitude I had. To face the man responsible for the atrocities I saw in the holding chamber struck a fear in my heart like I had never known.

"Once more, I stood before Vellix. Begrudgingly, I bowed, in my continued attempt to convince him I wished to repent for my foolish behavior. I played my part well, and in the end, I fooled the most powerful and evil man in all of Rohwen.

"Vellix gave me a job to do. A job I never intended to carry out … that was, until I realized something. In his feeling of superiority over me, he had given away too much. He leaked an emotion: fear. He told me he had become aware of a boy whom had arrived in our land. Vellix sought to confront this boy before he had a chance to linger. He told me the boy would be a danger to all who dwell here, which I knew, inadvertently, meant a danger to him. I knew I must find this boy before the Mirthless did. Surely, Vellix would have them searching as well.

"I believe his reason for using me is because I have remarkably sharp senses, which makes me an exceptional tracker. Things were playing in my favor. You see, I knew Vellix would be keen to give me all the information he had in order to make my search for the boy — you Conner — as easy as possible. 'My lord,' I said convincingly, 'I wish for nothing more than to rid Rohwen of this threat. What is it that will give the boy away?'

"Vellix answered without hesitation. 'He will be clad in strange garments. This should be his biggest giveaway. I am also aware that his name is Conner. My Mirthless have spotted him. They say he looks to be the age of coming into manhood.'

"When Vellix was done giving me the information he had, he warned me that if I so much as strayed, marginally, from the job he'd given me, I would pay dearly. He attempted to make mind-piercing eye contact with me as he spoke, as if hoping to see intent or truth in my eyes. I stared right back into his dark, sunken eyes. The fool! Didn't he understand that I am a wolf?" Zelimir inhaled, and his chest puffed up with pride.

"Vellix then told me he would be informing Rais of my mission, knowing it would put my mind at ease about being attacked. I was told to bring you straight to him and to keep you alive at all costs. Obviously, this meant he must want to speak with you before dispatching you.

"Our conversation was done, my deed ready to be carried out. The Mirthless brought me to the outskirts of these woods. I watched as they flew east, toward Iden. My mind was buzzing with curiosity. Why was the most powerful being in all of Rohwen scared of a boy? I had to know. I had to find the boy ... help him if I could... Whatever his power was ... whatever he could do to purge Rohwen of Vellix's evil... I knew I must help. The downfall of Vellix is the only hope for my kind to return to our, once, proud stature, rather than be servants of filth.

"You see, about twelve hundred years ago, Vellix approached Faolan — leader of the wolves during the age — with a bribe he could not resist. Vellix promised him, and all his descendants, the ability of human speech. In return, he asked for the unfaltering service of the pack. Ever since that day, the wolves have been at his service. I am appalled by some of the evils my ancestors achieved under his reign.

They became lustful for human meat — something that had been a last resort of survival. They brought innocent creatures before Vellix to become subject to his foul will... This behavior is still the way of my kind..."

"Would you like a few more frog legs, Zelimir?" Medwin asked, trying to sound understanding of the shame Zelimir must feel being directly related to such evil creatures.

"Yes, that would be great. Thank you... You are most kind."

Conner looked straight at Zelimir and said, "I can tell you why Vellix fears me." The wolf listened intently as Conner began explaining about the ancient scrolls of Hylan, Vivek, and cognition.

"So let me get this straight," Zelimir said, interrupting Conner's story for the sake of curiosity. "You have a power called cognition? And this is the same power that gives Vellix the abilities he has?"

"Yeah, and the scrolls said I would have a power others had only dreamed of," Conner told him, still trying to get used to the way this knowledge made him feel.

"This is a most interesting piece of information. Can you give me a demonstration of this power?"

A nervous feeling moved through Conner as the wolf put him on the spot. "Sure," he answered, brushing aside the unwanted sensation. He stabbed the stick with his last remaining frog leg on it into the ground. A second later, the ground around the stick rose up, rotating to bring the leg to a position that faced him. He pulled it off and took a bite, smiling.

"Incredible!" Zelimir exclaimed. "Now I understand Vellix's fear of your lingering. He doesn't want you to discover your true identity."

Conner nodded and continued his story. He came to the point where Vivek had told him he was destined to befriend the lone wolf. A thought entered his mind that bugged him. "Wait a minute. Something doesn't add up."

Medwin and Zelimir both stared silently and waited for him to divulge.

"If Vellix knew to fear my arrival — then he must have seen the scrolls. Why would he send you to find me if he knew we were destined to meet? That makes absolutely no sense."

"Indeed, Conner, your point is valid," Zelimir said. "Could it be that as I believed myself to be fooling him, he had a plan beyond my knowledge?"

"Why would he want to fulfill our destinies though?" Conner asked, looking bemused.

"Good question. My thoughts are that after such a short time in Rohwen, he thought you would know not of the scrolls. He assumed you would be blind to this knowledge, as he knew I was. Maybe he decided that if it was already our destiny to meet, he would be the one to control it. He is arrogant beyond any level I have ever seen. It would be like him to think he could control something like that. He must have thought his plan to be a brilliant one. Send me to find and bring you before him, and kill us both together."

"Well that isn't going to happen," Conner said, grasping instinctually at the handle of Scarlet. "What he has done is unforgivable!"

Medwin stood up. "Calm down," he said, placing a hand on Conner's shoulder as he surveyed their surroundings cautiously. "We mustn't be heard. Speaking of which, I feel vulnerable out here. I know we've got the trees for cover, but I think we should sleep in my underground room."

Conner gestured in agreement, and moments later, they were heading below Rohwen's surface.

"Wait," Zelimir said, leaping down into the room. "You have this power as well, Medwin?"

"I do," Medwin answered. He told Zelimir about how Vivek had chosen the Satria to pass down his knowledge of cognition.

Conner went and settled onto his bed. He watched Medwin do the same as Zelimir curled up on the floor. His mind was spinning with thoughts of Zelimir's story. The idea of using cognition to experiment on innocent people and creatures was sickening. Not only that, but what was the point? Did Vellix just do it for fun? What good were hundreds of deformed creatures going to do him? As he lay there, fuming with anger, it became clear that Vivek was right: he had to face Vellix. Any man capable of such evil could not be left unchallenged. But, before he could do anything, he would need a plan.

"So, Zelimir, now that you've found me, do you have a plan?" Conner asked, sounding hopeful. "I mean for going after Vellix," he added to make sure he and the wolf were on the same page.

Zelimir took a moment before he replied. "To be quite honest, no... I expected my search for you to take much longer. I haven't really had time to think of anything except how I was going to find you. I have to admit — the speed in which I located you was like — like..."

"Destiny," said Conner.

CHAPTER 15

The Pons

The following morning brought with it warm summer sun. Its brilliant rays found their way through the treetops and patterned the wooded floor with cheerful light.

As Conner and the others exited the room, the sunlight revealed Zelimir's appearance properly. The wolf — even in his half-starved state — was gorgeous. He stood nearly three feet tall and had thick fluffy fur, varying in color. His underside, legs, and snout were a tawny color, as opposed to his body, which was predominantly gray, with browns, darker grays, and white speckled in. There was a black streak running along his spine, and the dark fur that decorated his face looked almost like a mask, accenting his golden yellow eyes.

The three travelers sat in a circle and plotted their course of action.

"I say we head north, directly toward Mt. Cirrus," Medwin proposed. "Any other route will take substantially longer and only lead to the same end result."

Zelimir wasn't so sure about this idea. "Yes, but there is very little cover in Edelan," he reminded Medwin. "That area of the world is nothing more than a desert wasteland at this point. It would be a grueling journey to cross it," he concluded in a tone that made it clear he felt this final piece of information was enough to solidify his point.

"There might be something in that," said Conner, rolling his eyes upward, as if they may be able to see into his mind and therefore help him get a clear picture of what he was trying to think. "I mean," he continued slowly, still trying to make sure his thoughts were in order, "if we're spotted with an extra companion, the Mirthless will be sure to know something isn't right." His thoughts started to flow freely now. "To me, it makes sense to take the least likely route. I doubt the Mirthless will even fly over the desert. Don't you think they'll be assuming no one would ever go that way? Honestly, it just might be the *best* way."

Zelimir explored Conner's face for a moment before he answered. "You make a good point, Conner." The wolf continued to look thoughtful as he went on. "I suppose there is no real safety for us now — no matter where we are or what we do..."

"So straight for Mt. Cirrus it is then," Medwin said as he grabbed his pack.

"It would seem so," Zelimir laughed. "You surprise me, Medwin."

"Really... Why is that?" Medwin asked, who didn't appear to have liked the tone Zelimir had used.

"Most people aren't so spirited about racing to their untimely deaths," Zelimir said, giving him a serious look.

Medwin frowned. "What, you're expecting me to die?"

"Please don't think I'm singling you out," Zelimir responded quickly. "I expect all of us to die."

"What about my power of cognition?" Conner asked, looking disheartened. "I thought we were going after Vellix because I am the one to defeat him..."

"Perhaps you are. Tell me, though, if Vellix came walking out from those trees over there, do you think you would defeat him?" Zelimir asked rhetorically.

This question was not a difficult one for Conner to answer, but he did wish Zelimir would stop looking at him as though he already knew what he was going to say. "No — I don't think I would," Conner replied reluctantly.

"So what exactly is the point then? What are you getting at?" Medwin flared up. "Are you saying we should just give up now — because, if you are, then —"

"I'm only saying this," Zelimir yelled, clearly finished listening to Medwin's outburst. Medwin looked like the wolf had slapped him in the face, but Zelimir appeared not to care. He ignored the look and continued. "Screw your heads on straight and we might have a chance of defeating Vellix… Yes, I know he is extremely powerful, and it will take a great amount of power to challenge him, but this is going to take more than brawn: it's going to take brains…" Zelimir paused to allow his words some mental impact. "…We can't just stroll up to Vellix's front door and win that fight. We need to take a strategic approach."

Conner and Medwin looked at one another sheepishly, both of them realizing that these facts should have made sense from the get go. They shifted their feet while becoming unable to look at anything but the twigs, leaves, and pine needles sprinkled across the ground.

Zelimir noticed their silence and wondered if he had been too blunt with them. "Do not get discouraged. You need that kind of passion to embark on such a mission. I only ask that you exercise as much mental strength as you intend to exercise physically. It is the only way we stand a chance."

Conner and Medwin nodded, displaying a unanimous expression of respect for Zelimir's wisdom.

"Shall we then?" Zelimir said with a head gesture to the north. The boys responded with gestures of agreement. And so began the true journey: a journey to free beings of all kinds from the reign of Vellix.

The morning air was pleasant and it soothed Conner's mind as he, Medwin, and Zelimir set forth from the woods and started their descent into the Forsaken Desert.

Sparse clusters of branchy plants clung diligently on to life around the outskirts of the desert, but the farther they went, the more barren the land became. Soon all that existed around them were hills of sand, rolling fluidly into the horizon.

* * *

For the first couple of hours, Conner and the others spoke very little. Conner's vision strayed off into the distance. The heat of the desert was so intense that there appeared to be vapors rising like steam from the horizon into the azure-blue sky. Conner enjoyed the illusion for a while before losing interest.

He wished there was a more diverse landscape to enjoy. Up until now, he hadn't realized how much it helped pass the time when he was busy enjoying the beauty of the land around him. Now, with nothing but sand for miles in every direction, he was already starting to wish they were through the desert.

He was delighted when a few small knots of plant life became visible in the distance. They looked to be made mostly of cacti, but a good number of branchy bushes speckled the general area as well. Perhaps these were the first signs of life that marked the desert's end.

Zelimir's nose twitched. He ran off at full speed, heading for the heart of the bushes. There was some commotion, causing a plume of dust to rise into the air. The dust quickly became thick and blocked Conner and Medwin's view of what was happening.

A minute later, Zelimir emerged with a jackrabbit in his mouth. He trotted happily back to meet up with the others.

"Nice catch!" Medwin exclaimed. "I can store that in my pack until we are ready to stop for the night... If you want," he added hastily, realizing he had been quick to assume Zelimir would want to share his kill.

Zelimir dropped the jackrabbit to the ground and told Medwin that would be fine.

Conner knew how difficult it must have been for Zelimir not to devour his kill on the spot. The frog legs from the night before had obviously been less than substantial for the wolf, who had said he hadn't had a decent meal for quite some time. A surge of appreciation for Zelimir ran through him. He gave the wolf a thankful nod. Zelimir returned the gesture before signaling for them to continue their journey.

No other signs of plant life appeared as the hours passed, and eventually, Conner conceded to the dismal facts: this desert was going to take far more time to cross than he had anticipated. He found himself wondering if it had been wise to take this route after all. Zelimir was right; the journey across this barren land was grueling.

A hot eastern breeze started to pick up, causing a sand cloud to form at an alarming rate. The wind gathered speed relentlessly. Soon it was reaching intimidating speeds.

"*Run! We must find cover!*" Zelimir yelled, making sure he was heard over the deafening sound of wind as it blew past them.

Conner tried to cover his face with the tunic Vivek gave him, but his efforts proved to be in vain. Sand pelted his arms and face with intense force. The pain of it was becoming excruciating. What they needed was to get below the surface of the desert.

"*Medwin, make your cognition room! Hurry!*" Conner watched as Medwin's face screwed up even farther than it already had from the pain the bombarding sand was causing him. Nothing happened. Medwin's pained expression contorted even farther as he concentrated with all his might on the room; still, nothing happened. It wasn't going to work for him. "*You try, Conner! I can't concentrate! I'm in too much pain!*"

Conner didn't blame him. Medwin was shirtless after all. The only thing he had to cover his torso was his pack. "*Okay, I'll give it a shot!*" Conner yelled. He tried to set his focus on being underground, free of the sandstorm and catching his breath, but pain fogged his mind. Nothing happened. He wasn't sure how much longer he would be able to breathe in the sand cloud. Telling himself that pain was nothing more than an illusion, a feeling he could choose to ignore, he closed his eyes.

'I need a place to escape this sandstorm!' he thought with all the mental strength he could rally. The ground around him and the others gave way, turning into a sort of sand slide. They rode it deep below the desert floor as waterfalls of yellow-brown poured from the edges of the surface.

Conner exhaled a grunt of pain as hard sandstone floor met his feet and brought him to a jarring halt. He glanced around to make sure the others were okay before looking up at the vicious storm blowing overhead. "It isn't much," he coughed, feeling sand scratch the back of his throat. "But at least we can breathe…"

"Yeah, and we're not getting pelted by sand anymore," Medwin said, spitting granules to the floor.

Zelimir was panting heavily. He shook himself like a dog fresh out of water, spraying sand everywhere. "That cognition is a lifesaver."

"Yeah, it has already saved us on numerous occasions," Conner said as he brushed off his tunic, still watching the fierce storm blowing overhead.

"So, I guess we wait," Medwin thought aloud, looking around the deep rectangular enclosure. He spoke again, this time addressing Zelimir. "How long do you think this storm will last?"

"It is hard to say. I do not claim to be an expert on desert conditions. Let's just hope it doesn't eat up the whole day."

They sat down and did the only thing they could do: wait.

* * *

An hour passed, and the sound of strong wind gusts started to lessen. Conner looked up and saw that the air was nearly sand-free. "I think we're probably good now," he stated, looking for confirmation from the others.

Zelimir looked up. "It would appear so."

Sand began to cascade over the edges of the enclosure at Conner's

197

will, and as it filled the void, the three travelers rose steadily back to the surface.

"It would seem that the sandstorm forced us nearly a mile west," Zelimir said as he absorbed the view of their current position. "We should continue to head north from here. Water is vital and to travel east in hopes of regaining our former course would prove pointless."

Medwin nodded his agreement. He turned to Conner. "What do you think, Conner ... ... Conner?"

"What? Oh — yeah, sounds good." Conner had barely been listening. He was staring at the faded peak of Mt. Cirrus in the distance. Images of faceless, tormented creatures swam through his mind, and terror filled his heart. At some point — most likely sooner than later — he would have to face the man responsible for countless evils... A man — no — a monster, who had experience in the art of cognition far beyond his.

'You need to practice,' he told himself. 'You need to use cognition as much as possible! It will be up to you to defeat Vellix in the end. It is your task, your burden.' He looked over at the others, who were chatting a few paces in front of him. 'You can't let them down. They're counting on you.'

For the next few hours, Conner walked in silence, listening to Medwin and Zelimir's conversations, nodding if he was required to respond.

"So let me get this straight," said Zelimir. "This, Vivek, taught a chief of the Satria cognition — and the art has been passed down from generation to generation of worthy candidates in your tribe?"

"Yeah. We have worked hard to become as practiced in the art as possible over the years. Our tribe's elders are very skilled..."

"I wonder if Vellix is aware that there are others learned in the art," Zelimir pondered aloud.

"It's hard to say," said Medwin, who seemed quite pleased that Zelimir was showing interest in his people. "I know he respects us as warriors. We made sure of —"

A nerve-splitting shriek washed out Medwin's words. Conner was cast into shadow. His stomach twisted as he realized something massive had blocked out the entirety of the sun. He looked up just in time to see the silhouette of a Mirthless in a ferocious dive, its wings stretched to their full and incredible span, its legs reared and talons ready to seize their prey.

Conner dove to one side, narrowly escaping the attack.

The Mirthless rounded, gaining position for another charge.

"*Run!*" Zelimir yelled.

Conner and Medwin took off running as fast as they could but, due to their being on sand, this wasn't all too fast.

Zelimir, who was a great deal faster than they were, was soon hard to see as he blended into the horizon. This proved to matter very little, as the Mirthless seemed to have eyes only for Conner. It was right behind him, on course for a fresh attempt at snatching him up. Conner dove forward in hopes that this would make him harder to grab, but these hopes were futile. The Mirthless seized him in mid-dive — one of Conner's arms in each of its feet. With one flap of its huge wings, the beast prevented itself from hitting the desert floor and gained altitude.

Conner had to do something quick, or he would be far too high to survive a fall. Instinct kicked in; he did the only thing he could do. He used cognition to manipulate the land.

A large pillar of sandstone shot out of the ground, as if an ancient, spring-loaded booby trap had been triggered. The Mirthless smashed into the stone pillar with a deafening *crack!* Conner's nose broke upon impact. Blood gushed down his face, and his eyes started to water blindingly, but his mind remained focused.

The massive bird released its grasp on him. He reached up and gripped one of its feet with all his might, pulling down on the beast with great effort as it twisted and turned in a plummet back to the ground. He knew he had to get above the Mirthless, or allow the beast to crush him. He only just managed it before they slammed into the ground.

Landing on the armor-plated underbelly of the Mirthless was hardly better than hitting the ground. The impact stunned Conner for a second, but only for a second. He unsheathed Scarlet. His aim had to be true. The gaps between each plate of armor were narrow. He clutched the blade firmly in his hands and plunged it into the heart of the beast, avoiding even a scrape on the plates of armor. The Mirthless' body gave a mighty jolt, twitched numerous times out of reflex, and became still. Conner rolled off the lifeless creature and landed on all fours in the sand.

"Conner, are you okay!" Medwin yelped as he ran up to Conner, who was trying to stand with little success.

Conner was shaking violently. Now that the moment in which he needed to stay focused had passed, the weight of what happened flooded his senses. "I — I think my nose is broken," he said, attempting to mop the blood from his face.

"It definitely looks broken. Here, let me set it for you." Medwin made to reach for Conner's nose.

"Are you sure you know how?" Conner asked, jerking away from Medwin's reach, not hiding the distinct concern in his voice. He wasn't so sure Medwin was the right applicant for the job.

"No — I'm not sure I know how, because I've never tried," Medwin answered, smiling in a way that made him look rather mischievous.

Conner appreciated his ability to find some humor in the situation and decided to let him give it a try. After all, he *was* the only one around to do it. "Okay, give it a shot then. Just remember — if my nose is maimed forever — I will be blaming you!" He laughed, only to find that this was a bad idea as a fresh wave of blood poured from his nose.

"Fair enough," Medwin replied, laughing and grimacing at the same time. He moved closer and put his hands up to Conner's nose. "Okay, on the count of three. One ... two" — there was a dull snapping sound, during which Conner flinched. Medwin had set his nose before he reached the count of three in order to catch Conner off guard. From his experiences in life, he knew this was a great method for reducing pain.

"Half of pain is in our anticipation of it," Medwin said, as if reciting something he'd been told his whole life.

"Well? How does it look?" Conner asked, his eyes watering.

"Looks fine," Medwin replied. "Minus the blood, of course," he added, still investigating Conner's face.

Conner laughed and said, "If Lenny was here, he could literally say I broke my bloody nose!" Medwin burst into laughter.

"Thank goodness you're okay!" Zelimir exclaimed as he hastened toward them. "I had hoped the Mirthless would come after me if I caught its attention." He looked over at the dead beast lying there. "We have a day — maybe two..." Conner and Medwin looked at him curiously. "...Before Vellix knows he has been reduced to two Mirthless," he added. "We are lucky he has them searching in separate locations. Had the three of them been together, I'm sure at least one would have escaped, and Vellix would know we are a party of three — not two."

"I think it would be smart to get rid of this," said Conner. He motioned in the direction of the dead Mirthless; a hissing noise exhaled from the ground around its massive body. Ripples of sand began to flow toward an ever-devouring center, taking the beast's lifeless body with it. Soon there was nothing more to see than a few feathers at the tip of one wing, a talon wielding foot, and a gaping beak. Then, as the sand let out a one last hiss of air, the beast was gone.

Conner stood, staring at his newly formed pit of quicksand for a moment before closing his eyes and forming an image of what the area had looked like previously. After focusing intently on the image, he opened his eyes. The quicksand had gone.

"Let's keep moving," Zelimir said, who looked impressed with Conner's skill but anxious to keep going.

* * *

The day was coming to its conclusion. As the sun sank into the horizon, the temperature changed drastically. It seemed to transform from scorching heat to bitter cold in the blink of an eye.

That night, Conner was more grateful for Medwin's room than ever. Their travels during the day had taken them almost halfway across the desert — this was quite remarkable considering the whole incident with the Mirthless, not to mention the fact that they waited an hour for a sandstorm to blow over.

Conner's legs felt like gelatin as he clambered onto his bed. Walking in the sand had worked his muscles far beyond their comfort zone. It wasn't until the next morning, however, that he could fully appreciate how sore they really were. He woke up to find that the simple act of lifting them and getting out of bed was incredibly difficult. Medwin showed him some stretches before they set out for the day's travels, but Conner's muscles didn't start to loosen up properly until they had been submitted to the natural stretch that only walking can provide.

The early morning sun wasted no time in becoming unbearably hot. It beat down upon Conner and the others as they continued their journey northward. Zelimir panted heavily as he trotted along — Conner on his left; Medwin on his right. What a sight it would have been if someone saw them? A wolf in the desert is strange enough, but flanked by two boys as well. That was just unheard of.

* * *

It was past mid-day. The fatigue in Conner's legs had returned, making every step he took absolutely torturous. On he walked, trying not to think, willing himself to keep putting one foot in front of the other. A sleepy, euphoric sensation stole over him without his realizing it. One minute he was walking along, teeth clenched and pouring sweat; the next, he didn't seem to care about the pain anymore. In fact, he didn't seem to care about *anything* anymore. He drifted like a drone to nowhere in particular. Unaware to him, Medwin was doing the same. The two of them continued this bizarre behavior until they came upon an astonishing phenomenon.

The ground was acting upon its own accord. A rugged oval-shaped rock foundation rose from the sand and sprouted a multitude of tiers — the topmost of which began issuing a gurgling sound. Water erupted out of the gurgling tier and proceeded to run down to the next. Once this tier's capacity was filled, it overflowed into the next tier and so on.

The last tier was three quarters full when something else happened. Water bubbles turned into small red objects. Finally full, the tier overflowed onto the desert floor, and the moment it made contact, the water began carving a creek into the land, which curved consistently to the right. As it went, the small red objects hatched — they had been fish eggs.

Plants started sprouting into life along the ever-developing creek bank. Beautiful flowers, trees, bushes, and cacti were among them.

The fish were aging at an alarming rate. Already, they had reached adulthood. The plant life followed suit in this curious time-line. Flowers bloomed and withered in one steady motion. Leaves on the trees changed color from green to red, yellow to brown. It seemed that the farther the creek shoveled its way through the land, the farther into each season the life became.

Leaves from the trees fell graciously to the ground as it started snowing, covering the, now, dead plants and bare trees with a pristine blanket of white that sparkled brilliantly in the bright sun.

Had Conner been in a normal state of mind, he would have realized how miraculous the arrival of snow was, considering he was in a desert.

The self-forming creek began to slow down. Its carving of the land was coming to a halt. The creek bank returned to consisting of only sand and then there was no bank at all: the lifecycle had ended.

Seconds later, a rugged oval-shaped rock foundation emerged from the ground and sprouted a multitude of tiers. Somewhere deep in Conner's mind this seemed oddly familiar, but he was undaunted by this thought. He continued to follow the creek — Medwin at his side doing the same.

Zelimir, who knew what they had stumbled upon but was mildly entertained by the phenomenon, started to worry. He realized that the boys were in some kind of a trance and, left to their own devices, would probably carry on following the creek as it made its course and re-formed endlessly.

"Conner — Medwin…" He called their names but got no reaction. "*Conner — Medwin!*" He yelled their names this time, and again, he got no reaction. Aware that there was only one way to get them out of there, he went up to Conner, who was enjoying the summer stage of the creek's circular life, bit down on his tunic, and pulled him away.

Conner's mind jerked back to reality as he broke the invisible plain separating normalcy from whatever the self-forming creek had been. The pain in his legs returned instantly. He sat down and started to rub them. Now that he was looking back at the phenomenon, he could see that he had been appreciating just one of several of these bizarre anomalies. It looked incredibly strange to see multiple mini climates all happening in such a close space. One would be in the spring stage

205

with an assortment of beautiful flowers blooming into life, while another would be in the winter stage with snow falling delicately onto the already dead plants.

Zelimir went back for Medwin. Once they returned, and Medwin was sitting next to Conner, the wolf explained to them what happened.

"I believe," he said, staring in the direction of a mini-climate that was in its summer stage, all of its plants bursting with life, "that we just encountered the desert Pons. As you saw, the Pons are like an extremely advanced version of a mirage. They're not only mentally in existence, they're physically in existence, and so visually appealing that they take all objective desire from the poor soul who encounters them. The only thing that matters is to follow them on their endless journeys. Given the state you were in, you may not have noticed, but there are small portions of exposed human skeletons in the sand all around them. No doubt from the poor travelers who were not lucky enough to have had an animal companion — the Pons do not effect animals," he added to clarify his last statement. "Are you ready to go on?" he asked, surveying them.

"I suppose so," Medwin answered, rubbing his legs. "We should probably reach the river before we stop for the day. Conner, you ready?"

"Yeah," he said as he got to his feet.

With one last glance at the Pons, the three travelers set off, leaving the incredible phenomenon behind.

CHAPTER 16

The Forces of Evil

Several hours later, life seemed to spring up all around them. Groups of trees were ahead. The sandy desert terrain had vanished. The ground now consisted of dirt, veiled by sparse patches of grass.

The east fork of the Brio River was nearly visible. Conner had been able to hear it for a short time now, and all he could think of was taking huge, hydrating drinks of water. He had never known his mouth to be so dry. Medwin had managed to get water from some cacti, but that was hours ago. A real substantial drink sounded amazing. Conner looked over at Zelimir, whose tongue was hanging so far out of his mouth it looked in danger of falling out entirely. 'Poor guy,' he thought. 'This must be torture for him.'

Upon reaching the river, Conner noticed the bank was unlike the one he had seen on the west fork of the Brio. It sloped easily down to the river's edge, where infinite ripples of water journeyed toward the ocean. Conner ran and jumped in, Medwin and Zelimir just behind him.

Cool, soothing water was like a gift after almost two whole days in the unrelenting sun of the desert. Conner had never appreciated a river so much in his life. He dove under the water and swam around, investigating the different rocks. It was extraordinary how varied in shape, size, and color they were. A fish swam by languidly as he went up for air. He made to grab it, but the moment the fish sensed danger, it replaced its slow movements with incredible speed, darting away from his closing grip with ease.

As Conner surfaced, he noticed that the sky to the west had burst into an extraordinary assortment of oranges, pinks, and reds. Medwin pulled himself onto a rock, which protruded a few feet from the water's surface, and stared at the colorful sky as Zelimir got out of the water, found a cozy spot to curl up, and began licking one of his paws.

Conner wanted this moment to last forever. So peaceful. So beautiful. It was as if nothing evil could ever exist here. How could it? To him, it seemed like these things would shun from such a place, like vampires do from the light. Of course, this was not true. He glanced up at Mt. Cirrus. Clouds revealed the rich colors in the western sky and formed a swirling ring around the peak.

Evil exists everywhere, seeking to stamp out goodness and love. It is up to the good to stamp it out first, just as it was up to him to stamp out Vellix. The thought of his inevitable battle with Vellix was not one he wanted to dwell on. However, it did remind him that he was supposed to be practicing his cognition as much as possible.

The longer Conner stayed by the river, the more he wanted to stay there forever and forget about battles and evil. He knew this was impossible, of course, so he settled for the next best thing "Hey, Medwin?"

"Yeah?"

"I want to stay the night by the river. What do you think?"

"Sounds good to me," Medwin replied. "What about you, Zelimir?" He turned to look at the wolf.

Zelimir stood up and stretched eccentrically before answering, "I had assumed we would stay the night here. It will give us the opportunity to fill up on water in the morning before we move on. Speaking of moving on, I think we should talk about the direction we are going to head from here."

"What do you mean?" Medwin asked. "I thought we already decided that."

Zelimir nodded. "We decided that we would head north through the desert... No other conclusions were made."

Medwin remained silent and arranged his face into an expression of attentiveness.

Zelimir replied with a thankful nod before he went on, knowing Medwin was being purposely polite. "We cannot continue to approach Mt. Cirrus from a northern heading. When I was taken to Vellix, I noticed that the mouth of his mountain-peak cave faces southwest. For that reason alone, I think we should approach from the east. However, the main reason we need to stay to the east is that the land to the west side of the mountain is home to the wolves. It would be unwise to head anywhere near their hunting grounds.

Conner and Medwin nodded; Zelimir continued.

"Approaching from the east will not be easy either, though. It will mean we have to enter the Morik Forest."

Medwin turned to face Zelimir, fixing him with the same dark expression he was receiving from the wolf.

"What's the Morik Forest?" Conner asked tentatively, noticing that Medwin and Zelimir's expressions had become instantly grim at hearing the name.

Medwin answered, "My father told me it is a forest full of evil creatures. He said that the forest itself is alive. Travelers have avoided it for centuries. Many call it the Forest of Deception…"

Zelimir piped in, "Vellix infects the land around the mountain. He has tampered with and bent it to his twisted will. I believe he has done so to keep unwanted opposition out and wanted victims in. All manner of dark creatures live within the forest. Of course, the fact that we have this knowledge going in is a huge advantage. At least we will be ready. Well — as ready as we can be, anyway."

When Conner and Medwin didn't reply, Zelimir went on.

"The city of Ryvel fringes Morik's northeastern border, and I do not wish to have any encounter with them, so we will have to make sure we keep to the western side of the forest."

Medwin, who had gone back to staring at the sunset, clearly deep in thought, nodded in acknowledgment of Zelimir's words.

"After tomorrow's travels we should start journeying by night," Zelimir continued. "It is important that we minimize visibility the closer we get to the mountain."

Conner and Medwin agreed.

Medwin swam back to the river's edge and stepped up onto the bank. I'll be back," he said as he wandered toward a group of trees.

"What are you doing?" Conner asked.

"I need to find a tree branch I can use to make a spear. There are many fish in this part of the river. It shouldn't be difficult to catch a few."

Figuring Medwin had enough to deal with, Conner decided he would try to create a room they could sleep in that night. After glancing around the general area, he decided the side of the riverbank stood out as a good point of entry. He stared at the bank, boring it with his eyes. Dirt shoveled itself away as he became a mental excavator. Conner followed his tunnel fifteen feet into the bank as he created it.

Next, he fashioned a spacious room equipped with two beds made of dirt that looked nearly the same as the ones Medwin made. To finish the room he created a sizeable circular fire-pit near the far wall with a small opening behind it that led to a smoke chamber. He looked up at the ceiling. Roots burst through it, intertwining to form a rotisserie directly over the fire-pit.

Conner stood and admired his handy work for a moment before leaving the room to go see if Medwin was having any luck fishing. As he arrived at the bank of the river, he said, "Hey, have —"

Medwin put his hand up to silence Conner, stabbed his spear into the water, and pulled it up with a large fish on the end, which wriggled and flailed as he waded back to the bank. "What were you going to say?"

"Well you just answered my question, actually," Conner said. "I was going to ask if you had managed to catch anything yet."

Medwin turned to Conner as he made his way toward a boulder near the riverbank that had a relatively flat surface. "Yes, I did manage to catch something," he said, grinning as he placed his latest catch upon the rock. Two other fish were already there, lying motionless. "Will you get my hatchet? It's in my pack, just over there." He pointed to one of the nearby trees.

"Yeah, sure," Conner replied. "Do you want me to just bring the whole pack?" he asked as he arrived next to the tree.

"Yeah, you might as well," Medwin said, shrugging.

The volume of Conner and Medwin's conversation woke up Zelimir, who had fallen asleep on the peaceful riverbank. He gave them a disgruntled glare before lowering his head back into a particularly soft-looking patch of grass.

Conner handed Medwin his hatchet and set the pack down on the ground near his feet.

"Thanks," Medwin said as he reared the hatchet back and cut off the head of the first fish in the row.

Conner watched as Medwin did the same to the other two fish before he asked, "So are they ready to cook?"

Medwin grinned again. "Yeah, they're ready."

"Good," Conner replied. "Follow me." He led Medwin down the tunnel, into the room he'd created, and gestured toward the rotisserie made of tree roots. "Will that work for cooking the fish?"

Medwin beamed. "Yeah, that will be perfect. Nice touch." He patted Conner on the back.

"Will we be eating soon, Medwin? I am quite famished." Zelimir had entered the room without making the faintest of sounds.

"I'm about to start cooking the fish right —" Medwin suddenly remembered who he was speaking with. "Oh yeah, you take your meat raw. Here you go." He threw the largest of three fish to the wolf.

Zelimir devoured it, making obnoxious chomping and smacking sounds.

Conner had a nauseating vision in which he became the fish, and the wolf was ripping him apart. This vision had nearly been a reality only two nights ago.

Glad to be off the wolf's menu, Conner went to go close the entrance of the tunnel. As he reached the opening, a petrifying screeching sound met his ears. One of the Mirthless flew overhead. He jumped back in shock, fear bubbling up inside him. Realizing how foolish it had been to leave the tunnel entrance open for any period of time at all, he focused his mind on closing it. Mingled strands of grass and dirt came together to form a natural mesh. The mesh continued to grow and thicken until the tunnel entrance was completely covered.

Conner re-entered the room. He whispered as he told Medwin and Zelimir what he'd seen, as if the Mirthless would hear him if he spoke too loudly.

Medwin and Zelimir looked equally frightened. "Do you think it saw you?" They asked at once.

"I don't know. I was at the edge of the tunnel, so it might have." His stomach still turning with fear, Conner sat down on his bed, leaned against the wall, and let out a low sigh of anxiety.

"Let's not dwell on the thought," Zelimir said wisely. "We can't change whether or not it saw you, now."

No one responded, but the statement set in.

Conner practiced his cognition while he waited for the fish to be ready, making blades of grass, which hadn't existed a second before, grow in length and then shrink again. Or causing sections of the dirt floor to rise up and change form from one thing to another as he thought of them: a pyramid became a spiraling cone, which turned into a shrub, morphed into a candle, and melted back into the ground.

Soon the wonderful smell of dinner was wafting under his nose. Medwin handed him a freshly cooked fish. He took his meal with great enthusiasm and devoured it greedily, stopping only for brief moments to pull bones out of his mouth. Shortly after he'd finished eating, a placid feeling of sleepiness came over him. He nodded off.

* * *

Some hours later, one of Medwin's particularly loud snores woke Conner up. He had no idea what time it was, but the fire had gone out. Small embers were all that remained. His mouth felt parched, so he decided to head out to the river for a quick drink. His fingernails filled with dirt as he guided himself down the pitch-black tunnel toward the mesh wall covering the entrance. He mentally requested the mesh to remove itself; the wall retracted, revealing the opening once more.

Down at the river he cupped his hands under the water to retrieve a drink.

"Go back to 'em then — if you're so worried. If you're stickin' with me then shut up about it!"

"It's just them damn Mirthless! If we're caught, who knows what he'll do to us..."

Two men were approaching the river from the north side.

Conner tiptoed back up to the tunnel. Grass grew quickly over the opening at his mental command, and he stood there listening intently.

"I ain't gonna be caught, 'cause I ain't an idiot! I'll be traveling by night 'til I've reached the southern coast."

"I suppose that's a good plan."

"Course it is! Better plan than goin' into battle against the Satria!"

Conner gasped. He covered his mouth, hoping it hadn't been audible.

"I ain't about to forget what happened last time we fought 'em. Damn near wiped out our entire army! And where was Vellix? Didn' even turn up to help us, did he?"

"…You don't think Emeric will notice we're gone?"

"Nah… He's leadin' all the soldiers of Ryvel into battle. He ain't gonna notice if two of us are missing."

The two men were in view now. Conner noticed they were squat, stout, and clad in armor. They got a drink from the river before trudging across it.

On their way up the south side of the bank, the man to the right came inches from stepping directly into the opening where Conner was hiding. Had the man been any farther to his own left, he would have.

Conner's mind was racing. The Ryvelians were on their way to attack the Satria! He had to tell Medwin. They needed to warn the tribe before it was too late. He ran back to the room.

"Medwin —*Medwin, wake up!*"

"Wha — what's going on, Conner?" Medwin asked groggily, propping himself up onto an elbow.

"We've got to go! Get up!" Conner yelled urgently. "Come *on!*" he yelled again, when Medwin didn't hop right out of bed.

"What are you talking about, Conner? It's the middle of the night," Medwin replied exasperatedly.

Zelimir, who had woken up from all the commotion, asked, "Are you okay, Conner? Has something happened?"

"We have to get to your village as quickly as possible, Medwin!" Conner exclaimed. "The Ryvelians are on their way to attack the

215

Satria, right now!"

"*What!*" Medwin cried, leaping out of bed so fast you would have thought he just realized he was sharing it with a king cobra. "How do you know that?" he probed, looking completely maddened by instant anxiety.

"Yes, indeed, I would like some explanation for this sudden knowledge as well," said Zelimir, his voice so calm that he received a vexed look from Medwin.

Conner tried to calm down so he could give a steady answer. "I woke up ... I was thirsty, so I decided to go down for a drink of water. Two men were walking toward the river from the opposite side. They were having a conversation, so I hid in the tunnel opening and listened. From what I heard, I gathered that the men were Ryvelian soldiers that decided to abandon their duties and flee to the southern coast; the reason they were fleeing is because the Ryvelian army is on its way to attack the Satria, and they didn't want to be a part of the battle."

"*We have to go right now!*" Medwin bellowed, his maddened expression thoroughly justified by Conner's account of what he heard. Medwin grabbed his pack and started toward the tunnel.

"*Wait!*" Zelimir demanded. If we go to the aid of the Satria our companionship will be discovered, and the entire pack of wolves will be instructed to hunt me once more! This will extend to you two as well! Do you realize how hard it will be to achieve our mission with a pack of wolves on our trail?"

"I don't care! That's my tribe! My family, my friends — *my life!*"

"If we go — it is very likely you won't have a life to be worried about much longer!" Zelimir spat. He appeared to be at war with himself. His brow didn't know if it wanted to crease in anger or tighten with pity.

"That's a chance I'm willing to take!" Medwin retorted, spit flying from his mouth in all directions. "If you don't want to come, I won't blame you — you either Conner," he added hastily.

"I'm going with you, Medwin," Conner said without hesitation, a resolute look in his eyes.

"Oh, alright, let's go," Zelimir muttered, giving up on his better judgment.

Without another word on the matter, the three of them took off, Medwin leading the way. Conner created a bridge as they came upon the river. It consisted of tree roots, mud, and grass and looked like strands of DNA coming together as it stretched across to the northern bank. Due to the speed in which Conner had thought to create the bridge, they didn't even have to slow down to cross it.

Medwin headed northwest, striving to run faster than his legs could carry him. More than once, he came threateningly close to falling, but on each occasion, he was able to regain his balance by whirling his arms like windmills.

Zelimir stayed in stride with Medwin, looking as if he was out for a pleasant jog. His tongue slapped the side of his face in time with each leaping stride he took, sending trickling strands of drool flying off the tip.

Conner struggled immensely to keep up with their accelerated pace, but he was not in shape like the son of the chief of warriors. Nor was he ever going to be as fast or fit as a fully-grown wolf. Searing pain ran through his side. It felt like someone wedged a knife in between his ribs and proceeded to give it a little twist every time he inhaled.

On he ran, combatting the pain with thoughts of bravery, conviction, and dedication. He knew his cognition could be of assistance in the battle. He had a serious amount of pent up aggression toward anything or anyone who chose to serve the monstrosity that was Vellix, and he knew that taking out some of his forces would quench his thirst for justice.

Mile after mile they ran. It was as if Medwin had received a shot of adrenaline. He had unrelenting amounts of energy, and as a result, the chunk of land they were able to cover over the course of the next couple of hours was truly a feat.

The sun was on the verge of poking its shiny face over the eastern horizon when the faintest twinkle of lights came into view, somewhere northwest of them. Medwin stopped running, and Zelimir followed suit. Conner fell to the ground and vomited uncontrollably. He had long since overexerted himself. It felt like there would never be enough air in his lungs again. His head was buzzing. He felt faint.

"Are — you — okay — Conner?" Medwin asked, his breaths coming in quick intervals.

Knowing he wouldn't be able to speak at the moment, Conner combined a facial expression and hand gesture that implied he was okay but needed a few minutes to catch his breath.

Zelimir, who had been panting lightly and gazing in the direction of the faint lights, turned to face Medwin. "Surely those will be the torches of the Ryvelian army," he said mournfully, hoping this information wouldn't be too hard for Medwin to bear. If he was right, it would mean there was virtually no chance of reaching the Satria before the Ryvelians.

Dawn broke, and pastel lavender splattered across the morning sky as if it were a canvas. Daylight revealed the landscape. Acres upon acres of open grassy field lay before them.

"Let's keep moving," Medwin urged his companions, obviously unable to think of anything but doing his best to warn his people of the coming danger, no matter how the odds were stacked against him.

Conner, who could only guess what it must be like to have your thoughts overtaken by images of losing loved ones, did his best to keep up as Medwin broke back into a run. Medwin ran until Conner was on the verge of passing out, stopped to take a short break, and was off once again.

Eventually, the hazy forms of trees in the distance told them that they would soon arrive at the main fork of the Brio River.

By the time they reached the river, Conner's running had become more like a mixture of stumbling and jogging. His heart would be bursting out of his chest at any moment now, he was sure of it. He looked across the river to the valley on the other side, and the sight that met his eyes almost made him forget how exhausted he was. A battle was about to take place — two massive armies, separated only by billions of innocent blades of grass, stood facing each other.

Conner gaped at the scene, feeling any of the courage he thought he had draining away like water from an unstopped sink.

The Ryvelians were not the only ones who came to attack the Satria. They were joined by all the forces of evil at Vellix's disposal.

CHAPTER 17

Duel of the Hylan

"Our lookout, Krikor, must have spotted the Ryvelians in time to warn the tribe," said Medwin, who seemed to be letting out the longest sigh of relief in recorded history. He turned his attention to the valley across the river as a man emerged from amongst the Satria army and started toward the Ryvelians. Conner heard Medwin say, "Father," under his breath as he, too, watched the man approaching the Ryvelian army.

An armor-clad man, mounted atop a huge boar, rode out from the Ryvelian front line to meet the approaching man. Two other men rode on either side of him. Conner noticed that both the other men were carrying a flag that bore some kind of image. He strained to catch a glimpse of what it was but from his distance, it was nearly impossible to see.

The armor-clad man signaled for the two men flanking him to stay back as he rode the last few paces that separated him from the Satria chief. Their conversation didn't last very long — a minute or less. They turned away from one another and headed back to their armies.

No sooner than the man clad in armor had reached his front lines was he signling for his archers to fire. Nayati signaled as well. Thousands of arrows, fired from opposing sides of the valley, met in the air, looking as if a swarm of insects had blocked out the dawning sun.

The valley floor trembled as the Ryvelian army charged, and as they reached the defending Satria armies, the menacing clatters and clanks of battle pierced the air.

"Come on, let's go help!" Medwin yelled, grabbing the hatchet from his pack.

Conner was staring intensely at the scene across the river. He'd never seen anything so vicious. Although it was hard to make out any detail from their distance, he could tell the battle was extremely violent. Men's yells and cries drifted on the wind, finding his ears with a whispered warning of the dangers that lay ahead.

"Conner, let's go!" Medwin pressed. "Make a bridge, so we can cross the river — *hurry!*"

Conner, who was becoming increasingly frightened by the fierce battle, fashioned the bridge and, feeling reluctant, he crossed — Medwin and Zelimir in the lead. Butterflies went crazy in his stomach as he approached the combat. It was as if they knew where he was headed and weren't all too keen on joining him.

The Satria held a strong line of defense against the first Ryvelian attack, their forward-most warriors used body-length shields to keep the onslaught of enemies at bay while others impaled them with barb-ended spears. Because they worked as a unit, very few Ryvelian foot soldiers were able to penetrate their lines.

It wasn't until the Ryvelian captains arrived that the Satria line of defense was broken. Riding upon huge boars, the captains bulldozed through the Satria's front lines, slashing or trampling the warriors who challenged them. The man leading their charge appeared more savage than the rest. Sharp horns elaborated his helmet, which had been wrought to make him look like a skull-headed demon. He wielded a spear in one hand and in the other, a sword that shimmered in the morning light. Upon his back was a large round shield, riddled with steel spikes — he was the same man who had gone out to meet with Chief Nayati before battle.

'That must be Emeric,' Conner thought, appalled by the man's appearance now that he was close enough to see him more clearly.

Large groups of Ryvelian soldiers plunged into the points of vulnerability created by the captains, but many of the soldiers met their ends shortly thereafter because they had entered a sea of combat-seasoned Satria warriors.

The deafening sound of breaking stone echoed around the valley as Satria elders rose up on self-made platforms of granite and began using cognition to combat the boar-mounted Ryvelian captains. Conner watched as an elder with skin so loose it sagged off his bones made a gesture with his hands, as if spreading the air apart. Again, the valley echoed with the sound of breaking stone as a gaping crevice formed directly in front of the last group of charging captains, five of whom were unable to stop in time to keep from falling into the huge fracture. Their boars' high-pitched squeals rang distinctly over the cries and yells of thousands of battling men.

Medwin reached the lines of battle, his hatchet drawn. He entered the fight with a low, swiping strike, taking out the legs of the first Ryvelian he came upon, followed by a high slice at the next. Two soldiers attacked from opposing sides. He ducked the attacks, rolled behind the soldier in front of him, jumped to his feet and struck him in the neck. The other soldier took a step back, looking frightened.

Medwin threw his hatchet with deadly accuracy, striking him in the head. The young warrior walked over to the man retrieved his hatchet and disappeared into the mayhem of battle.

Zelimir closed in on a charging boar from behind and rammed the beast's hind-leg in stride, throwing its rider brutally. The boar slammed to the ground with a bone-breaking thud and lay still. Zelimir darted over to the Ryvelian captain who'd been flung from the boar before he could get to his feet, bit down on his neck, and shook violently until the man's flailing limbs ceased to move.

Conner withdrew Scarlet. The dagger suddenly looked tiny and insignificant. What was he supposed to do with a knife? The weapons of the Ryvelian soldiers were double-edged swords, bows and arrows, and gnarled wooded spears with ends like machetes. He needed a better weapon. 'Use cognition,' he reminded himself.

The sound of rushing air blocked out the battle cries as he rose twenty feet above the valley floor on a circular platform of rock, carpeted by grass. From this vantage point, he saw that Vellix's dark creatures were making their way to the front lines of battle. They were diverse in shape and size but all shared the distinct look of something unnatural and hideous.

The first of the creatures to arrive forced their way into the Satria defenses, tackling and ripping apart warriors with their dagger-sized claws and piercing fangs. Their black, leathery hides provided them with enough protection from the Satria's weapons that trying to kill them with arrows or spears proved to be nearly useless.

"*Break into small groups and team up on them!*" screamed one of the Satria warrior captains, pointing his sword at the beast closest to him. The warriors carried out his orders with precision, forming groups of two — one to distract the beasts; the other to decapitate them.

Screeching winged creatures with decaying flesh swooped down from the sky and attacked the Satria elders, clawing at them savagely with their hands and feet in a malicious attempt to knock them off their platforms. Satria archers picked them off one by one with incredible skill, hitting them in their heads and hearts.

A group of creatures that nearly looked human slashed their way into battle. Their flesh was gray with red markings, their hair long, sleek, and dark. Each one of them wielded a saber in both hands, with which they were exceedingly skilled. One of them started barking orders.

"Izel, take a group to the right flank! Boden, take a group to the left! The rest of you, follow me!"

Conner had a morbid thought. These savage beings looked like they could have been Satria at some point — their red markings were in the same places as the Satria's white ones, and their hair was very similar, draping down their backs like smooth hangings of silk. This disturbing thought dissolved as something else caught Conner's attention. The creatures were nothing but the arms and torsos of two beings fused together to form one monstrosity. The way they walked was repulsive. They arched their upper-halves forward, which caused their skin to stretch tightly around their bony frames, revealing one abnormally long spine that connected opposing rib cages. As their hands reached the ground, they assumed the duties of their feet, while their feet became hands in their assent back up to a standing position, at which point their skin sagged lamely.

Conner couldn't tell if these grotesque beings had eyes, but he realized they clearly had mouths as one of them arched over a Satria warrior and started to devour him. Conner couldn't let the man die this way. Thousands of blades of grass began to grow rapidly next to the foul beast, braiding as they went. The rope-like braids wrapped themselves tightly around the creature and ripped it to the ground.

The vision of the warrior that met Conner's eyes as he came back into clear view was one he would never forget. He had not been able to save him. A newfound hatred for these foul creatures sprang up inside Conner like a roaring fire.

A dull snapping sound filled the air as the creature broke free from its bonds. The grass had not been strong enough to hold it.

'You need to make it stronger!' Conner demanded of himself. The grass braids formed again; this time, instead of remaining the less than durable form of grass, they transformed seamlessly into wood. The transformation started at the roots and worked up to the tips of each blade. The newly formed wooden bonds snatched the creature and threw it back to the ground. It struggled wildly, contorting its deformed body into even more grotesque postures than ever in a mad attempt to break free. But the wood was fresh and supple. The creature had no chance of escape.

The fact that his cognition was good enough to assist the Satria in battle gave Conner an elated feeling of purpose. But he quickly abandoned that feeling, knowing it would cause him to lose concentration. He took a deep breath, closed his eyes, and focused intently. Thousands of blades of grass sprang up from the ground, turning to wood as they braided together and detained other creatures across the battlefield. The Satria warriors noticed this and wasted no time slaying the repulsive beasts.

"Arrr, kill the bloody lot o' 'em, yeh scurvy dogs!"

Conner's heart leapt. He knew that booming voice could only belong to one person. He scanned the scenes of battle frantically, searching for the source. It wasn't long before he found it.

Captain Bellamy was charging the enemy lines, accompanied by his crew. Among them was a strong, agile-looking man. It was Ammin!

'How is that possible?' Conner thought, completely bewildered but ecstatic to see them. 'How are they here? ...And isn't Ammin supposed to be dead?' he could hardly fathom their arrival, which could not have come at a better time. The Satria gained the edge they so desperately needed.

Bellamy and Ammin fought back-to-back, slashing down anything that was foolish enough to attack them. Their skills with a cutlass were of men who spent countless years wielding the weapon.

"Oi, Ammin, yeh won' 'ave enough fingers an' toes ter count yer kills if yeh don' slow down a bit!" Bellamy thundered, laughing heartily as he ran through the most recent Ryvelian to approach him.

"I'll just have to use yours then, won't I?" Ammin yelled back, a huge smile drawn across his blood-splattered face.

"Arrrr!" Bellamy roared in response.

Lenny noticed Conner on his rock platform as he headed for the battle. He gave him a heroic nod before diving into the chaos. *"Come on yeh filthy blaggards! I'll kill the lot o' yeh!"* he cried, swinging his blade skillfully at the oncoming enemies.

227

An arrow zoomed past Conner, coming so close to hitting him that he felt the small flurry of wind it created. The archer would soon regret firing the arrow as the ground around him sprang to life and launched him a hundred feet into the air, leaving him in a deadly free fall.

As Conner watched the man fall helplessly to his death, he felt an unpleasant sensation wash over him. He had just killed a man. It was odd to think he'd taken a life. That man would never laugh again — love again — live again. Conner had to fight back a strong sensation of nausea as the true impact of what he had done set in. 'This is a battle,' he reassured himself. 'That man tried to kill you. It's kill or be killed.' He looked back down at the battle and saw that Chief Nayati had made his way into view.

Using cognition, the chief manipulated the ground around his enemies, mentally ordering it to snatch at their feet and legs, which rendered them helpless against his attacks. He slayed huge groups of Ryvelian soldiers with apparent ease, leaving them piled up and limp-bodied in his wake. Not only did he take on the Ryvelians and foul creatures that were attacking him, but more than once, he protected nearby warriors from what would have been fatal strikes.

"Watch it Thane!" he barked in his deep, powerful voice. "These Bazza are clever," he signaled the beasts he spoke of by engaging the grey-skinned creature nearest to him. "They're quicker and stronger than the rest!"

The man named Thane received a grazing slash across the length of his chest from one of the Bazza, assuring him that his chief spoke the truth. After a quick glance at the wound, which caused his face to contort with fury, Thane retaliated with the skill of a man whose senses had heightened tenfold. He drove his sword through the heart of the Bazza warrior that attacked him and didn't slow down as he met the next enemy in his path.

Emeric was the last of the Ryvelian captains still mounted upon his boar. The battle had taken its toll upon him: one of the horns on his helmet had snapped off, and there were dings and dents canvasing his shield and armor. His resolve to destroy the Satria, however, had not faltered. He was taking on groups of them at a time, blocking enemy strikes and countering with devastating attacks.

"Emeric!" Nayati boomed.

Emeric turned his attention toward the chief, who was holding his hands up as if to welcome a challenge. A malicious grin grew across the evil captain's face. He jabbed the butt end of his spear into the side of his boar. It started to charge toward the chief. Emeric lowered his spear, pointing it directly at Nayati's heart.

At first Nayati didn't move — Emeric's evil smile grew wider still — then, remaining completely composed, Nayati knelt down, grabbed a spear from the hand of a fallen warrior, and closed his eyes. Without warning, the valley floor leapt up and grabbed Emeric's boar by its front hooves. The boar crashed to a halt, flinging Emeric high into the air. Nayati braced his spear firmly in an upward position and let gravity do the rest. Emeric's torso was impaled by the spear as he came barreling down upon it. His eyes grew wide with horror as Nayati released the spear and let him fall to the ground. He gurgled a few words of hatred at the Satria chief through the blood that had filled his mouth and attacked the Satria no more.

Medwin saw his father standing over Emeric and joined him. They looked down at his dead body for a moment before jumping back into battle. And, as father and son, they fought to protect their tribe.

Zelimir dashed in and out of view, dodging attacks as though they were part of an obstacle course he had mastered, biting the Ryvelian soldiers in the backs of their legs to disable them, leaving them helpless to the Satria warrior's attacks.

"*No!*" Ammin cried out at the top of his lungs.

Conner whipped around to see what had happened just in time to watch as one of the Bazza withdrew their saber from Captain Bellamy's heart and stepped back, looking triumphant. Bellamy staggered forward a few steps before dropping to his knees. The jolly look that fighting alongside his first mate had given him was permanently etched onto his face as he fell forward to the ground and lay motionless.

The rage that filled Ammin after seeing his captain slain was fearsome. Blinded by tears of grief and hate, he engaged the Bazza warrior that had taken the life of his captain, but his anger got the better of him. He was no match for the skill of his enemy. The Bazza kicked him square in the chest and moved in for the kill. Lenny slit the beast's throat from behind before it had a chance to strike and helped Ammin to his feet.

"Now's no' the time fer losin' focus, mate!" he said after glancing quickly at Bellamy's dead body. "There'll be plen'y o' time fer grief if we live though this!"

Ammin's face hardened. He gave Lenny a thankful nod and dove back into battle.

Conner shifted the unblinking gaze he had placed upon Bellamy's dead body to the sky as a terrifying screech filled the valley. The two remaining Mirthless had arrived. They soared down, lifted Satria warriors out of battle, and released them to their deaths. The Satria archers attempted to bring them down, but the beast's armor-plated undersides deflected the arrows as if they were nothing more than twigs. Horror struck Conner as he realized one of the most recent warriors to be dropped was Chief Nayati. His mind reeled. This couldn't be happening.

Medwin watched in a daze as his father fell from a height that far surpassed what a human could survive. His body hit the valley floor and broke. Medwin stood there, transfixed. He would die if he didn't defend himself.

Conner's platform receded into the land. He sped toward Medwin, pulled out Scarlet along the way, and killed the Ryvelian that was about to attack him.

Medwin was barely able to see Conner through his tears: tears that didn't know if they were due to sadness or rage, so they settled for being due to both. "Use cognition on me and give me wings, Conner!" he cried.

Conner heard Medwin's words, but initially, they didn't sink in. "What are you talking about?" he asked with a tone of uncertainty to match his baffled expression.

"Use cognition on me and give me wings!" Medwin yelled again, his eyes so wide that he looked deranged. "We know it can be done! Look at the beasts Vellix created!"

"But — I don't even —"

"*Conner, you are the one with power others have only dreamed of, so act like it! Give me wings, so I can kill the monster that took my*" *father from me!"*

The words Medwin yelled weighed heavily on Conner. He had to do this. He had to do it for Medwin. The Mirthless had just taken his father's life. "Okay, Medwin, I'll do it," he said firmly. He conjured an image of Medwin with magnificent white wings in his mind, focusing on the image until it was clear and vivid.

Medwin fell to his knees, screaming in agony. The skin over his shoulder blades started to lump up disturbingly. His flesh looked in danger of bursting at any moment. It did. Dazzling white wings were born into life on his back, unfurling gracefully. Medwin got to his feet without a word and launched into the sky, hatchet in hand.

As Conner watched him soar into the air, he had a gut-wrenching realization. Had he just enabled his friend to fly to his death? He looked up and watched as Medwin figured out how to make the wings work for him; to his immense relief, Medwin seemed to be a natural. He moved through the air with such skill that it appeared as though he'd been flying his whole life.

* * *

Medwin's mind was clear, his vision set. He would kill the Mirthless that took his father or die trying. He flew into the beast's line of sight so it would become aware of his presence in the sky. Although it was incredibly frightening, he was delighted to see that the Mirthless made an immediate course change to intercept him.

He went straight into a nosedive, hoping the beast would take the bait. Without a moment's hesitation, the Mirthless followed, throwing back its wings and becoming as sleek as possible. It reached full speed with absurd quickness, a black streak in the sky, gaining on its soon-to-be prey. The beast yelled out to Medwin in an attempt to provoke him and hinder his concentration. "You don't stand a chance! I will end you — just like I ended the foolish chief of your pathetic tribe!"

Medwin's fury at hearing these words was unmeasurable. He opened his wings wide, and his rate of speed slowed dramatically. The Mirthless, who was far heavier, couldn't react quickly enough to make an evasive maneuver. Calling on all his strength, Medwin thrust his hatchet into the neck of the Mirthless. Sparks rained down on him as his steel blade met the beast's organic armor plating with a reverberating clang and continued plowing through its neck until the creature's head was severed entirely. He watched as the huge Mirthless' now headless body spiraled down to the valley floor in one direction, while its head plummeted like a heavy stone in the other.

As Medwin attempted to catch his breath, a boulder, which seemed to appear from nowhere, hit one of his wings. The hollow bones broke, causing him to lose all dexterity in it. Another boulder pelted him, this time in the side. He lost altitude in a grim plunge back to Rohwen's surface. With his remaining wing, he was able to level himself out before hitting the ground, but the landing was still harsh, furthering the damage to his already broken wing and mangling the other beyond recognition.

* * *

As Conner sprinted toward Medwin, he noticed the sounds of battle dying behind him. "Medwin!" he yelled. "Are you okay?" As far as he was concerned, the landing had looked terrible. When Medwin gave no sign of movement or response, the worst kinds of thoughts started to swirl around Conner's head. He held his breath as he approached Medwin's motionless body, wanting more than anything for him to reply any second.

Medwin's chest heaved; Conner exhaled a breath of relief. "Are you alright, Medwin?" he asked anxiously.

"I will survive," Medwin replied distantly. He propped himself up with a grunt of pain and focused his attention on something that stood beyond Conner.

Relieved that his friend was going to be okay, Conner turned around to investigate whatever it was in which Medwin was showing so much interest. What was left of the Ryvelian army had parted and formed a path, at the end of which stood a man, hooded and cloaked. The trailing folds of his black robes whipped and lashed threateningly in the wind.

Vellix stood there, surveying the body-littered valley floor.

The Satria stood quietly, staring at the dark figure.

Another hooded and cloaked man emerged. Unlike Vellix, who stood on the side of the Ryvelians, he came from amidst the Satria.

Every other man in the valley was silent as the two men approached one another.

Vellix pulled his hood back and spoke. "So ... you're still alive then?" The hatred he felt for the man he spoke to was visible on his aged face.

The other man pulled back his hood and replied. "Yes ... I am still alive, Vellix..." It was Vivek.

'How is this possible?' Conner thought. 'First Bellamy, Ammin, and the crew show up! And now Vivek's here, too? How did they all get here? How did they even know the battle was taking place?' Conner's curious thoughts were broken when Vellix spoke again, his voice exuding arrogance.

"My skills far exceed yours, Vivek. I am master of cognition; therefore, I am master of Rohwen and all who dwell here."

"You have mastered nothing but evil, Vellix," said Vivek, sounding disgusted. "You disgrace our ancestors! They would never have condoned such appalling acts as yours."

"How can you be so sure? The Hylanian race became extinct before we had a chance to find out, didn't they?"

Vivek was silent.

"Yes, I know we are the last of the Hylan, you fool! Is that why I haven't so much as heard a whisper of your existence for the last seven hundred years?" Vellix laughed, and it was full of a cruel, mocking tone. "Because you've been trying to make sure I didn't find the scrolls?" He laughed again, filling the core of Conner's very being with pure hatred.

"I see you learned nothing from them!" Vivek retorted scornfully.

Vellix stopped laughing. He looked angry, but when he spoke, his voice was calm. "I learned a great deal from the scrolls," he said with a sneer, which caused no less than twenty deep lines in his face to tighten. "I have overtaken the skill level of any of our ancestors. Even Neksis is unable to overlook my abilities."

Vivek stood silent for a moment, as if Vellix's last words had affected him in a different way than any other's he had spoken. Finally, Vivek said, "I would not call using cognition to experiment on people and animals in an attempt to create an army of foul creatures the works of a skilled man… I would call those the works of a scared man, who feels insecure and miserable, so he builds strength off the fear of others. *You are pathetic!*" Vellix's face twisted with rage. Vivek continued, "What, you thought nobody knew what goes on in Mt. Cirrus? You are not the only one with a winged messenger, Vellix." Vivek held out his arm. Moments later, a powerful-looking hawk landed on it and screeched aggressively at its master's enemy.

The land broke in a circle around Vellix, emitting loud cracking sounds as deep fissures shot sporadically in all directions. Vellix launched into the air on a podium of rock.

More fissures carved through the land as Vivek launched skyward as well. The two men — last of a dead race — started to duel.

Vellix raised his hands until they faced Vivek and shot an onslaught of blazing red fireballs from his palms, aiming for Vivek's head.

A slab of rock broke free from Vivek's platform and rose up in front of him, blocking Vellix's fiery attack. Vivek countered. A massive oak tree sprouted and grew to its full, towering height as he raised his hands above his head in one fluent motion. The tree wrapped its hard branches firmly around Vellix and began to crush him.

A small pond of corrosive purple liquid bubbled up from beneath the surface all around the tree's root-base. Within moments, the tree began to wither and die, releasing its prisoner. Vellix looked shaken, but not as much as he looked furious. He aimed a hand at the slab of rock that was shielding Vivek and it shattered.

As Conner watched the two masters of cognition duel one another, it was like watching two composers, the land as their orchestra. Every fiber of the valley obeyed their mental command.

New slabs of rock grew from the surface of Vivek's platform as Vellix made a swift gesture with both hands. Just as the walls of stone grew taller than Vivek, Vellix clapped his hands firmly together. The rock encased Vivek's whole body and began shrinking back into the platform.

The stone capsule began to shake intensely. Vivek screamed with fury as he destroyed his prison, shooting fragments of rock in all directions. He looked up and, once again, his granite platform launched skyward. Vellix pursued.

It was nearly impossible for Conner to see what was going on now, due to the height in which the battle was taking place. The suspense was torture. His heartbeat was in his throat. It felt like someone had gone in and started rapping vigorously on his Adam's apple.

The valley floor began to vibrate. Seconds later, a vine-like plant burst from beneath the surface. Strange berries that glowed a poisonous green grew all over the vine as it coiled and slithered through the air on a journey toward Vivek: its master. Vivek gestured toward Vellix, and the vines shot straight for him, wrapping their tendrils firmly around his body.

Vellix let out a high-pitched scream of agony and dropped to his knees. He clutched his face, howling in pain as neon-green fumes began to pour from it. More vines wrapped themselves around him until the majority of his body was covered in the acidic foliage. Thick clouds of fumes drifted from the tangle of vines. Vellix grunted loudly, as if he had found resolution in the deepest depths of his core. He stopped sobbing, grunted again, and retaliated. The vines released him and lunged toward Vivek. But before they could reach him, Vivek raised his hands and entered a wide-legged stance, as if he were about to push something extremely heavy. The vines stopped and shot back in Vellix's direction. Vellix entered a stance similar to Vivek's and the coils of plant began to tremble violently in midair.

For a moment, it wasn't clear who had more control, but it wasn't long before it became obvious that Vivek was losing. Unable to match Vellix's power any longer, he dropped to one knee and was instantly wrapped up in his own vines. He roared in painful fury as hundreds of poisonous berries burned through his cloak and smoldered against his flesh. The plant turned a sickly shade of brown and withered as Vivek destroyed his own creation. He slowly got back to his feet, but it was more than apparent that fatigue was beginning to overcome him.

The ground bellow Conner's feet began to shake. He watched in horror as dozens of boulders erupted from beneath the grass and hurtled toward Vivek, leaving faint streams of brownish-grey behind them.

Vivek held off the attack, stopping the boulders before they could reach him and heaving them back at Vellix, all of which Vellix destroyed before they could hit him. But Vellix's rock projectiles started coming from all angles. The intensity was too much for Vivek's exhausted body. Finally, one of the boulders found its target and knocked him down, crushing one of his legs. Vivek shrieked in pain and clutched at the broken leg.

Vellix sent another torrent of fireballs at Vivek as he attempted to get back to his feet. Vivek didn't have the strength to defend himself, and the fire attacks pelted him relentlessly until his blackened body fell from the rock pillar and landed in a shattered heap on the valley floor, leaving behind it a spiraling trail of dark smoke.

A loud screech filled the valley as the last Mirthless arrived at Vellix's side. He jumped on its back and they headed for Mt. Cirrus.

Conner couldn't believe it. Vivek was dead... He had hardly known the man, but the sense of loss he felt watching the ancient man die was that of losing a close family member. He didn't want to believe it was true, but the evidence would not allow him to think otherwise. The man that had told him of his fate was gone...

The Ryvelians, with their leader slain, and abandoned by Vellix, fled for their lives. A large group of Satria warriors gave chase to make sure they crossed the river and did not return.

Now that the majority of the living had cleared away, Conner was truly able to digest the full picture of carnage that the battle had caused. Hundreds — possibly thousands — of men lay slain, their bodies scattered across the valley. He saw one of the Ryvelian flags lying in taters upon the ground and went over to it. After a quick investigation, he realized it bore the image of a falcon in a majestic pose.

Conner left the flag behind and went back to scanning the horrific scenes around him. He saw the creatures he had detained, still wrapped in their wooden bonds. He saw the crevices that the Satria elders had created to rid the battle of boar-mounted Ryvelian captains. And then... Then he saw something he wanted to forget.

Bellamy's body was lying there, never again to give orders to his crew, never again to take another swig of rum, never again to breathe. Loathing for war — for what it cost — welled up inside Conner. It was like something toxic that made him sick and had no cure. He continued to look around, even though he knew the images he would see were sure to sicken him further.

Medwin was knelt next to his father, his shoulders shaking as he mourned his great loss.

Conner saw the maimed wings that were still somehow attached to him and removed them. All that remained were two bloody gashes where the skin had ruptured. He focused in on the gashes and soon the wounds had healed enough to stop the loss of blood.

As he walked up to Medwin, Conner realized he didn't know what to say. Words were empty. They could not bring his father back, nor could they make the magnitude of his loss any easier to bear. Conner settled for putting his hand on Medwin's shoulder, which stopped shaking when it felt his touch.

Medwin turned to face Conner, tears still streaking freely down his face. "I am chief of the Satria now" — his face hardened — "and my first act as chief will be to hunt down and kill the last Mirthless!"

CHAPTER 18

Ammin's Explanation

Conner nodded firmly and looked over at Ammin, Lenny, and what remained of the crew. They had all gathered around Bellamy to say their farewells.

Zelimir arrived next to Conner. There were a few patches of his fur missing, which blood had replaced, but other than that, he appeared to be fine. "Do you know those men?" the wolf asked curiously, noticing the telling look of sadness on Conner's face.

"Yeah — I know them..." Conner replied quietly. "They're the ones Medwin and I sailed to Rhona with. The captain was just killed in battle."

"...I am sorry to hear that."

"Bellamy is dead?" Medwin asked, turning quickly to face Conner. He had been so absorbed in the loss of his father that he hadn't noticed.

"He is," Conner answered, still speaking quietly.

Medwin's head fell. He now had the burden of another death to mourn.

"Bastard!" Ammin screamed as he drove his sword through a sailor that had bent over Bellamy's body and was in the process of standing back up.

Conner watched, alarmed by Ammin's sudden act of violence. The first mate hadn't struck him as the type that would act so viciously

241

toward one of his own.

"Wha' the 'ell was tha' fer?" one of the other sailors yelled, checking to see if his shipmate was still alive.

Ammin crouched down next to the man he'd stabbed and pried something out of his right hand. Conner recognized it as the key Bellamy wore around his neck as Ammin held it up and said, "That bastard was trying to steal this." He threw a disgusted look toward the man. "Until there is an official vote for captaincy of *the Colossus*, this key stays with me. A few of the crew began to object, but Ammin yelled over them. "It was Bellamy's will that I take possession of the key in the event that he died. I was his first mate. If you have a problem with that, step forward now, and we can settle it." Not one of the bickering men stepped forward, nor did they reply.

Lenny glanced over at Conner and Medwin, as if he wanted to approach them, but the presence of Zelimir seemed to deter him.

"It's okay, Lenny, you can come over," Conner said reassuringly. "He's our friend," he added with a head gesture toward Zelimir.

Lenny moved toward them but still seemed slightly reluctant. "Oi, mates," he said insecurely, "glad ter see yeh made it ou' o' tha' palaver alrigh'."

"You too," Conner replied.

Medwin didn't speak. He just made a lame gesture of acknowledgment as a fresh wave of tears rolled down his face.

Conner gave Medwin a sympathetic glance, which he hoped would let his friend know how badly he felt for him, and turned to introduce Lenny and the wolf to each other. "Lenny, this is our friend, Zelimir; Zelimir — Lenny."

"Good to meet you," said Zelimir with a friendly nod of his head.

"Bloody 'ell, 'e talks an' all," Lenny blurted out rudely. His eyes widened, and his face clearly stated that he had not meant to say this aloud. "I — uh — I mean — uh, nice ter mee' yeh ... mate," he uttered in an attempt to repair the damage he'd already done.

Zelimir saw that Lenny greatly regretted blurting out his first sentence and said, "It is okay that you are shocked. I am aware that talking animals are not common."

Lenny looked a great deal more at ease after that.

Ammin finished paying his respects to the captain. He hailed Conner and came over to the group.

Conner was eager to know how Ammin survived back when he had keel hulled himself. Not to mention how he and the rest of the crew just happened to show up at a battle they should have known nothing about. But he decided he should console Ammin before he battered him with questions.

"I am sorry about your loss. I know the captain must have meant a great deal to you."

"Thank you, Conner. His death was not in vain. I am glad to say he went out with the blood of many enemies on his sword." Ammin's reply was formal, but it did not conceal the true sadness he felt.

There was a short silence before Conner asked, "Ammin, how —"

"Did I survive?" Ammin said. He had obviously been assuming that this question would come up. "I would expect nothing less than for you to wonder. You're probably curious about how the lads and I just so happened to show up at this battle as well, am I right?"

"I was definitely wondering that," Conner replied, his lips curling to form the first hint of a smile since Medwin had served him his fish dinner the night before. The muscles in his face got a shock when they realized their owner had called them into action. He stared at Ammin intently and waited for him to begin his story.

Zelimir appeared to be interested in what Ammin had to say. He remained seated where he was. Lenny, who already knew the whole tale, seemed eager for Ammin to get to the part where he came in. Medwin stood motionless. It was hard to tell if he was even aware of what was happening around him. Conner was sure his mind was miles away, drowning in misery.

Ammin surveyed them all for a moment before starting his explanation. "Well, as you know, I keel hulled myself in order to save *the Colossus* from sure destruction."

"Thanks for that by the way," said Conner; there was a murmur of agreement from Medwin and Lenny.

Ammin waved his hand as if to say, "Think nothing of it," before he continued. "Elandra cut the rope that I had tied around my ankle in order to stay at pace with *the Colossus*. I was left wading in the ocean with no chance of ever catching up with you lot. I scanned my surroundings and realized I was most likely closer to Rhona than I was to the mainland, so I floated on my back to conserve energy and headed for the island. That trip is not one that I will cherish." Ammin paused for effect, which worked because Conner's mind exploded instantly into contemplation of what it would be like to be stuck in miles of open water and have to swim to shore.

"I estimated that I was about twenty miles from the island's shores," Ammin continued, pulling Conner back to reality. "That is no small jaunt when you're in the ocean… The moment I noticed that the tide was helping me in to the beach was one of the greatest feelings I have ever experienced. Needless to say, I was ecstatic. Hours upon hours of staying afloat in the ocean is *not* my idea of a holiday."

Conner and Lenny laughed at the obvious truth in this statement.

Ammin allowed their laughter to die down before he continued. "Once I had reached the island, I headed into the jungle in search of nourishment. I knew that all my work to stay alive thus far would have been for naught if I didn't find some food. The jungle is abundant with edible life, but it was like the animals knew I was coming and decided it was a convenient time to vanish. I couldn't find a single thing. Well — I found some coconuts," he added as an afterthought, "but what I mean to say is: I couldn't find any meat.

"Soaked to the bone and starving, my first night on Rhona was an uncomfortable one. The sun had gone down long before I'd reached the island, so, obviously, there was no hope for me to get dry without its warmth — unless I had fire of course. Unfortunately, I had no way to start one. All I had on me was my pistol and my sword. My pistol is a matchlock, so without a fire source, the gun was useless to me. I will be sure to carry my magnesium rod and striker with me at all times from now on. You can be sure of that!

"A few hours of sleep is all I got that night. I awoke at the break of dawn with a stomach so angry I wasn't sure if I'd ever be able to please it again. But, now that I could see properly, I decided to go a bit farther into the jungle on my hunt for food; I was rewarded with a bird lunch. With my belly full, I set to work and chopped down the largest stocks of bamboo I could find, in order to build a raft. My goal was to get back to Beach Bay, where I hoped to meet up with Bellamy and the crew. I will admit, I was quite doubtful about whether or not they had survived the attack from Elandra, but I remained hopeful. I worked until the sun went down and forced me to quit for the day.

"The next morning, I got right back to work. Around mid-day, I saw a large hawk that was headed for the central region of the island. I marked this in my mind — where there is predator, there is prey. I would head to this location on my next hunt. What I didn't realize was that that hawk was about to become the reason I'm standing here telling you this story."

Conner and Medwin looked at one another with similarly confused expressions.

"It was the early hours of evening the following day. A rustling sound on the edge of the jungle alerted me to the fact that I was not alone. I drew my sword and waited. Something I would have never expected to see emerged. It was an extremely old man. When he saw me, he looked very pleased. 'Do you believe in fate?' he asked me. 'Or, perhaps, unbelievably convenient coincidence?' I didn't know how to take the insane oddness of these questions. The arrival of the man was strange enough, but then his questions were, to say the least, peculiar."

* * *

"I am Vivek, and I believe in fate, for it never fails to reveal itself." A red-tailed hawk landed on his arm. "You know what to do, Lolani," Vivek told the huge bird. The hawk puffed out its chest majestically and took flight, heading north. Vivek continued. "You see, I am in need of a ride to Beach Bay, and here you are with a half-built raft. Would you like a hand with that?" He gestured in the direction of the unfinished raft.

"I am not so sure you —"

"Do not judge me based on my age," said Vivek as perfect lengths of bamboo grew in front of Ammin in a matter of seconds. "I believe that should be enough to finish — don't you think?" he asked, assessing Ammin's astonishment with a satisfied smile.

"Yeah, it seems to be about the — perfect — amount," said Ammin, investigating the freshly grown stalks of bamboo more closely. "How did you do that?"

"I am skilled in an art called cognition. It enables me to bend the land to my will."

"Well that must come in handy!"

"Quite."

"The name's Ammin by the way," said Ammin, extending his hand to shake Vivek's.

"Very pleased to meet you, Ammin," Vivek replied as he clasped both his knobby-knuckled hands around the one Ammin had extended toward him.

The two men worked and chatted until the raft was completed.

"So tell me, why is it that you need to get to Beach Bay?" Ammin asked, wondering why this old man would want to travel at all.

"I seek a crew that is willing to die to save Rohwen," Vivek replied mildly, as if stating something as simple as wanting to go for a change of scenery.

Ammin took an interested viewpoint to this statement. This old man had just gone from strange to stranger. "Do you mean to imply that Rohwen is in need of being saved?"

"That is exactly what I just implied, Ammin." When Ammin continued to stare at him vaguely, Vivek asked, "Shall I explain?"

"Please do."

"You are familiar with the Satria tribe, I take it."

"I am."

"They are about to be invaded by the forces of Vellix," said Vivek, looking suddenly grim. "Normally I would say they could fend for themselves, but Vellix has, I believe, a most cunning plot — my hawk, Lolani, has just gone to confirm it — but, based on the information she has already given me, I believe my theory to be quite accurate."

Ammin had become instantly attentive. Now he was taking in Vivek's every word with great interest.

"Vellix has the whole of the Ryvelian army at his disposal, not to mention the evil creatures of his creation. He has sent these armies to attack the Satria from the east. Meanwhile, he has a ship harbored in the Thanos River. It is my belief that he is going to send this vessel to the mouth of the west fork Brio River, in order to attack the unprotected village of the Satria." Vivek stopped talking for a moment to see if Ammin had digested the full severity of his theory. "You see, while the Satria warriors are out in the valley, fighting to protect their village," he went on to clarify himself, "a small band of soldiers will be demolishing the very thing they are fighting for."

Ammin looked appalled. "That is the most cowardly, sickening, disgusting thing I have ever heard in my life. Mind you, that is saying something coming from a sailor."

Vivek nodded. "Vellix fears the Satria because they are an incredibly skilled warrior tribe. So, what better way to wipe them out than to destroy their village, and all within, while the men are in battle? With their women gone, they won't be able to reproduce, and the Satria will become a dead breed."

Ammin stared at Vivek thoughtfully for a second before saying, "There's just one thing that I don't understand."

Vivek gestured for Ammin to continue, arranging his face into an expression of curiosity.

"Well, I thought you said you wanted to find a crew willing to die to save Rohwen."

"I did."

"But from what I've gathered, it sounds like you need a crew willing to die to save the Satria."

Vivek eyed Ammin seriously. "You don't understand. If the Satria are wiped out, all hope is lost."

Ammin didn't really know how one civilization could have such a drastic impact on the rest of the world, but there was one thing he did know: as long as he had breath in his lungs, he would always fight against the killing of innocent women and children.

"Get some sleep, Vivek," he said. "At dawn, we sail for Beach Bay. I'll find us a crew. I promise. In fact, if you want to go on that fate stuff you believe in, I think our crew is already there waiting for us."

"I am glad to see that you have accepted that the chance of fate could, indeed, be fate in itself."

Ammin gave Vivek a puzzled look. "Right... Good night then."

* * *

At daybreak, the two unlikely companions sailed for Beach Bay. It was early in the afternoon when the harbor came into view, and what Ammin saw made his heart leap. Anchored there, and looking as marvelous as ever, was *the Colossus*.

"Well, it looks like we shouldn't have any trouble finding a crew!" Ammin exclaimed. "You see that ship there?" he asked, pointing toward the harbor. "The one that says *Colossus* across the stern?" he added.

"Yes, I see it," Vivek said after a brief moment.

"That is my captain's ship," Ammin told him, smiling toothily. "He won't turn down our proposal. For one, I'm his first mate, and for two, the idea of slaying the men, or creatures, on course for such evil deeds will suit him."

"This is most pleasing!" said Vivek, who truly did look pleased.

The two men docked their raft, and Ammin headed straight for Osman's — the rundown old beachfront pub. As he entered, Ammin saw the majority of the crew gathered around circular tables. Bellamy saw the figure of the first mate he thought dead in the doorway. His eyes grew to twice their normal size. *"Ammin — is that you?"* he asked, as if seeing a ghost.

"Aye, Captain," Ammin answered.

"Ammin!" Bellamy thundered, looking, if possible, more jolly than ever. *"'Ave a drink, mate! Bartender, another round on me!"* A loud,

joyous applause from the crew followed Bellamy's words.

Lenny was quite vocal in his approval of another round. "Come on then! Le's make a righ' bender o' it!" he yelled, already slurring his words a bit more than usual.

Ammin had to cut their cheers short. "Captain … captain … *captain!*"

Finally, Bellamy heard his first mate over the noisy cheers of the crew. He fixed Ammin with a disappointed stare.

"There is no time for drinks," Ammin said, sounding stern. "We need to set sail straightaway!"

Bellamy looked slightly bemused. "Wha' are yeh on abou', Ammin?"

"We need to go to the aid of the Satria," Ammin said, and he dove into his explanation of the plot revealed by Vivek.

Once Ammin had finished, the captain looked sickened. "Are yeh sure 'bout this?"

"Just trust me, Bellamy. Have I ever led you astray?"

"Nah, yeh 'aven't, mate," Bellamy replied seriously. And, after looking at his first mate for another second, he said, "Alrigh', lads, yeh 'eard Ammin. We're settin' sail!"

The crew looked let down as their captain made this announcement. They had just returned from misty cove and fancied a good day or two at the pub.

"*Look lively!*" Bellamy screamed as his men moved toward the door more slowly than he would have liked, a few of them muttering under their breath.

"Wha' was tha', Mikkel?" Bellamy interrogated one of the griping men. "Go' a problem?"

"No — no problem, Captain."

"Tha's wha' I though'."

"Captain, I would like to introduce you to Vivek," said Ammin as they exited the pub. "I know he comes off a bit strange," he added in a whisper because Vivek was nearly within earshot, "but he seems to be a good man. He definitely has the welfare of Rohwen in his best interest."

As they arrived in front of Vivek, Ammin introduced the two men. "Bellamy — Vivek. Vivek — Bellamy."

"Good to meet you, Captain," said Vivek.

"You as well, Vivek," Bellamy replied. "So, Ammin," he began, as they boarded *the Colossus*. "I take it we're headin' fer the western coas' line?"

"Aye, Captain," Ammin replied with a nod.

"How long do you think the trip will take?" Vivek asked, looking concerned.

"*The Colossus* can do twenty-three ter twenty-five knots when 'er sails are brimmin' with wind," Bellamy answered proudly.

"That will make it about a fourteen hour trip to the mouth of the west fork," Ammin added.

Vivek looked anxious. "I hope we are not too late."

As Bellamy gave the orders to get them underway, Vivek heard something that made his ears perk. It was the screeching cry of his hawk, Lolani. She landed on his arm and spoke. "Your theory is confirmed, master. The Ryvelian vessel has set sail. Fortunately, all hope is not lost. I would say that you are on course to intercept them, somewhere near the mouth of the west fork. If you tell the captain to travel without any of his ship's lights lit, you will gain the element of surprise."

"Very good, Lolani. The whole of Rohwen is indebted to you." With that, the hawk took flight.

Vivek flagged Ammin, who had watched his conversation with the hawk from a distance, to come over. "Ammin, my hawk has just informed me that, as it stands, we are on course to intercept the enemy vessel."

"Right, I will inform the captain."

"Oh, and, Ammin — one more thing."

"Yeah?"

"I think we would be wise to travel without any lights lit. I know it won't be dark for quite some time, but you should probably tell the crew now, so they can get their weapons prepared. Tonight is new moon; once the sun has gone down, it will be extremely dark."

"I will make sure the crew is informed."

"Very good."

* * *

Just over thirteen hours had passed since Vivek's hawk had come and gone.

"Ship lights dead ahead!" yelled the sailor in the crow's nest.

Ammin handed Bellamy a spyglass. He looked through it and said, "Aye, that there is. Hoist the sails on the mizzenmast," he ordered his crew more quietly than usual, aware of how far his voice would carry in the deep silence of night.

Lenny ran by at top speed to fulfill the order.

Ammin praised his captain. "Good thinking. We won't want to get too close."

"Aye," Bellamy grunted.

Vivek had heard the captain's order. He headed for the bridge. "So you've sighted the enemy ship then?" he asked eagerly.

Ammin answered. "Yeah, their ship lights just became visible."

"They've jus' made a course change. They've turned portside," said Bellamy, still holding the spyglass up to his eye. "Looks like they're gonna 'ead up the river 'n' sail righ' inter the heart o' the forest."

"We've got to hurry and get up there!" Vivek urged.

"Lower the sails on the mizzenmast. An' don' take all year abou' it, yeh duffers."

With the rear sails lowered, *the Colossus* instantly gained considerable speed. Bellamy steered his ship into the mouth of the Brio River's west fork. His control was immaculate. He stayed perfectly centered in the river as he entered it.

Just visible up ahead was the enemy vessel. Bellamy and crew followed at a safe distance. Eventually, their target slowed and anchored. A crew of Ryvelian soldiers disembarked and headed into the forest.

Bellamy gave silent orders for his crew to get them anchored; moments later, they were creeping slowly into the forest behind their unsuspecting prey.

Lenny stepped on a twig. He heard a voice just ahead of him and stopped to hide behind a tree, holding his breath while the rest of the crew found their own ways to become invisible.

"Did you hear that, Miles?"

"Hear what?"

"I thought I heard the snap of a twig."

"Your senses are just on edge, Rodney. Keep quiet! Do you realize what will happen to us if we're caught by the Satria warriors before they head to battle? You might as well fall on your sword, 'cause I can promise, it would be a damn shade better that what they'll do to yeh!"

Rodney was sure he'd heard something. He went back to check while the rest of the soldiers carried on through the woods. Soon he reached the tree where Lenny stood, still as a statue. The moment he walked by, Lenny came to life and silenced Rodney permanently. Then he signaled to Bellamy that it was safe to continue their pursuit.

As the Ryvelian soldiers reached the tree line around the Satria village, not a single one of them suspected that as they sought to mount a surprise attack, the true surprise attack waited behind them in the form of a group of sailors.

It wasn't long before the loud resonating note of a horn blasted through the silent air. Twice the horn sounded, followed closely by the voice of a man. "Nayati — *Chief Nayati!*"

The chief emerged from his hut. "What is it Krikor?" he asked uneasily.

"Ryvelian armies, approaching from the east!" exclaimed the Satria lookout that had seen exactly what Vellix had wanted him to see and was now responding accordingly.

"Round up the warriors," yelled the chief.

Krikor took off running though the village, blasting his horn as he went.

A group of ten men were the first to wake. They grabbed their weapons and gathered around Nayati. "Captains," boomed the chief, "prepare to lead your companies. We're headed for battle."

Soon, over a thousand warriors had gathered around their chief.

Women and children stood at the doors of their huts and watched on as Nayati spoke to his men.

"Krikor has informed me that the Ryvelian armies approach. We head for battle to protect all we know and love! The Ryvelians seek to take that away from us. For that, they will pay!"

Every Satria warrior raised their weapon in salute of their chief's inspiring words. They marched out of the village to fight for what they held most dear. What they didn't know, was that they had just left what they loved in more jeopardy than they could have ever guessed. For, as soon as they were out of range, their village was to be invaded. If it wasn't for Vivek's efforts to find a crew, and Bellamy's faith in Ammin, unspeakable atrocities would have taken place on that morning, and the warriors would have returned to a smoldering village of death.

Bellamy and Ammin made meaningful eye contact as they silently drew their swords. The rest of the crew followed suit.

Lenny licked his lips in anticipation — surely, this would repay Medwin for saving him from those three men that were going to rob and kill him. He clutched his sword tightly, ready to strike.

Vivek stood there, breathing calmly and preparing his mind to turn the forest into a weapon with cognition.

Vellix's forces attacked, but before they could reach their first victims, they realized something was very wrong.

Bellamy had already slain five. He wasted no time in adding a sixth.

Ammin had taken out seven.

Lenny caught up quickly. He dispatched two soldiers at once with one powerful slash.

Dale and Landon seemed to be enjoying themselves immensely. They were making crude jokes about the pathetic way in which their unsuspecting enemies were attempting to defend themselves.

James made sure to let Gavin know that his most recent kill had been the fiercest of the bunch, and on top of that, he still had the higher kill-count.

Gavin responded by dropping to his knees, evading the attack that was aimed for his head, grabbing the sword of the Ryvelian that James had killed, jumping back to his feet, and killing, not only the soldier whose attack he had evaded, but the one that James was currently engaged with.

Bellamy roared with laughter. "Taugh' 'im a bit too well, eh James?" he cackled.

"Aye," James responded as he struck down the next enemy in his path.

Vivek's cognition proved ferocious. Trees from all around the village became animated: roots burst from below the surface and snatched up his enemies, crushing the life out of them or wrapping around their legs to hold them in place while branches arrived to deliver devastating blows. Poisoned ivy sprouted up around soldiers and pulled them into the dirt as they let out wild screams of fear and pain. Vivek's kill-count increased so fast that he didn't even bother to keep track of it.

Vellix's malignant plan was foiled as dawn broke, and as the sun rose and cast away the darkness, it was a symbol of the darkness that had been slain in the Forest of Elders.

* * *

"Vellix's forces were defeated before they could carry out their dark deed," said Ammin. "In the end they only took five of our crew with them. After that, we headed for the battle and, of course, you know the rest."

Medwin's skin was pale and chalky. Hearing that his mother — and all the other women and children in his tribe — had come so close to sure death made him look as though he was physically ill. When he spoke, his voice sounded feeble. "We are forever in your debt. Ammin ... Lenny ... how can I ever repay you?"

"Think nothin' o' it!" Lenny exclaimed as he clapped Medwin on the back. "We're even now, mate!"

"It was my pleasure, Medwin," Ammin said.

Conner looked as shocked as Medwin did. He couldn't even begin to think what it would have been like for the Satria warriors to return to their village, only to find that it had been massacred at the very same time they risked their lives to save it. "You are good men," Conner said sincerely. "Ammin, I know my opinion doesn't matter to the crew, but I vote you next captain of *the Colossus*. I can't think of a better man for the job."

CHAPTER 19

Willow Grove

Ammin gazed at Conner for a moment before turning to look at the crew, who were digging a grave for their fallen captain with their swords, knives, and bare hands. "We will see," he said quietly. "I would be honored to captain the Colossus."

"Yeh go' my vote, mate," Lenny said. With that, the two of them went over to the partially dug grave to help their crew.

Conner had a realization. Vivek was still in need of a proper burial. It wasn't hard to locate him. His body was lying at the foot of the stone pillar he'd created during his duel with Vellix. As Conner walked up to him, and saw the ancient man's lifeless eyes staring into nothing, he knew that the Hylan were now truly extinct. Vellix did not deserve the title. He didn't even deserve the title of "human."

Conner used cognition to dig a grave deep below the surface. He gently closed Vivek's eyes as he laid him to rest. For a solid minute, he stared at the body, lost within the depths of thought. His eyes started to burn, urging him to look away. He blinked a few times before sinking into a state of concentration.

Dirt began to pour back into the grave, continuing until it had filled. Conner looked at the mound that covered Vivek and noticed that one of the last acts of cognition the ancient man ever performed was casting it into shadow. An idea struck him. The ground quivered as the large granite pillar began to recede into the valley. Soon all that remained of it was a headstone-sized portion. Conner thought for a minute about what to put on the headstone. Eventually, words began to etch themselves onto its rocky face. When they had finished, the headstone read: *Here Lies Vivek: Last of the Hylan.*

Conner, pleased with his work, but thoroughly saddened by the fact he would never speak with Vivek again, headed back over to Medwin and Zelimir.

"I need to address my people," Medwin said as he wiped fresh dirt off his hands. "I do not look forward to informing mother of my father's death. She will mourn this loss greatly."

Conner stared at the grave that he knew belonged to Chief Nayati, feeling like he should find some words of condolence. The problem was that nothing felt sincere enough. He settled for saying nothing at all.

"Let's go," Medwin said, finally prying his eyes away from his father's grave as he started toward the Ancient Forest.

Feelings of sadness for Medwin continued to smolder inside Conner as he followed his friend. Again, he wished there was something he could say, something that would sound as honest and genuine as he felt. But every time he came to the verge of speaking, all the things he'd been about to say sounded suddenly pathetic in light of Medwin's loss. His father was gone. Nayati would never be able to look his son in the eye and tell him how proud he was again. He would never be able to pass down another lesson for life. He was gone.

Just when Conner was finally about to try his best to console Medwin, Zelimir spoke.

"I am very sorry for your loss, Medwin," the wolf said solemnly. "Your people are unlucky in one sense, for they have lost a fine leader. Yet, they are lucky in another, as they have just gained a great one in his stead. You have the makings of a great chief, Medwin. Wisdom, loyalty, pride, and compassion are characteristics you have shown that cannot be overlooked. I know that the pain you feel right now probably seems as though it will never subside. You probably feel like you will never be whole again because a part you is missing that can never return. And, while this is partially true, it is not wholly true. Time heals wounds and wisdom knows the path to acceptance. Eventually, you will learn to find your father within yourself. He will always live in your memory."

Tears streamed down Medwin's face as he listened intently to Zelimir's speech. "Thank you, Zelimir," he replied when it became clear that the wolf had reached his conclusion. "Your words give me much needed strength."

In Conner's opinion, no words of condolence could have been better than those that Zelimir had just spoken. He was glad, now, that he hadn't said anything. Zelimir had done a much better job of finding the right thing to say.

Medwin led his companions into the forest. Conner remembered entering it when he had first arrived in Rohwen. It seemed so long ago now. So many things had happened since then. A thought suddenly found the front of his mind — he was near the gateway back to his world. He could search for his way home. He stopped walking.

"Is there something wrong?" Zelimir asked when he realized Conner had come to a halt.

Conner looked up at Zelimir, his expression confused, as if the wolf's question had baffled him. He shifted his gaze to Medwin, who had turned around to see what was going on. Guilt consumed him as he made eye contact with the friend he had just considered abandoning. Medwin needed him. Rohwen needed him. If he left now, his act of cowardice would haunt him for the rest of his days.

"Conner... Are you okay?" Medwin asked seriously when Conner didn't reply to Zelimir.

"Yeah, I'm fine. I just... It's nothing. Let's keep moving." Medwin and Zelimir looked at him speculatively. "Seriously, I'm fine," he said again. This time, the others gave him a nod and they continued their journey toward the Satria village.

As they drew closer to the village, Conner saw the dead bodies of the Ryvelian soldiers piled up on the outskirts of the huge clearing. It wasn't hard to tell which ones Vivek had slain, their bodies were nearly broken beyond recognition. It felt strange to Conner, but he didn't have a single ounce of pity for these fallen men. The deed they intended to carryout was so unspeakably heinous that it removed any compassion he normally would have had.

Conner, Medwin, and Zelimir stepped into the village. A woman saw them as they entered. She ran to Medwin, flung her arms around his neck, and pulled him into a loving hug. Conner knew instantly that this woman was Medwin's mother. Her eyes sparkled with the same pride as her son's, and her hair shared the look of black silk as it fell elegantly below the middle of her back.

Medwin met his mother's eyes with a telling gaze of sorrow. She fell to her knees and started to weep. The look Medwin had given her said all the words he could not.

Conner stood a short distance away, feeling this wasn't a moment he should intrude upon.

Zelimir sat down next to him. "It is always hard to lose a loved one..." he said, looking on at Medwin and his mother with great sadness. "Especially when that loved one should have had many more years to spend with their family. It seems like you can find nothing good in a situation like this... But good things can come from any situation, if you let them... I believe that Medwin has the ability to find positive elements in his premature appointment as chief. It may take some time — and I would not blame him if it does — but eventually, he will."

"Yeah, I agree," Conner replied slowly as he watched Medwin comfort his mother.

Medwin waved his friends over. "Conner — Zelimir, this is my mother, Minna," he introduced them as they arrived next to him.

Conner met Minna's eyes with a look of condolence and nodded his acknowledgment of being introduced. "I'm sorry for your loss," he said, breaking eye contact with her quickly. She seemed to have composed herself to a certain degree, but her eyes were still puffy and red. It saddened him greatly to look at her.

"Mother, will you tell Krikor to sound the horn?" Medwin asked. "I need to address my people."

Minna looked at her son, and it was obvious how much admiration she had for him. The fact that he was ready to take on the responsibilities as chief, even though it was a constant reminder of his father's death, proved that he was qualified for the job. She hurried off and returned a moment later with Krikor. He sounded the horn and everyone in the village began to gather around.

Medwin took a deep breath. His face hardened as he repressed his emotions in order to assume his role as chief: a role that didn't afford him the luxury of showing weakness. "I am saddened to inform you that my father, Chief Nayati, was killed in battle," he started, determined not to break back into tears.

Many of the women put their hands over their mouths; others began to weep.

"I am your chief now," Medwin continued, "and I vow not to rest until Vellix and his Mirthless have paid for their crimes against us ... and all the people of Rohwen!" He turned to his mother and hugged her again. "I have to leave," he said as he released her and signaled to Conner and Zelimir that it was time to go.

Minna gazed at her son, a mixture of pride and pain warping her features. But she did not speak.

"Come on," Medwin said, his voice harsh with emotion. "I made a promise to my people. I'm in the mood to fulfill it."

Conner saw Medwin's fists clench. He gave him an understanding nod as they left the village and headed east.

On the way out of the forest, Medwin picked some edible berries and mushrooms. "Sorry Zelimir," he apologized with a shrug, "I know this isn't really what you would prefer to eat, but it's convenient."

"It is better than nothing," Zelimir replied, not hiding the scowl that thoughts of such food gave him.

* * *

For the next five days, they traveled east. There was no sign of the last Mirthless or of the wolves. They journeyed by night as Zelimir had suggested. The new moon had been six days ago, and now the lunar night light was just larger than a sliver in the star-flecked sky.

Shortly before dawn on the sixth day, a dark mass in the distance came into view. At first, Conner assumed it was trees, but as he drew closer, a scent of the sweetest nature drifted pleasantly across the crisp air. He realized with an overwhelming sense of awe that it wasn't trees he'd seen. It was massive flowers. A pale blue morning sky provided just enough light to reveal their striking beauty.

The flowers varied in color, with shades of pink, white, orange, and lavender being the most common. Spots of stunning colors that always complimented the dominant shade of the flower sprinkled each petal. Long pointed leaves grew almost evenly off both sides of each stem, giving them the look of an odd kind of ladder.

Conner suddenly recognized the flowers. His mother had grown these every spring for his whole life. They were huge versions of oriental lilies. He continued to look around, unable to stifle the grin that had spread across his face. Wildflowers riddled the field-grass shadowed by these huge lilies. Being dead tired from the night's travels, Conner lied down in the grass. It was just tall enough that he disappeared into its depths.

Medwin and Zelimir gazed longingly at the comfortable grass and could not resist it. They lied down next to Conner, and all three of them floated away into euphoric sleep.

* * *

"No, Azalea! Don't get any closer. That's a wolf!"

"So...? If you haven't noticed, it's sleeping right next to two boys, *Flora*."

"Well ... yeah, but —"

"But what? I'm getting a better look."

Conner thought he'd been dreaming about the two girls, but then the deep shade of red behind his eyelids fell into blackness. He opened his eyes to find a girl standing over him. The sun that hid behind Azalea illuminated her figure, making her look angelic. She stepped back when she noticed that Conner had woken up.

"It's okay," Conner said quickly as he sat up and saw the girls more clearly. "You don't need to worry."

The girls looked at one another cautiously.

"My name is Conner. What's yours?" he said to further his effort of convincing them he meant no harm.

The girl that had approached Conner initially looked down at him with emerald green eyes that set off her vibrant pink dress and replied, "I am Azalea, and this" — she gestured to the girl, whose sky blue eyes went perfectly with the bright yellow dress she wore — "is my twin sister, Flora."

"Pleased to meet you," said Conner, wiping his dew-soaked eyes as he began to take more notice of the girls' appearance. Their carefully tailored dresses made them look remarkably like flowers, and daisies, strung delicately together in the shape of crowns, topped their long wavy hair.

Conner felt sure that these girls must live near here. It made perfect sense, due to their extraordinary resemblance to flowers.

Medwin sat up and stretched. The moment he saw the two girls, he looked taken aback.

Azalea and Flora swapped flattered looks and started to giggle. The loud noise woke up Zelimir. He yawned widely, revealing his vicious-looking canines.

Both the girls took a step back, a look of fear on their faces.

"It's okay," Conner said convincingly. "He's our friend. He won't harm you."

Zelimir sat up. "Yes, you have nothing to fear."

The girls' jaws dropped. "You — you can talk!" they exclaimed.

"Yes, and quite well, if I don't say so myself."

Conner burst into laughter. Medwin attempted a grin, but he didn't seem able to find it in his heart to truly enjoy anything just yet. His feelings of bitterness and loss were still too great.

Azalea looked to be somewhere between confusion, embarrassment, and anger, and Flora was staring at Zelimir as if he was bound to lunge at her at any moment.

"You must be Botanicans," Medwin said, looking around at the tree-sized lilies.

Flora found her voice. "Yeah," she replied simply, not looking at Medwin as she answered.

Conner looked up at the same lily that Medwin was still investigating. "You live in a very beautiful place," he told the girls with a tone of admiration.

Azalea seemed quite pleased to hear that Conner appreciated the beauty around him. "Would you like to see our village?" she asked with a tentative smile, turning almost the same shade of pink as her dress.

"Well — uh — I guess so, sure," Conner replied with a carefree shrug of his shoulders, while returning Azalea's smile.

"Conner!" Medwin snapped sharply. "Don't forget our mission! I" — he lowered his voice to a whisper — "I want to end this!"

"So do I," Conner whispered back. "But… But — you're right." He knew he didn't have a rebuttal. There was no time to get side tracked. Every hour that Vellix was still alive was an hour too many.

"You guys are on a mission?" Flora asked, becoming suddenly curious and animated.

When Conner, Medwin, and Zelimir all failed to respond, it became obvious that the answer was "yes."

"What kind of mission?" Azalea probed, getting close enough to Conner now that he could smell the sweet fragrance of her hair.

Conner and the others exchanged hesitant looks, none of them sure if it would be wise to tell these girls the details of their mission. The girls seemed to be innocent enough, but that didn't mean everyone they were in contact with was.

Conner studied Azalea's shining face. She seemed to be itching with curiosity — a feeling he was extremely familiar with. After another moment's contemplation, he just couldn't see the harm in answering her question. "We are on a mission to destroy Vellix," he said bluntly.

Both girls gasped.

"You're going to" — Azalea lowered her voice to a secretive whisper much like Medwin's had been — "try and kill Vellix? …But he is so powerful! How do you, I mean, how *are* you going to do that?"

Conner looked down at the grass in front of her feet. A stem started to grow there with delicate elegance. As the stem grew taller, leaves unfurled from it. Soon tiny buds started to form. They continued to grow until seams of violet became visible all around them. Finally, the buds reached a point where they could no longer retain the flower within, and they bloomed into delightful irises.

Azalea shifted her eyes from the flowers back up to Conner, the look of wonder imprinted upon her face, but Flora didn't seem nearly as impressed. She crossed her arms moodily.

"How did you do that?" Azalea asked, now staring intently back down at the irises.

"I used a power called cognition," Conner answered with a slight sign of arrogance in his voice. He made eye contact with Medwin right as he said this and blushed immediately.

Flora clicked her tongue impatiently. "So that's how you plan to defeat Vellix?" she said disrespectfully. "Using that power?" she added with a short glance over at the flowers Conner had created.

"Yes, that is the plan," said Conner, the arrogance in his voice now replaced by humility.

"I don't really know that *flowers* are going to do much to Vellix," Flora went on rudely. "You would think someone planning to take on Vellix would actually —"

Thorn covered vines burst forth from the ground where the irises had just been, interrupting Flora's rude comment. They started to strangle the huge stem of the closest tree-sized lily.

"Stop it!" Azalea yelled imploringly, putting a hand out as if she could save the lily. "Flora" — she punched her sister in the shoulder — "didn't mean it. She can be really *rude!*" Azalea shot Flora the dirtiest look Conner had ever seen.

The vines retreated at Conner's will, and as they did, a guilty feeling crept up inside him. He noticed the damage he had done to the flower's stem. There were deep lacerations, bleeding moisture and spiraling at least twenty feet up it. He knew that the flower didn't actually feel anything, but he was also painfully aware of the fact he had just done cognition out of spitefulness for the first time. He did it to shut Flora up. Her words hurt his pride. He wanted to show her how stupid she was to assume the power could only create flowers.

"Sorry," Flora uttered, still looking shocked and frightened by the appearance of the vines. "I shouldn't have been rude," she continued, not looking at Conner, but throwing occasional glances at her sister's furiously expectant expression.

Hoping that Flora's apology had been enough to put them all back on good terms, Azalea said, "We would be forever grateful you know — if you were able to defeat Vellix."

Conner wasn't sure if Azalea was just trying to repair the damage her sister had done, or if she actually meant what she said.

"Vellix has caused our people to live in fear for centuries," Azalea continued, and her expression became blank, as if she had entered a place in her mind that caused it to freeze.

Conner knew that look. He had seen it on Medwin's face, and he had felt it on his own. He was sure, now, that Azalea could not have been more serious. "I will certainly do my best to defeat him," he said quietly.

Zelimir, who had been watching the interaction between Conner and the girls as though their levels of ignorance were causing him a minor amount of pain, finally chimed in. "We will succeed or we will die trying…"

Conner knew that the wolf had more reason than living in fear to want Vellix dealt with: his kind were actually servants of Vellix's evil.

"Why don't you come to our village," Azalea proposed again, looking from Conner to Medwin to Zelimir with hopes that one of them would accept her offer. "Come on," she pled. "Everyone would be so pleased to meet you."

"We really need to keep moving," Conner replied reluctantly. The truth was — a little break would have been a nice change of pace.

"We will have a feast in your honor," Azalea added raucously, now seeming to enter a world in which the word "no" didn't exist.

This was a very tempting offer. They hadn't had much to eat the last few days, and a good meal would provide needed energy. Conner got a nod from Medwin. He looked over at Zelimir, who told him sunset was at least a few hours away, which meant they had time before setting off on that night's travels. Conner nodded and said, "That is an offer we can't pass up."

"That settles it then," Azalea replied, looking pleased. Without another word, she grabbed Flora by the arm, and together, they skipped off toward their village, Conner and the others following a few paces behind them.

A combination of scent and scenery made the journey through the forest of lilies delightful. Eventually, a village full of colorful huts appeared up ahead. As Conner got closer, he noticed that the huts were blooms from the huge lilies turned upside down. He couldn't help but smile.

The village was quite active. Women were chasing their children or going down to the creek to fetch water, while men stood in varied places: some chopping wood, some clutching fishing rods, whose lines were cast into the creek, others were gathered around a fire-pit that marked the center of their community.

One of the men spotted Zelimir. He yelled "*wolf*" as he unsheathed a large knife and threw it at Zelimir with all his might. The knife never found its target because a shield of dirt and grass formed in its path before it had the chance.

"Thank you," said Zelimir gratefully with a polite gesture toward Conner.

Azalea ran over to the group of men. "Please — don't attack him!" she yelled pleadingly. "He won't hurt you!"

The men looked confused. They were taking in the scene in front of them more clearly now. Surely if the wolf was dangerous, he wouldn't be accompanied by two boys... And, how did the ground just rise up of its own accord like that?

"He's a good wolf!" Azalea said sincerely.

Before the men had a chance to reply, someone else butt in. "*Azalea — Flora! Where have you been?*" bellowed a man walking toward them.

"Just out exploring, father," Azalea explained, while Flora became suddenly interested in the blades of grass at her feet.

"You know the rules! How many times do I have to tell you! It is not safe to go out exploring at your age! You're only thirteen! If the Mirthless had seen you" — the man's enraged expression softened — "I could have lost you ... forever."

Azalea joined her sister in her investigation of the grass at their feet. "I'm sorry, father," she said with conviction. "Guess what though?" she asked, jerking her head up quickly, her face radiant.

"What?" asked her father, the hint of a smirk threatening to break into an amused grin.

"We met some travelers," Azalea waved the three of them over. "They're on a mission to destroy Vellix!"

"What are you talking about?" her father asked doubtfully as Conner, Medwin, and Zelimir made their way over to the man and his daughters. He looked at the wolf for a moment but didn't react as the other men had. He was wise enough to realize that the beast must be friendly.

With the help of Conner and the others, Azalea and Flora explained to their father of the mission to destroy Vellix and return peace to Rohwen. Conner gave the man a demonstration of cognition, telling him it was this very skill that had enabled Vellix to achieve his level of power.

"So you share the same power then," the man muttered thoughtfully. Conner nodded.

"We haven't had news this good for years! This calls for a celebration! I will inform Jonquil straight away. I am sure he will want to have a feast in your honor!"

Conner chanced a look over at Azalea and wasn't at all shocked to find her giving him an "I told you so" look, which she followed up with a beaming smile.

* * *

The feast that night was incredible: a main course of honey-glazed boar, accompanied by grilled fish, corn on the cob, sweet dinner rolls, stuffing, mashed potatoes, and some kind of pudding for desert.

The news of the three travelers and their mission spread through the village like a wild fire. Soon it was on the tongue of every man, woman, and child.

As dinner ended, the celebration continued with joyful music and dancing. Conner wasn't much of a dancer, so he sat and watched the others.

Medwin, on the other hand, was great at it. He danced energetically around the fire, finally able to expel some of the sadness and anger that burned within. Flora approached him and asked if he would like to dance with her. At first, he looked speechless — Flora was very pretty — but then he smiled, and they danced together, arm in arm.

Conner felt a tug on his hand. He looked up to find Azalea smiling down at him.

"Come on, Conner! Dance with me!" she said in her cutest voice.

Conner's face started to burn. He looked around for some excuse to get out of it, but all he saw was Zelimir, who gave him an approving nod that quite plainly said, "Go on. Dance with her, you fool!"

As Conner stared into Azalea's smiling face, he thought, 'This might be your last chance to let loose and have some fun.' He took Azalea's hand. She gave him a big, glowing smile and, as they danced around the fire, a great feeling of joy came over him. Thoughts of confronting Vellix left the front of his mind for the first time in days. He felt so light that he might float away.

It seemed all too soon that the music stopped. A man stood up and raised his hand to get the attention of his people.

"Who's that?" Conner asked.

"That is our leader, Jonquil," Azalea answered in a whisper.

"Botanicans…" Jonquil began. "Tonight is a special night… It is a night of hope, not only for our people, but for all the people of Rohwen!"

The whole village roared its approval of these words.

"Let us offer these brave heroes as much hospitality as we can!"

The village cheered again, and the sound of it was like poison in Conner's veins. It was already hard enough to think about how much Medwin and Zelimir were depending on him, but then, as he looked into the ecstatic faces of hundreds of people who were all counting on him for their liberation from Vellix's evil reign, the reality of the task overwhelmed him. The truth of the matter was that he was a fourteen-year-old boy, who'd only been doing cognition for a short time, whereas Vellix had been practicing the art for nearly two thousand years. Conner no longer questioned the fact that he was the one to have special abilities in the art, but he still felt like he needed more time. Time to hone his skills, to make sure he was ready.

He left the celebration, seeking the peace and quiet of the forest. After wandering aimlessly for a few minutes, he sat down in the tall grass and allowed the tranquil fragrance of the flowers to sooth him.

"Conner?"

Someone had come up behind him. He turned to look and saw that it was Flora and Azalea's father. "Oh, hello," he said with what he hoped was a casual tone.

"Abram — that is my name… May I have a word?"

"Sure."

"I couldn't help but notice that you seem burdened by the task before you."

Conner continued to stare into space. Abram went on.

"It is wise of you to fear Vellix. Without this emotion, you lose respect for your opponent, at which point you have lost the fight before it has even begun... I will not claim to have the answer to your question, which is 'how do I defeat him?' I am sure."

Conner thought for a second and realized that he hadn't really been looking for a specific way to win the fight with Vellix. He had just been wishing he was more skilled than his enemy. The idea of finding a weakness seemed so obvious now. Abram spoke again, interrupting his thoughts.

"There is a grove northeast of here. Within that grove lives a most ancient weeping willow tree. It is said that all of the knowledge and wisdom of this land's many years resides within that tree."

Conner turned and looked at Abram. "What do you mean — like the tree is alive or something?"

"Of course the tree is alive!" Abram said exasperatedly. "Everything around us is alive. The flowers, the grass, the trees... They all breathe as we do — need water, sun, and love as we do. It is sad to say, but most people disrespect the land in the same way Vellix disrespects people, maiming and punishing it for their own personal gain: cutting down trees that have been alive since before they were even a shadow of a thought; damming rivers because it will make life easier; killing animals for pleasure rather than necessity. These acts are of pure ignorance, Conner."

"I have never really taken the time to think about that before," Conner replied honestly. "Those words will stay with me, Abram. I will do my best to respect the land in all I do."

"That is very good — very good indeed. It is these things that will separate you from your enemy: respect, compassion, honor, and love."

Conner absorbed Abram's words before he asked, "So about that willow tree... Where is it again?"

"You will find it if you travel northeast of the village," said Abram with an approving smile.

"I will make it a point to find this tree," said Conner, whose words could not have been more truthful.

"Very good. Shall we head back to the festivities? They are, after all, in your honor."

Conner laughed awkwardly. "Yeah, let's go," he replied. "Thanks for talking with me. I feel a little better now."

"Oh, you are more than welcome, Conner. Thank *you* for what you are doing for Rohwen. It takes a great deal of bravery to face a man as powerful as Vellix."

Conner smiled at Abram, and they went back to the celebration.

* * *

"Do you have to go already?"

"It's still early!"

"Stay a while longer."

"Yeah!"

Flora and Azalea were trying to persuade their guests to stay. Since they had arrived, the whole village was buzzing with excitement.

"We really can't," said Conner, while Medwin filled his pack with enough food to last them for the next few days. "It's already a couple hours past nightfall, which means we've lost time as it is. Thanks again for everything, but we really need to be going."

The girls looked let down, but in an understanding way.

Conner, Medwin, and Zelimir said their goodbyes and headed north out of the village. They were just on the outskirts of the lily forest when Abram yelled to Conner.

"Don't forget, Willow Grove!"

"I won't," Conner replied with one last wave.

"'Willow Grove?' What's 'Willow Grove?'" Medwin asked as he joined Conner in his final wave of farewell.

"It is the home of an ancient weeping willow tree," Conner answered.

"I have heard of such a place," said Zelimir. "The tree is said to hold some kind of mythical power."

"Abram told me that the knowledge and wisdom of this land's many years resides within the tree... I'm not exactly sure what that means, but I want to check it out."

"I see no harm in investigating the tree," Zelimir admitted. "As long as it isn't too far off course."

"Abram said it was northeast of the village, so we will have to go out of our way — but not too far, I don't think."

"Medwin, what do you think of visiting the tree?" Zelimir asked, noticing that Medwin had become suddenly silent.

"Whatever you guys want to do," he replied in a tone that clearly stated his mind was elsewhere.

Conner looked over at him. "Are you okay?" he asked.

"No, not really," Medwin answered honestly. "It's just so hard! It isn't fair!"

Conner knew where the conversation was headed.

"My father was such a good man! He had knowledge and wisdom that I will never gain now — because he is gone..."

Conner saw the corner of Medwin's eye glisten. "I — I'm ... sorry, Medwin... I don't know what to say."

"You don't have to say anything. I shouldn't need anyone to say anything! If there's one thing my father taught me, it's that when the living mourn the dead in excess, they become as dead as the one they mourn for."

"It is only natural for you to mourn the loss of your father, Medwin," said Zelimir with his most calming voice. "To be wise is to use your feelings as fuel. Allow the memories of your father's greatness to guide you toward becoming a man deserving of the same respect and honor."

"Once again, Zelimir, your words give me needed strength. You are very wise."

Zelimir didn't reply, but he looked pleased to hear Medwin say this.

In the darkness of night, Conner was just able to see that the tree-sized lilies had begun to thin. Fir, oak, and birch trees replaced them.

* * *

The three travelers walked on in silence as the hours passed, and eventually, they came upon a clearing.

As Conner stepped into Willow Grove, he was unable to suppress a grin. Faint moonlight illuminated the scene that lay before him. An ancient willow tree stood near the center of the grove; around it grew the most incredible grass he had ever seen. It looked as lush as a plant could possibly be. Purple, white, yellow, pink, blue, and red wild flowers spackled the grass, giving it perfect contrast.

Conner walked up to the willow tree. Its leaf covered branches wept down to the point that they brushed along the grass. It was for this reason that he couldn't even see the tree's aged trunk. He pulled apart the curtain of branches and stepped into the depths of the weeping willow. The moment his body entered the umbrella of foliage, thoughts erupted into the front of his mind.

'Never undervalue those who appear unimportant. Do not judge what you do not know, lest be judged yourself. Only a fool takes another living creature at face value. An enemy is only as strong as their greatest weakness. To gain power by force is to lose pride by choice.'

The thoughts were not his, but his voice was speaking them. It was as if the tree was talking to him but only on brainwaves.

'Pity the evil, for they know not of love or happiness. Respect all forms of life. Beware arrogance, as it has befriended ignorance…

'Conner, your journey is a brave one.'

Conner was shocked when the tree addressed him personally, now speaking in a cool, female voice, rather than his own.

'Your acts thus far have been honorable. Rohwen has awaited your arrival for many years, and the time is coming when Vellix will have to pay for his corruption. You are wondering, maybe, how I know these things… If so, I do not blame you. The answer is not an obvious one. It is this: I am the one who foresaw all that you know of your destiny…'

Conner's mind began to race, but he didn't reply. The willow tree continued.

'That was thousands of years ago. The time has come now for you to fulfill your purpose. You face a man who is extremely skilled, but you have something he does not. You have honor, respect, and love for the life around you. These are mighty tools. Vellix is a fool to underestimate them. Yes, he is powerful, but he is drunk with that power. In the end, it will become his downfall...

'I only have two more things to say, and then it will be time for you to continue your journey. The first being, keep your friends close, and always remember that they share your goal. Lastly, I implore you to give any living creature a chance to prove itself, no matter how they may appear. Do you understand these words?'

"Yes," Conner said aloud, which felt odd because the tree had been talking to him in his head. When he got no reply, he took this as a sign that their conversation was over. The weeping willow had given him all the advice she had to offer. Conner stepped back out into the grove to find Medwin and Zelimir wearing expectant expressions, both of them anxious to find out what happened.

"What was it like under there?" Medwin asked.

Conner didn't know how to reply. He'd just had one of the oddest experiences of his life. A tree had just spoken to him with the voice of a woman. And, among other things, she had said she was the one who predicted his future so many years ago. "…It was really weird…" he finally replied. "Let's keep moving."

CHAPTER 20

An Underwater Passageway

The sounds of countless creatures' mourning cries twisted and bent as they traveled through the pitch-black depths of the small lake at the center of a deep hollow. A wiry little hunchback broke the lake's surface gasping for air, and the cries came back into sharp, echoed focus. "Must be a way! Must be! Got to find it! Keep searching!" he wailed miserably. He'd been strategically searching every inch of the lake for years, hoping to find some way of escaping. So far, the only result was that his state of mind had become increasingly manic.

Thousands of creatures that had given up, and now settled for voicing their sorrow in a demented chorus of cries, filled the hundreds of rock shelves above, but he would never give up. He didn't care if the rest of the creatures had given up. He would never resign himself to this life of captivity. There had to be a way out. Some way to escape Vellix's holding chamber.

After inhaling the biggest breath he possibly could, he dove back into the lake and swam his fastest to the next spot he hadn't yet searched. His lungs in desperate need of oxygen, he resurfaced, took another massive gulp of air, and dove once more into the deep, black water. Something caught the corner of his beady eyes. One miniscule ray of light flashed briefly across the edge of a rock along the lake's northern wall. 'Get air first! Must get air! Then I go check,' he thought, full of the kind of excitement he hadn't felt in ages.

A quick breath later, he was swimming his fastest in search of the small shimmer of light. His eyes widened as he found it once more.

His arms and legs worked furiously, pushing him ever closer to his destination. 'Yes! Yes yes *yes!*' That was the only word that played through his mind as a small tunnel came into view. He swam into it, giving every drop of energy he had to his extremities. The tunnel forked, forcing him to make a quick decision. 'Go up, or follow the light? Go up or follow the light?' he thought frantically. His lungs beseeched him to give them air. 'Go up,' he told himself. The decision was a good one. Within seconds, his head broke the surface of the water. He had swum into a tiny air pocket in the tunnel. He took a few more breaths, dove back under, and resumed the path toward light.

As the tunnel came to an end, he entered a large body of water, and his mind exploded with dark thoughts that doubted everything he was doing. It was as if his brain had become his worst enemy, saying things like, 'you'll never reach the surface,' or, 'what's the point of escaping? You're a freak! No one will ever want you around. You should have just stayed in the chamber with all the other freaks!'

Strong-willed as the little hunchback was, he fought the terrible thoughts and pushed for the surface. The moment his head broke the plane of water, all the morbid and demeaning thoughts ceased to exist.

Dazzling light from the dawning sun blinded him as he swam to shore, climbed out of the water, and fell to his hands and knees. Fatigue attempted to overwhelm his body, but the elation of escaping his prison filled him with adrenaline. He was so happy that he could hardly contain it. "Hehehe! Free! I am! That is what I am! *Free!*" He bellowed.

He scanned the scenery around him, and it quickly became clear that the best way to travel would be southeast. There was a forest off in the distance and its trees would be a useful cover from the eyes of the Mirthless. The last thing he wanted was to be caught and thrown right back into the holding chamber. The very thought of it made him tremble.

His adrenaline levels settled, and as he set off for the tree line, feelings of joy replaced them: joy felt only by free beings — free to breathe the clean air and feel the breeze wisp across their face. Free to smell the fresh grass and flowers.

His eyes were used to the morning light now. He marveled in the landscape around him as he made his way toward the forest.

He reached the tree line some hours later, and upon entering the forest, his eyes swept from one thing to the next, overjoyed to soak it all in. But it wasn't long before fear took over those feelings of joy. There was something unsettling about this forest. He couldn't shake the feeling that something was watching him. It felt like the very trees were staring him down with evil intent.

A whispered voice broke the, otherwise, silent air. The little hunchback dove into a bush in an attempt to conceal himself. The owners of the voices were just beyond a mossy old tree.

CHAPTER 21

Morik Forest

Conner explained to Medwin and Zelimir all he had learned from the willow tree as they left Willow Grove and headed north.

Medwin was just as astounded by the revelations as Conner had been. "That's unbelievable. The prediction of your arrival came from a tree?" He shook his head disbelievingly while Conner nodded in response to his question.

Zelimir remained silent for a minute before stating that the real phenomenon was not that a tree could predict the future but that it could have conscience thought.

Conner and Medwin both gave the wolf curious looks, but neither of them chose to reply.

A field lay just beyond the woods that enclosed the grove. Its level scape revealed the dark forms of the trees that made up the Morik Forest.

"There it is," Medwin said darkly as he pointed toward the forest.

Zelimir gazed at the forest for a moment before turning to Conner and Medwin. "It is safe to assume that we will face trials which require quick wit. We must be prepared to work together and watch one another's backs — six eyes are better that two."

Conner and Medwin nodded.

The sky to the east began to turn fire red as the rising sun prepared to peek over the horizon.

"So should we stop here?" Conner asked, noticing that dawn was quickly approaching.

"No," Zelimir said, "not this time. It would be very foolish to travel into Morik in the dark of night. We will carry on through the day, and with any luck, no unwanted eyes will spot us."

Over the next few hours, the forest became steadily more visible, and as Conner approached it, fear rose in his heart just as steadily. He wasn't sure if his mind was playing tricks on him, but it looked as though the trees were casting shadows of ugly faces and skulls upon the field that lay before it.

As they reached the outskirts of the forest, the three companions exchanged serious looks before entering its murky depths. A thick fog that appeared as though it never lifted hovered ominously over the forest floor, consuming the life underneath. The trees looked threatening, as if they were all on the verge of snatching up the next thing to come too close. Their branches resembled bony arms with claw-ridden hands, and the knots on their trunks formed wicked faces.

With the exception of the distant squawks of ravens, the forest was dead quiet. It was a nerve-piercing, eerie silence that made Conner feel as though he was being watched.

All three of them were on high alert. Medwin's hatchet had never looked more ready to strike. Zelimir's nose twitched restlessly as he used his greatest sense to search for enemies. Conner pulled out Scarlet and looked at its blade. He whipped around swiftly to investigate a tree that was right behind him.

"What is it, Conner?" Medwin asked nervously. "Did you see something?"

"I could swear I saw that tree move in the reflection of Scarlet's blade," said Conner, still staring at the tree, which remained as motionless as he would expect a tree to be, when not being battered by wind. "I guess I was just seeing things," he concluded.

"I wouldn't be too sure about that," Zelimir said seriously.

"Keep your guard up!" Medwin added, his hatchet still poised to strike at any moment.

They crept through the forest with their senses heightened to twice the ordinary level. Every single sound they heard made their insides squirm.

The forest's trees grew close to each other, and as a result, their canopy blocked out a large majority of the sun's bright rays. Due to the gloomy darkness, Conner's pupils dilated, allowing his mind to play tricks on him. Twice since the time he thought he'd seen that tree move, similar things had happened. He swore something darted from behind one tree to another.

The hair on his arms stood on end as a raspy breathing sound disturbed the menacing silence. He and the others craned their necks in search of the source to no avail. They saw nothing but trees, rocks, dirt, and fog.

Conner whispered over to Medwin and Zelimir. "This place is creeping me out!"

Medwin turned to face him, his expression tense. "I know what you —"

"*Ahhh!*" Conner cried out. The creature that had been watching him for some time now seized its chance to attack, while its prey was busy talking.

Human flesh made up the creature's head and torso, but its arms and legs consisted of wood. Its fingers and toes were like long, sharp spears. Green, dingy dreadlocks grew from its scalp, looking remarkably like moss.

The creature had jumped on Conner before he knew what was happening. Its piercing fingers and toes stabbed deeply into him, injecting a deadly poison. Conner froze immediately. He felt his body seizing further with each passing second that the powerful poison coursed through his bloodstream. The creature looked him straight in the eye with malicious intent, and Conner could see his fear-stricken face reflecting back at him in the black pupils of his attacker. His focus shifted as a silver blur blazed across his vision.

The creature's face became blank as its body fell to the ground in two separate pieces. Medwin came into view, still in the pose that follows a fierce strike.

"Conner, are you okay?"

Conner wanted to warn Medwin that two more of the creatures were creeping up behind him, but at this point, whatever poison the creature injected him with had made a full circuit through his bloodstream; he couldn't move a muscle.

Fortunately, Zelimir saw the two creatures. He leapt at the nearest of them, latching his fangs onto its throat and shaking his foe violently before releasing it to the forest floor.

Medwin wheeled around at top speed. He used this motion as his first attack. His hatchet skimmed the last of the creatures across its mid-section. A trickle of green blood seeped from the wound.

The creature looked down at the cut and then back up at Medwin.

It bared its sharp teeth before launching itself at him, full of rage.

Medwin rolled under the attack, stood up, turned quickly, and struck the creature in the neck. It fell to the ground rasping and clutching at the wound. Medwin struck the creature again to put it out of its misery before scanning the area in search of others. When none appeared, he rushed over to Conner.

"What are we going to do?" he asked Zelimir, sounding worried and anxious.

"I am not sure," Zelimir replied as he arrived next to Medwin. "We need to find some way to revive him."

Medwin's eyes lit up. He reached into his pack and pulled out a glass jar. It took some work, but eventually he was able to pry Conner's mouth open and pour Vivek's reviver down his throat.

After what felt like an eternity, Conner started to cough uncontrollably. Some of the liquid had gone down his air passage, but the fact that he could cough at all meant the reviver had worked. He was getting dexterity back in all his limbs. He took slow, timed breaths until it felt as though his lungs had recovered a comfortable amount of oxygen. "What *were* those things?" he asked as he rubbed feeling back into his arms.

"Dryads," Zelimir answered darkly.

"Dryads?"

"Yes… They are part human, part tree. The one that stabbed you must have injected some kind of poison into your system. That is why you were unable to move. If Medwin hadn't thought to give you that reviver, you would have been stuck here until the poison shut down your heart."

"That's twice since we left Rhona that Vivek's medicines have come in handy," Conner said gratefully. "I definitely wouldn't like to think of where we would have been without them."

"Yeah, let's hope there's not a third time," Medwin replied.

Zelimir surveyed the forest anxiously. "Let's keep moving. The sooner we get out of here, the better."

They traveled more quickly now, their eyes darting from side to side in order to keep pace with their feet.

Medwin turned to the others. "I wonder how much farther it —"

The sound of crumpling leaves drifted from the other side of a mossy tree

"What was that?"

Conner wasn't going to wait for whatever it was to attack him. He was going to take the offensive this time. With Scarlet clutched in his hand, he passed the old tree and saw something curled up in a clump of bushes. He dove onto it with his dagger reared back.

"*Please!* Please — don't hurt me!"

Conner looked into the pleading eyes of a deformed little hunchback; the last words that the willow tree had spoken to him floated across his mind. He lowered Scarlet and released him.

"Oh, thank you! Thank you — *thank you!*"

Medwin and Zelimir arrived at either side of Conner. Medwin pointed his bloodstained hatchet at the hunchback. "Do you serve Vellix?" he interrogated bluntly.

"No — no! Hate Vellix! I *hate* Vellix!"

"Then what are you doing in the Morik Forest?" Medwin went on, his hatchet still poised aggressively.

"Escaped — found a tunnel. Couldn't take the chamber any longer!"

"Wait, you were in Vellix's holding chamber?" Zelimir asked, his expression changing to one of pity.

"Oh yes! Yes, for years the chamber was my prison," the hunchback answered with a crazy look in his eyes. "Free now, though! *Ha!*"

"Sorry about jumping on you like that," said Conner, who now pitied the poor thing. "What is your name?"

The creature gazed at him strangely, as if he couldn't believe that anyone would ever care enough about him to ask his name. "It — it is Moxie," he replied, becoming instantly shy.

"Well, I'm Conner, and these two are Medwin and Zelimir," Conner waved a hand at each of his friends as he said their names.

Moxie acknowledged them with a bow.

"So how did you escape the holding chamber?" Conner asked.

"Found a tunnel between lakes. Used it to get to the lake on the outside..."

The wheels in Conner's head started to turn. 'A way out means a way in' he concluded. If he could use the tunnel to enter the mountain without Vellix being aware of it, he would gain the ability to ambush his vastly more experienced enemy. This could be vital information. "Do you think you could find the tunnel again, Moxie?"

"Never going back! No! Not going back in the lake! It made me think bad things!" Moxie shook his head dramatically as he answered.

"Well, can you at least tell me how, or where, to find it?" Conner asked, feeling somewhat deflated.

"Yes — I can tell you. The tunnel is in the wall of the southern bank, deep below the surface."

"Thank you!" Conner exclaimed. "You have no idea how much you just helped us!"

"Why do you want to go? Don't go there! Vellix ... does things ... terrible things to the those he captures."

"I'm going because I must destroy Vellix," Conner said.

"You ... want to ... fight Vellix?" Moxie asked quietly.

"Yes," Conner answered.

"Oh no — bad plan. Vellix will kill you... He has special power."

"I have the same power," Conner replied seriously. "That is why it has to be me to destroy him. Thanks again for your help, but now we need to go and find that tunnel."

Moxie stared up at Conner, transfixed as he started to walk away. "Wait! I will show you. You kill Vellix, so he never hurts another like he did me." Moxie's expression became pitiful as the words he spoke represented his disturbing appearance.

Conner's sheer pity for Moxie increased but not on the level as the respect he gained for him. To go back to the place, which had been his living nightmare for so long, took the kind of bravery most people only dream of possessing.

"Come on. Follow me. I will show you the tunnel," said the little hunchback as he started to march back in the direction he had come.

They followed Moxie in his northern heading for a half an hour before Conner started to notice that Moxie's head was turning from left to right as if he was lost.

"Where are you taking us?" Medwin probed as he peered up through the dense treetops. "Why are we heading west — straight for the mountain?"

Moxie didn't reply, but his head began turning from side to side more frantically than ever.

"But, Medwin," Conner interjected, "we haven't changed course. We've been heading north the whole time."

"Well, then explain why I can see the sun through the trees directly in front of me," said Medwin, whose frustration seemed to be rising steadily.

Conner looked up in front of him and saw the tiny bright dots of light that he knew were rays of sunlight attempting to penetrate the thick treetops. He realized he had no answer.

Zelimir seemed to be trying to riddle out the cause of this strange phenomenon as well. He knew they hadn't changed course, but Medwin was right. The sun was directly in front of them.

"I swear! I'm not bad!" Moxie cried, obviously thinking Conner and the others were on the brink of deeming him untrustworthy. "I am not! I thought I was going the way I came!"

With their focus placed so intently on Moxie, Conner and the others didn't notice the tree roots that had started to slither noiselessly toward them. Loud cries of fear mingled as the roots bound their ankles.

Conner tried to use cognition to free himself. The root around his ankle vibrated strenuously, but it would not release him.

Medwin used his hatchet to chop at his bonds, but every time he got through one and moved on to the other, a new root detained his previous foot.

Zelimir, having seen these failed attempts, did not waste his energy.

"Gorenduals!" Moxie cried out, pointing through the trees.

Before Conner had a chance to contemplate what a Gorendual was, he had his answer. No less than five of the hideous creatures, fused at the torso, moved toward him in a freakish fashion. As the creatures approached, it reminded Conner of how disgusted he had been by the way they walked. He was closest to them, and as they got within range of an attack, he had the answer to his question from back at the battle. They did have eyes; they glowed a greyish blue in the dark forest.

Fear numbed Conner's mind. The creature would be right over the top of him with its next step. He remembered how they had devoured Satria warriors during the battle, and a nauseating sensation stole over him. The Gorendual pushed him over and opened its mouth wide. He saw inside the beast. Two rows of yellowing teeth grew in a circle. Filthy green saliva seeped off its jowls and landed on his face.

The creature was so close now that Conner could feel its hot, rancid breath on him; the stench of it was foul. He wasn't going to die like this. He grabbed Scarlet and stabbed it in the direction of the Gorendual's open mouth. The blade extended in length by five times its original size, puncturing straight through the beast and out the backside of its deformed body. Conner's root bonds released him at once. 'They must be the ones controlling the roots,' he thought as he turned around and slayed the Gorendual that was inches from doing to Zelimir what the wolf had almost done to him on the night they met.

Zelimir, free of his bonds, lunged at the first Gorendual he could reach, and as it died, Medwin's bonds released him.

Medwin leapt up and killed one Gorendual before running past Conner to claim the last of the five that had come to attack them. But, before he had the chance, two new roots ripped him back to the ground, creating a whirling plume of thick fog.

Conner ran forward, jumped over the roots that lunged at him, and stabbed the beast with his newly formed sword-version of Scarlet. As the beast sighed its dying groan, Conner turned to find Moxie curled up in a ball on the ground, shaking and muttering, "No — no — no."

"It's okay now, Moxie," said Conner reassuringly. "We've killed them."

Moxie poked his head up and surveyed the area hopefully. "Hurry! Get out of here!" he yelled as he began to run.

Conner noticed that he ran straight in the direction of the sun. "Moxie! Moxie, wait! You're still heading west!"

Moxie yelled over his shoulder. "The forest is evil! It's deceiving us!"

Conner took off after him, knowing that if he didn't, they would lose him altogether. Medwin and Zelimir followed.

Within ten minutes, the trees started to thin. The moment they exited the forest the sun they had been running in the direction of was on their left. Moxie had been right. The forest had created the illusion that they were traveling west with the sole purpose of keeping the travelers stuck within its boundaries.

"Wait!" Zelimir yelled, his nose twitching furiously. "Rais..." he whispered darkly.

"What?" Medwin asked, confused. Then his expression grew with comprehension. "You mean — the wolves? They're near?"

"Yes... they're somewhere east of here... Conner — Medwin, you carry on without me. I must confront Rais."

"*What?*" Conner cried hysterically. "Are you crazy? I thought you were avoiding the pack! You'll be outnumbered! You'll die!"

"It is the only way, Conner... If the wolves catch up with us, which is inevitable — if I smell them, they smell us — then you will both be killed. The pack is very large. I'm not saying you wouldn't put up a valiant fight, but in the end, you would be overpowered."

"But, Zelimir, we —"

"No 'buts', Conner! You have a mission. That is your destiny... I know now that this is mine. It is the act of a coward to run from their battles. The pack will allow Rais and me to battle one on one. It is tradition. If I challenge him, he will not refuse me... I don't expect to win the fight, but it is the only way to make sure you get to the lake safely."

Conner and Medwin looked searchingly at the wolf. He stared back, his expression unbending.

"I'll miss you, Zelimir," Conner said honestly.

"Focus on your goal, Conner. If you succeed, we may see one another in the future. Medwin... take care." With those last words, Zelimir departed.

CHAPTER 22

Dive Headfirst Into Sorrow

Zelimir ran at top speed until he saw multiple columns of smoke floating across the sky. He knew they must be coming from fires in the city of Ryvel. As he slowed to catch his breath and sniff the air, the scents of around forty wolves filled his nostrils from every direction. The pack had already surrounded him but none showed themselves. "Rais! Show yourself. I have come to put an end to your rule."

Rais stepped out from a tight-knit group of trees and bushes. The rest of the pack started to emerge from hiding as well. They formed a circle, enclosing their leader and his challenger.

"So, you've come to challenge me?" said Rais, his confidence overflowing. You're more of a fool than I thought. I will make sure not to kill you too quickly. I want you to have time to think about how pathetic you are."

Zelimir's wisdom kept him from replying to the pack leader.

The two wolves started to circle one another, baring their teeth, neither of them willing to break eye contact.

Zelimir focused his mind. Rais was larger than he was, so to overpower him was not an option. Zelimir would have to use cunning to win this fight: a fight that was more important than anything had ever been in his life. The outcome would determine the fate of his pack. If Rais won, the title would remain his to keep, and the wolves would continue to live under the control of Vellix. But if he won, the title would shift and he would become the new leader of the wolves.

Rais made the first move, charging at Zelimir aggressively. He sidestepped and the wolves circled each other once more. Zelimir lunged forward — Rais dodged the attack, bit down on his neck, and dropped him to the ground. Zelimir yelped in pain before breaking free. He got to his feet and retaliated, sinking fangs deep into his enemy's left leg. Rais sliced Zelimir's face, forcing himself free. Zelimir attempted to strike back and got his leg bitten for the effort. The wound was deep, but he blocked out the pain, directing all of his energy into the task before him.

The wolves lunged at each other. Both of them delivered heavy blows, striking viciously at every inch of their opponent they could reach. It was a brutal fight, and soon splatters of crimson-red covered the green grass around them. They fought proudly, neither of them willing to go down.

But one of them did.

Zelimir collapsed to the ground, his chest rising and falling rapidly, blood seeping from the deep wounds that littered his body.

Rais walked cockily to his side to finish him, but his lack of focus betrayed him.

Zelimir latched onto Rais's throat and ripped him to the ground in one bound so quick that Rais had no chance to react. The evil pack leader struggled heavily at first, flailing his legs in an attempt to strike Zelimir, but it wasn't long before his motions became meager and slow. Zelimir shook Rais forcefully until his movements ceased completely. He released his dead opponent and fought the urge to collapse with exhaustion.

After allowing himself a moment to recover, he glanced around at the pack. They looked shocked at the outcome of the fight. He let the silence between them reach its peak. Finally, he spoke, and into his words, he poured the same emotion that lived within his heart.

"It is time," he began, shifting his gaze from one wolf to the next. "Time that we lived with the pride we once had: a pride unrivaled... ... ...Shameful — that is the only word to describe the feeling that has clutched me, as it is the only word to describe the actions of my kind." He paused, but continued to eye each wolf that encircled him in turn. "From this day forward, we no longer live under Vellix, whose rule is at an end; we no longer feed on human meat; we no longer thrive off the fear of others. We will work to regain the respect of our long departed ancestors. We will reclaim the pride that once attached itself to every wolf in Rohwen."

The pack remained silent as Zelimir's speech came to an end. They waited a brief moment to ensure that he had finished before bowing to their new leader: a leader that had just removed the dark shroud that had shadowed their kind for so long.

* * *

"Moxie, slow down," Conner yelled as he and Medwin followed the hunchback at a run.

"We must get to the lake quick!" Moxie yelled in reply. "I don't want to be seen!"

Conner grit his teeth and did all he could to keep up. He focused on one breath at a time, trying not to think about the pain in his legs

301

and side, or of the fact that each breath he took felt less effective than his last.

Relief soothed him as they reached the edge of the lake. He wasn't sure how much farther he would have been able to run without stopping. He drew large, steady breaths until his heart rate returned to normal.

It was nearly nightfall, and the lake's placid surface mirrored a purpling evening sky, the image only broken by the occasional ripple of water as it met land.

Moxie started to walk along the lake's southern bank, mumbling something to himself. His scarcely decipherable words were drowned out entirely as a chilling screech consumed the warm, evening air.

Zarmena — last of the Mirthless — landed just beyond Conner and Medwin. The band of clouds that spiraled around Mt. Cirrus' towering peak were just visible over the top of the beast.

Moxie ran off into a cluster of trees, but Zarmena paid him no attention. She was staring straight at Conner and Medwin. "You will pay for what you did to Zedge and Saura!" she spat. "I am going to take you to my master, and he will show you the true meaning of pain and suffering!"

Conner wasn't afraid of Zarmena. The only emotion he felt toward the last Mirthless was hatred. "You're the one who will pay," he replied, his voice carrying the loathing he felt for the creature that stood before him. "You won't make it back to your master. We killed the other two. Now it's your turn!" He pointed at her accusingly. "Acts as terrible as yours never go unpunished! You should have known your time would come."

"You really think that you have a chance against Vellix?" said Zarmena condescendingly. "You're a child," she sneered, "and he is the most powerful man to ever walk this land!"

While Zarmena was talking, she didn't notice that the ground had risen up around both of her feet and was ready to snatch them at any second. At the same time, the branches on a tree right behind her stretched out past their original length and positioned themselves over each of her wings.

Medwin saw that Conner was preparing to detain the huge beast. A broad smile spread across his face.

"What is so funny, boy? You find your fate to be amusing?" Zarmena asked with an incredulous tone.

"No, but I find yours to be!" Medwin replied, now laughing at the beast.

His laughter put her over the edge. Her massive wings spread wide as she made to attack Medwin, but as soon as they had moved away from her body, the branches wrapped quickly around them. Zarmena fought desperately against the bonds, but her efforts were no use. It wasn't long before she realized that her feet were unable to move as well. "How dare you!" she screeched as grass, dirt, and clay clawed their way up her legs, ripping her down. She screeched louder still as more and more of her body sank out of sight.

Conner grabbed a staff-sized branch from the ground and threw it to Medwin. As it flew through the air, one end whittled itself into a deadly point.

Medwin snatched the spear out of air and heaved it at Zarmena. It struck her in the throat, just above her armor-plated chest. She shrieked horrifically, choking in pain as blood began to seep from the wound and drizzle from the corners of her beak. The ground continued to swallow her, muffling her cries. It wasn't long before her body was lost from sight entirely. The land shifted and stirred for another moment, then became still.

"Conner is most powerful!" Moxie exclaimed as he came out of hiding. "That was the Mirthless that took me to Vellix, years ago." He appeared to be exceedingly justified as he spoke.

Medwin stared down at the spot where the ground had swallowed Zarmena. "Thank you, Conner…"

Conner turned toward Medwin and gave him a curious look.

"For understanding that I needed closure, that I needed to be the one to kill it," Medwin said to clarify himself.

"You're welcome," Conner replied.

My father is avenged," Medwin said passionately. "Now, let's get the monster that created those horrible beasts!"

Conner glanced at Medwin, whose expression was hard with determination before turning to face the lake. A thought had struck him — a thought he was almost positive he'd been suppressing for days now. He couldn't let Medwin come with him. Medwin would almost surely be killed. He had to say something. "Uh — hey, Medwin," he started awkwardly.

"Huh?" Medwin replied, using a slightly different tone than usual because he noticed Conner's discomfort.

"I think … you … should stay here," Conner said timidly. "I think I should go it alone from here out…"

Medwin didn't reply right away. He seemed to be mulling over

Conner's words. Finally, he said, "I was wondering if you might say that. I don't blame you for your reasoning. You expect me to die if I enter the fight with you and Vellix... But, I made a promise to my people: that I wouldn't stop until Vellix was dead."

"But, what good will you be to your people if you die?" Conner asked. "Think of the toll it would take on your mother if she lost you just after losing your father?" Before the words had even left his mouth, Conner hugely regretted saying them.

"Do you think that the name 'chief' is just a title, Conner? You expect me sit here like a coward? I thought you knew what it meant to be a *leader! A warrior!*" Medwin's face was hard as stone as he stared Conner down.

"You're right," Conner muttered quietly.

"What was that?"

"You're right," Conner repeated loudly. "You've been with me the whole time, and if you hadn't been ... I would be dead..."

Medwin's expression relaxed. "If I die, it will be with the same honor as my father. It will be fighting for the freedom of my tribe! That is what my people deserve from their leader. They may mourn my death, but not as they will celebrate if Vellix is defeated!"

Medwin's outlook inspired Conner. He suddenly realized that just because he was the one destined to defeat Vellix, it didn't necessarily mean he would survive. What if they killed one another in battle? It wasn't really about living or dying at all. It was about honor. To die with honor was more important than to live without any. He nodded to Medwin and turned to Moxie. "Show us the tunnel."

Without a moment's hesitation, Moxie dove into the lake. Conner and Medwin followed.

The second Conner's head plunged under the water's surface, his mind erupted with terrible thoughts. 'Why are you trying to save Rohwen or its inhabitants? What has it, or any of them, ever done for you? You're going to die trying, and no one will even care that you're gone. Give up now, while you're still ahead.'

Conner swam on, following Moxie, but the sorrow that began to fill his heart was immense. 'How do you know that Moxie isn't just leading you into a trap?' his mind continued vindictively. 'What if Vellix sent him to lure you right where he wants you? You're just a foolish boy that thinks he can change what he doesn't understand.'

Moxie reached the spot he was searching for. He pointed toward a section of rock, then toward the surface, and began swimming up frantically.

Conner realized he was going up for air and made to follow, but his mind urged him to remain where he was, saying, 'Why would you go up for air when you could remain here and die? Death would be an escape, an outlet. It would free you. Nothing could harm you.' He fought the lies he was telling himself with images of his parent's smiling faces and pushed to keep up with Moxie. It seemed to take an eternity, but finally, his head broke the water's surface. A sensation far beyond relief came over him as he realized his mind was no longer under attack, yet he couldn't help but feel depressed. Did he really think those things he'd thought? Were those thoughts his own? Were they thoughts he chose to bury deep beneath his pride and integrity?

The water's surface broke somewhere behind him. He turned to find Medwin gasping for air. As he watched Medwin breathe in life, he was reminded of how much his friendship truly meant. It was then that he had his answer: those thoughts were not his. They were blatant lies. Rohwen had done a great deal for him, as had its inhabitants. And Moxie couldn't be leading him into a trap, because he was taking him exactly where he wanted to go. And dying wouldn't be easier, because if he died now, Vellix would have won, and he could think of nothing harder than standing aside and allowing Vellix to win.

"Are you ready?" Moxie asked, noticing that Conner and Medwin both seemed to be breathing calmly once more.

"Yeah," they said in unison, both of them sounding resolute.

Moxie inhaled a massive breath and dove below the surface. Conner followed, telling himself to ignore the horrible thoughts that would attack him. He tried to force his mind to focus on keeping up with Moxie, but it wasn't long before he lost the battle.

'What a useless effort this is,' said the deceitful voice in his head. 'Vellix is just going to kill you, so what's the point?'

Moxie swam into a tunnel and headed straight for the pocket of air that he knew existed from his first time using the underwater passage.

Conner entered the tunnel, found Moxie's feet, and went up for air. As he gasped in great breaths, he noticed that Medwin was no longer by his side. He dove back under to search for him, fearing the worst.

The moment he made it back to the lake, he saw Medwin drifting to the bottom, as though he'd given up. 'Leave him. He's just dead weight.' Conner ignored his rancid thoughts, grabbed Medwin's arm, and swam with avid determination back to the pocket of air.

He slapped Medwin in the face once they surfaced, but the young chief didn't respond. Instead, his head just lulled around every time

Conner struck it. "Come on, Medwin!" he yelled, squeezing him numerous times around the chest. "Come on! You can't die! I won't let you!" He squeezed him again. "Please don't die! Please!"

Moxie looked on sadly as Conner did all he could to revive Medwin.

Just when Conner was on the verge of breaking into tears, Medwin coughed up a mouthful of water. His eyes were blood red, his skin pale.

"Thank goodness," Conner sighed. He waited for Medwin to stop coughing before asking if he was okay. When Medwin didn't respond, he asked again.

Medwin nodded and looked Conner in the eye. "I'm sorry," he suddenly blurted out. "I — I just gave up... I had ... the most terrible thoughts! I don't even want to repeat them."

"I know," Conner said, understanding exactly what Medwin had felt. "The same thing happened to me... Catch your breath, and then we'll carry on."

Moxie allowed Medwin a moment to recover before he dove back under to lead them into the smaller lake in the center of Vellix's holding chamber.

Conner heard the strangest sound as he swam closer to the surface. It was beyond melancholy. It was like the most sorrowful song he had ever heard. Being underwater, he guessed that mermaids might be singing, but as his head broke the water's surface, the song was amplified — not just in volume, but in its agony. He realized that the sounds had not been a song at all. They were the woeful cries of thousands of creatures that had given up all hope. Medwin surfaced next to him.

"What is that?" he asked, sounding disturbed. "It's the most depressing thing I've ever heard."

"It must be the creatures that Zelimir told us about," Conner replied. "We're in the holding chamber..."

"I can barely see a thing," said Medwin.

Moxie replied from somewhere far closer to Conner than he realized he was. "It's always this dark. Never see much in the chamber." He told them as he headed for the bank of cold stone with which he was far too familiar. Conner and Medwin swam blindly behind him, using the splashing sounds he made as a guide.

"Nearly there," Moxie called back to them.

As he climbed up onto the rock shore, Conner could just make out the basic shapes of the poor, deformed, hopeless, and abandoned creatures that once had normal lives — lives that Vellix had demolished while attempting to create his army.

"We need some kind of a light source," Medwin told Conner, glancing around the chamber pointlessly. "Try to create a flame — you know, like the ones Vellix used..." Medwin broke off because he realized he was about to delve into the subject of Vivek's death. "...Anyway ... I'm sure you'll be able to do it without a problem — create the flames I mean. I'm certain you can do it. After those wings you gave me, it doesn't seem like there is anything you can't do. They were perfect. I can't even explain exactly what I mean. It was like I was born with them or something. Every mental command I gave, they obeyed without hesitation."

Conner looked down at the black form of his hand. He willed a flame to appear within his palm. A little spark flickered with a total lack of conviction. He wasn't discouraged, though. He knew it might take a try or two to get the hang of it. He tried again, willing himself to conjure the flame.

The holding chamber burst into a dim flickering light as a ball of flame came to life in his palm. Seconds later the amount of light in the chamber doubled as Conner ignited a ball of flame in his other hand as well.

Unlike Vellix's flames, which burned a threatening red, his were a vibrant shade of cyan-blue. He looked up to find the ceiling of the chamber, but darkness still sheathed it. Shadows, thrown by the miserable creatures dwelling upon the shelves of rock swayed menacingly as the flames flickered in cadence.

Moxie glanced around the enormous chamber, truly, for the first time; anger and despair seemed to be battling in the look of horror expressed on his face. His little fists clenched up with fury.

"Moxie, do you know how to find the stairs that lead to Vellix's chamber?" Conner asked delicately, knowing that Moxie was in no state to be pushed.

"Stairs? There's no stairs," Moxie replied, still staring upward.

"They must be hidden," Medwin said as he began his search of the nearest wall.

Conner pondered for a moment. 'What would be a good way to hide something as obvious as stairs?' he thought to himself. 'I guess it is nearly pitch black down here. Maybe Vellix thought the creatures wouldn't ever find the stairs, even with its entrance exposed. Or maybe he welcomed the chance to exploit superiority over his inadequate experiments if they ever found their way up,' he thought in disgust.

Like the spark that preceded the flame he conjured moments ago, an idea came to him. He started to fling fireballs in every direction, watching intently to see if a notch or out-of-place shadow would appear. Bright blue patches of sparks lit up the stone walls and reflected vividly off the surface of the lake, but he saw nothing out of the ordinary. His luck changed with the next set of flames, however. Two of the fireballs vanished as they went right through a small section of the wall.

"Did you see that?" Medwin asked excitedly.

"Yeah," Conner replied, "that has to be it." No sooner than the words had left his mouth, his stomach lurched heavily. Vellix was just up those stairs...

Moxie shifted slightly and it reminded Conner of his presence. "Moxie, you have been more helpful to us — to Rohwen — than I can ever give you praise for. Thank you — for everything. Now, I suggest that you get away from the mountain."

"Go and start your life of freedom," Medwin added, giving him a warm smile.

Moxie looked from Conner to Medwin; he was unable to express his appreciation for their kindness. With one quick smile, he dove into the lake and out of sight.

CHAPTER 23

Fools and Freaks

Using his blue flames to locate the secret entrance, Conner, with Medwin beside him, passed effortlessly through the false section of rock wall and stepped onto the stairway that led up to Vellix's mountain-peak chamber.

They traveled in silence, both of them lost within their own anxious thoughts, and hours passed without the faintest sign that they were nearing the top.

Conner thought of how Zelimir had been right about the stairs feeling endless but instantly wished he hadn't. He couldn't bear to think about the wolf. He didn't want to think about him being dead. Before he could stop them, images of the wolf lying dead on the ground, mangled by wounds, had corrupted his mind. Tears began to streak freely down his face. He wiped them away as if tending to a pestering itch in order to hide his grief from Medwin. A heart-wrenching jolt reminded him of what he was approaching as faint hints of red light started to show themselves on the staircase walls. He held his breath as he reached what appeared to be the last bend before Vellix's chamber.

Medwin crouched down and started to crawl forward slowly.

'Good idea,' Conner thought, not daring to speak aloud. He peaked around the corner to find a dimly lit cavern chamber.

An empty throne of elegant stone stood before them, rising from the cavern floor as if molded from the very ground around it. All was still and quiet. Vega — the deformed creature that had shown Zelimir to the holding chamber — was gone. The room seemed abandoned.

Conner's feelings of fear, elation, and purpose slowly began to ebb away. He started to survey the chamber in further detail. Polished onyx pillars stood every twenty feet, each one home to a gracefully wrought iron sconce containing Vellix's cognition flames. Carved into the handsome stone floor was an intricate pattern of lines that emanated from the throne to a large mirror on the opposite side of the room. From that point, the pattern broke into two sections and continued in opposing directions until they were lost in the chamber's deepest shadows.

The chamber was nothing short of the most elaborate and beautiful work with cognition Conner had ever seen. He wondered why a man like Vellix would have gone to the trouble of surrounding himself with such beauty, but after a moment's contemplation, he felt that the answer was actually obvious. Vellix had surrounded himself with the beauty of his own power.

Feeling that he had spent enough time observing the room, Conner decided to chance a few whispered words. "I don't think Vellix is here..."

"I think you might be right," Medwin whispered back.

"What should we do? I didn't expect this at all..."

Medwin stood up and entered the chamber cautiously. Conner followed, wondering what they should do next.

The room held a feeling of cold neither of them had ever experienced. Conner felt it was extremely fitting of the man whose heart was colder than ice. Even the red flames that gleamed threateningly within their torches seemed incapable of giving off warmth.

Conner and Medwin moved over to the ledge outside the mouth of the chamber and looked down upon Rohwen. The view was even spectacular at night. A vague hint of the ocean was visible; miniscule sparkles of moonlight twinkled and bent with the unpredictable motion of the water, disappearing and reappearing in an elegant dance of white.

"Vellix doesn't deserve to look upon such beauty," said Medwin in conclusion, after he had drank in the gorgeous view. "He doesn't even —"

Crack!

A chunk of stone struck Medwin square in the back. He dropped to his hands and knees, wailing in pain.

"Is that so?" sneered a man hooded and cloaked in black robes as he materialized from the deepest shadows of the chamber. The dull thud of a body hitting stone issued from behind him as the lifeless face belonging to Vega became visible in the firelight.

Conner whipped around far too late to react — Vellix had already shot multiple fireballs at him. They scorched his skin, leaving nasty burns across his chest. Conner retaliated, throwing a cluster of his blue flames back at Vellix. The cognition master lazily lifted one hand, and the flames dematerialized into wisps of smoke inches from his palm. Smirking, he swiftly raised both his hands into the air and a thick layer of the stone floor encased Conner up to his neck. He struggled to free himself, but it seemed to be pointless. He thought intently about the rock crumbling — still, nothing happened. 'How could we have been so foolish?' he thought hysterically. 'Why did we just waltz into Vellix's chambers so willingly?' He looked down at Medwin, whose eyes were blazing with purpose.

As Medwin got to his feet, Vellix raised his hands again — the young warrior had extraordinary reflexes. He dove, rolled away from the stone that was to become his tomb, and was back on his feet.

Vellix appeared taken aback before he started to bombard Medwin with fireballs.

Medwin used the steel blade of his hatchet to deflect the onslaught of fire attacks, running toward his enemy all the while. He swung a well-aimed strike at Vellix's throat and the cognition master had to move quickly to evade it. The hood fell from his head and exposed his gnarled face. A large portion of it was burned so badly that the flesh was appallingly warped: the result of Vivek's final attack. His acidic berries had been so powerful that even Vellix's superb skills with cognition had not been enough to repair the damage.

Medwin took another careful swing but again, he missed his target. This time Vellix made him pay. The bones in both of Medwin's arms broke involuntarily, while Conner watched on in horror. "*No!*" he yelled furiously as a strong surge of loathing for Vellix boiled within his core. The stone that held him captive shattered, and before the jagged chunks and slivers of rock could find the floor, they hurtled toward Vellix.

The master stood stationary, his expression indifferent as the jagged chunks of rock turned to dust around him and drifted to the floor — now completely harmless. Conner focused his mind on the last granules of dust as they were about to settle; they melded back together, creating one shard of stone that slashed Vellix's leg just above the ankle.

Vellix exhaled a grunt of pain. "You are powerful, Conner..." he admitted as if he were enjoying himself immensely. A timely silence followed his words, during which all that was audible were Medwin's piteous sobs.

Conner couldn't stand that Vellix knew his name; he couldn't stand the fact that he wasn't able to help Medwin. His fury toward Vellix was so strong — it filled him so much — that he thought he might explode.

"However," Vellix continued, still sounding entertained, "you were a fool to attempt an attack on me... And even more so for coming here to do it. I am in control of this mountain in ways you could scarcely imagine. It would have been wise to lure me out of my comfort zone."

"You know nothing of wisdom, Vellix!" Conner spat. He didn't even know where he was going with the statement, but he decided to elaborate, due to the instant look of rage on his opponents face. "If you had any wisdom you would have used your power to gain the love and trust of the people of Rohwen. Instead, you oppress them with your evil. They would have been happy to serve a man of your power — had you treated them with respect. But you don't even respect yourself, do you? So how could you respect them?"

Vellix replied with another wave of fire attacks; Conner countered with his own, and the fiery orbs met in the middle of their creators, sending showers of blue and red glowing embers to the cavern floor, where they scattered in all directions, flickering like fireflies before burning out.

317

Conner pulled Scarlet from his belt and charged Vellix. The cognition master flicked his left hand toward Conner while lifting his right hand toward the ceiling. Conner rolled under the boulder that was hurtling for the right side of his body, leapt to his feet, sidestepped the section of cavern floor that attempted to snatch his legs, and thrust his sword at Vellix's midsection. Vellix allowed the sword to plunge into his robes, wrapped it up with a quick flick of his wrist, and pulled it out of Conner's grip. It spiraled off, hitting the ground with an echoing clang, far from Conner's reach. Vellix smirked evilly.

Conner thought fast. The floor beneath Scarlet came to life and flung the sword back into his hands. He caught it and rammed the blade straight through Vellix's stomach. Blood began to soak the front of his robes where the sword pierced through him. Conner gave Scarlet's hilt another violent shove, making sure the sword could sink in no further, and then took a step back. To his horror, Vellix's evil smile was broadening, making him look more deranged than ever.

He grabbed the hilt of the sword, ripped it out with a harsh grunt, and threw it across the room, where it smashed into the mirror, sending small shards of glass in all directions. "*Fool!* I cannot be killed by things so petty as flesh wounds!" he closed his eyes and took a deep, stabilizing breath.

Conner's heart sank as he saw that Vellix's wound was healing itself.

"You have learned nothing of cognition," Vellix hissed darkly, pointing a hand in the direction of Conner's mid-section, a look of twisted pleasure spreading across his faintly illuminated face.

Conner fell to the ground, feeling the invisible vice of Vellix's cognition clamping down on his insides as the evil master began to torture him. He screamed in the kind of agony he had never known. It was beyond pain — it was worse than death — he wanted to die.

Vellix slowly closed his open hand, forming a tight fist; the pain in Conner's core increased just as slowly, making the experience he was enduring feel as though it was lasting a lifetime. He began thrashing and jerking desperately as the agony became more than he could bear.

"You are going to die, Conner," Vellix told him with a morbid sense of enjoyment. "You never should have put so much faith in the scrolls," he scoffed as Conner writhed on the floor, shrieking. "You are no match for me, pathetic by comparison!"

The pain Conner was enduring was unbelievable — the vice cranked tighter still — his organs, rib cage, and spine squealed in a painful fury. He was on the brink of passing out, his vision steadily becoming nothing more than a blur.

A faint sound produced by dozens of pattering footsteps filled the chamber, accompanied by the familiar voice of a little person who was so big on the inside that it was incredible all of it fit within his tiny shell.

"*Get him! Get Vellix!*" yelled Moxie as he led no less than fifty of Vellix's freakish and defected experiments into the chamber to overpower their oppressor.

Vellix's immense skill with cognition became more apparent as he fought off the onslaught deftly, using the surrounding walls and floor of the chamber to detain numerous creatures as he dealt with others. But now that he was busy battling his own creations, he wasn't able to continue torturing the boy he had wanted to toy with before killing.

Conner slowly got to his feet, still clutching at his stomach. He fought the urge to throw up, looked over at Medwin, who had passed out from the pain he'd gone through, and then turned to face Vellix. He wanted to hurt the pathetic excuse for a man, whose evil had done so much damage, so badly that killing him didn't seem good enough. He wanted him to suffer for longer than death would allow; suffer as so many had at *his* hand. It was at that moment, when his loathing for Vellix was at its peak, that he conceived a plan that never would have come to him otherwise.

With his gaze fixed upon the cloaked monster, still fighting off his own creatures as they attempted to subdue him, Conner uttered a few words under his breath, his face full of fury and intent.

Vellix stopped fighting instantly — his hands went to his head as his face twisted in convulsion, his eyes and mouth twitching uncontrollably before becoming blank and expressionless. The freakish creatures detained him and paid no mind to his body colliding with every step of the stairway as they dragged him into the depths of his holding chamber. He would suffer the same fate he had sentenced upon so many others.

Moxie walked toward Conner, looking pleased. He was holding Scarlet in one hand and Medwin's hatchet in the other. Together he and Conner went over to Medwin.

Conner reached into Medwin's pack, pulled out what he now realized was the last reviver, and poured it down his throat. Medwin's eyes opened blearily. His arms were still broken, but at least he had regained consciousness.

"I'm going to fix your arms," Conner said, feeling completely assured that he was capable.

"Wait — what?" Medwin became instantly alert.

"On the count of three," Conner went on, brushing aside Medwin's obvious concern. "One — two —"

"Arrgh!" Medwin cried out.

"Sorry, but someone told me that half of pain is in our anticipation of it," Conner laughed, grimacing as his bruised insides squirmed with pain.

Medwin rotated his arms to test them. "Thanks Conner," he said gratefully, "They feel good as —" He cut his sentence short, suddenly becoming worried and looking frantically around the chamber. "What happened? Where's Vellix?"

"He won't be bothering anyone ... ever again," Conner replied seriously.

"What did you do to him?"

"Well" — Conner paused for a moment to give Moxie an admiring glance — "Moxie arrived with a hoard of creatures, and it distracted Vellix long enough for me to form an attack."

Medwin remained silent, listening intently as Conner continued.

"I focused my thoughts and said to myself, 'I want his brain to suffer a trauma that leaves it just functional enough to understand who he is, dwelling only on the reason for his punishment.'"

Medwin marveled in the cleverness of the idea. "So, he is still alive, but only enough to suffer a fate worse than death?"

"Exactly!"

"Conner — you are brilliant!"

"The praise should really go to Moxie here," said Conner, patting the little hunchback on his shoulder.

"So, tell us, Moxie, why did you come back? And how did you get that many of the creatures from the holding chamber to come up and attack Vellix?"

Moxie looked at them kindly for a moment before he spoke. "The lake — that makes nasty thoughts … told me you were both going to die. I couldn't — couldn't let you die! Not after you were so nice! Nicer to me — than anyone … ever..." He stared blankly at his feet for a second. "So I came back," he continued, looking up at them with a determined gaze. "I knew I couldn't help alone, though. I spoke to all the creatures in the holding chamber. Told them it was time to fight back, to get the justice they deserved. Most of them just sat there and moaned … but not all of them. A group followed!"

"And they were the ones that attacked Vellix," said Conner happily, wincing because in his excitement he had flexed his muscles, and the tiny amount of pressure this put on his organs caused him pain. "Moxie you saved us both. You are a true hero. You will be remembered in Rohwen for your deeds today."

"I would personally like to thank you on behalf of the Satria tribe, Moxie," Medwin said, placing a hand on his shoulder. "You are welcome to stay with my people, as my personal guest, for as long as you like," he offered wholeheartedly. "My people can learn from someone with courage like yours," he added.

Tears of joy trickled over Moxie's deformed little face and glistened in the red torchlight before they dripped off his chin. "Oh, thank — thank you!" he sniffled. "I accept!"

"Good! I am honored to have you," Medwin replied. "Come on, let's get out of here."

CHAPTER 24

Can I Keep Him?

Night still blanketed the land that was now free of Vellix's cruelty and domination, but there was plenty of moonlight to help Conner, Medwin, and Moxie find their way as they descended Mt. Cirrus.

"What do you think will become of the Ryvelians now that their master is no longer able to guide them?" Conner asked Medwin curiously.

"Who knows? I highly doubt they will be trying to attack us any time soon, though," he said happily. "...There fate's really going to come down to the elders in the end," he mumbled as an afterthought.

"What?"

"...Nothing..."

Conner eyed Medwin for a second before he decided to forget about whatever he had said and move on to a new question. "How are you going to let all the other people know that they are free of Vellix?"

"I will send messengers to each of them. It may be difficult to locate the Edelish because they are in hiding, but we will try. This news will mean that they can start their lives over."

Conner got an unsurpassable feeling of achievement as he pictured all the people who would be able to live their lives free of fear. Then a thought came to him that he had known would come back up sooner than later. 'What about Zelimir?' Before he could stop himself, he had delved back into thoughts about how Zelimir had headed into a battle that he would most likely lose. Conner felt sick thinking about the fact that the wolf had probably died in order to give him and Medwin time to make it to the lake. 'Why did he have to sacrifice himself? Why couldn't we have just run for it?' His tormented thoughts must have shown on his face because Moxie noticed that he looked upset.

"What is wrong?" he inquired. "Are you not happy? You have done a great thing!"

"I am just thinking about Zelimir," Conner replied. "You know, the wolf we were with when we met you," he added, noticing the quizzical look on Moxie's face.

"Oh ... you are thinking ... he is dead?" Moxie asked carefully.

"Yes ... I think he is dead." Conner hated his answer because it had just confirmed the question for not only Moxie, but for him as well.

Medwin took a more positive outlook. "What makes you so sure he's dead? Zelimir is very wise. I wouldn't be that shocked if he won the fight against Rais."

Conner wasn't sure if Medwin was trying to make him feel better or if he really believed the words he had said. Either way, Conner was grateful for his optimism. The idea that Zelimir might still be alive made his victory over Vellix much sweeter. "I hope you're right, Medwin," he said, feeling considerably better.

They had only made it a short distance down the mountain when Medwin suggested that they stop and get some sleep. Night had long since reached its blackest hour. Conner looked up at the stars that had become faint in the ever-brightening sky. A few of them gave him a wink as they shimmered happily. His gaze moved downward. He watched as the sky's deep shades of blue faded perfectly into a cold steel grey that rested upon the thin strip of orange bordering the ocean, growing consistently more vivid as it reached its eastern expanses.

The peace that was coming over Conner's mind as the truth of his victory set in was unbelievable. It was over. He had really done it. Vivek's face glided across his mind. He wished he could share the news of his triumph with the man who had spent so long waiting to see Vellix overthrown, but Vivek was just another casualty of Vellix's reign, another good person that had to suffer — to die — in Vellix's quest for power and control. Conner forced the thoughts out of his mind. He felt that he had had enough of thinking about Vellix to last him a lifetime.

He started to smile as he pictured Azalea and Flora, free to explore to their heart's content without the unnerving thought that the Mirthless would carry them off to Mt. Cirrus worrying their father sick.

Medwin sat down with a grunt. "I'm really tired," he yawned

"Yeah, me too," Conner said, realizing how exhausted he was as well. "Moxie, you want to help me gather some fire wood?"

"Oh yes! I can help!" Moxie replied with far more enthusiasm than was necessary.

Once they had a neat little teepee of wood set up, Conner shot a fireball at the center. It ignited immediately.

The three of them sat around the fire, staring at the mesmerizing flames as they twisted and swayed to a beat that only they knew. One by one, Conner, Medwin, and Moxie drifted to sleep.

* * *

"Wake up ... Conner — Medwin! Wake up!"

Conner opened his eyes to find an energetic Moxie pouring over him.

"Come on, guys! Let's go!"

Medwin stretched and yawned drowsily. "Give me a second, Moxie. I feel like I got hit by a brick!"

"Well, actually, it was a huge rock, but — same difference," Conner laughed. His injuries felt unbelievably better this morning. In fact, he felt as if he were full of helium and might glide away. Everything looked brighter. The breeze felt crisper. The scents in the air smelled sweeter. He gazed back up Mt. Cirrus. It was really quite beautiful the way the clouds spiraled around the peak. He took a long, deep breath. "So, you ready yet, Medwin?" he asked, unable to contain the grin that felt like it might get stuck on his face if he didn't stop smiling soon.

"Yeah, I'm ready," Medwin replied after one last stretch. "Let's try and get to the Brio River as quickly as possible. I need some water."

"Water would be amazing right now," Conner agreed, smacking his dry lips and wondering why he found this to be funny.

As they descended the mountain, their conversation revolved almost entirely around the battle with Vellix. Conner had no problem reliving the feeling he'd gotten when Vellix's face had gone as blank as his mind had become.

"I'm just glad it's over," said Medwin seriously.

"Me too," Conner replied with a natural sigh of relief.

* * *

Night had fallen by the time they reached the Brio River. They were all so ready for a drink that they submerged their whole heads into the water to guzzle it down. The water was extremely cold as it hit Conner's throat. It felt like his brain was going to freeze, but he kept drinking anyway. It was as if he couldn't get enough to satisfy his thirst. Soon he was uncomfortably bloated. He stopped drinking, lied down in pain on the riverbank, and wishing he had taken more care not to overindulge, he nodded off.

The next morning, the three of them sat happily on the bank. Six sets of toes grazed the water's surface while they swapped stories of their favorite parts of the journey.

"Remember when Bellamy and his crew celebrated the victory over Elandra a little too heavily?" Conner laughed.

"That was hilarious," said Medwin, a reminiscent gleam in his eye. "They were so out of it, they didn't even wake up when *the Colossus* slammed into the shore of Misty Cove!"

Moxie laughed even though he had no idea what they were talking about. It was just that their laughter was contagious.

"You should have seen the look on your face when you lost concentration and let the path you formed across the marsh break apart," Medwin said, grinning. "Yeah, we got soaked and had to get more firewood ... but the look on your face was worth it!" he finished, still smiling.

Conner returned his smile, even though the memory didn't really bring him the same joy it obviously did for Medwin. "I still remember how crazy it was for me," he said, moving to a new topic, "when I found out that I was destined to befriend a wolf. I think I pretty much yelled at Vivek when he told me."

"I wonder what Ammin, Lenny, and the rest of the crew are up to?" Medwin said, staring off in the direction of Beach Bay.

"I hope the crew voted Ammin as their captain," Conner said earnestly. Medwin nodded.

Moxie, who didn't really have any stories to swap, asked, "You want fish?"

Conner and Medwin looked down at him quizzically. "What?" they asked in unison. The question was a simple one, but it was so out of context that it still made no sense.

"You want fish?" Moxie asked again, looking at Conner and Medwin as if unable to understand how his question was hard to answer.

"Sure!" they both exclaimed now that it had become clear that Moxie was offering them food.

Moxie dove into the water; the shadow of his little body made a few quick movements before he resurfaced, each of his hands clutching a large fish. He threw them on the bank as he clambered back out of the water.

"Wow!" said Medwin, impressed. "You are really good at that! How did you catch them one-handed like that?"

"I had a lot of practice," Moxie answered as he proceeded to smash the two fish against the nearest rock. "I lived by a lake for years."

"Oh, I guess that does make sense," Medwin replied sheepishly.

Conner got a fire going, and before long all three of them had bellies full of fish. With the energy it gave them, they continued the journey toward Medwin's village with an added spring in their step.

* * *

Two days of travel passed seamlessly, and nothing more eventful than Moxie being chased by an extremely disgruntled bird, whose eggs he had tried to steal, had happened. They were well into the valley of gently rolling hills now. Shadows, sculpted by the few clouds in the sky, moved slowly over the hills, adding interest to the green grass. Conner distinctly remembered the view from here; it was nearly identical to the one he'd had the moment he arrived in Rohwen.

As they walked past a small wooded area, a short distance from the Ancient Forest, something faint that almost sounded like a voice found Conner's ears. "Did you hear that, guys?" he asked, but before he got an answer, he heard it again.

"Shhh," he told Medwin, who was about to respond. It *was* a voice: a familiar voice. Suddenly, he knew what it was. They were standing near the gate back to his world, and he could hear his mother calling him from the other side.

"What is that?" Medwin asked in a bemused sort of way, while Moxie stood there with his ear perked, hoping to hear the sound again.

"It's — my mother," Conner said, well aware of how weird his statement might sound.

"Your — mother?" Medwin looked at Conner as if he was delusional.

"This is where —"

"The gate!" Medwin said quickly. "We're next to the gate between our worlds, aren't we?"

"Yeah … and … I think it's about time for me —"

"To go back to your world," Medwin said, finishing Conner's sentence again and trying not to look as though the thought of Conner leaving pained him as much as it did.

"…Yeah…" Conner looked down at the ground. Not so long ago, he would have been ecstatic to be going home. Now, however, he realized that Rohwen had become like his home away from home. What if leaving meant he couldn't get back and he never saw Medwin again? Medwin was the best friend Conner had ever known. The thought of never seeing him again was completely depressing. The faint sound of his mother's voice met his ears again, forcing him to come to grips with the fact that he had no other option: it was time to go home.

Medwin heard it, too. "I will truly miss you," he admitted, staring at Conner sadly.

"You too," Conner replied wholeheartedly. "I really can't thank you enough for sticking with me through everything, and for being such a good friend."

Medwin nodded.

"Moxie, I want you to have this," said Conner, pulling Scarlet out from his belt. "It was given to me by a great man, and now I would like to pass it on to you." Before he handed Scarlet to Moxie, he gave it one last look of appreciation and shrank it back to its original length — a dagger seemed much more fitting for little Moxie.

"Thank you, Conner!" Moxie exclaimed, overjoyed. "It is — beautiful…" he whispered, looking as though receiving the gift was going to bring him to tears.

"You deserve it, Moxie," Conner said honestly. "Well, I guess that's it then… Take care guys," he said with a wave as he stepped into the woods to start his search for the gate.

The urge to look back came over him almost immediately. He fought it, knowing it would just make saying goodbye even harder if he did, but the urge overwhelmed him, and he lost the battle miserably.

Medwin and Moxie stood there watching him as he glanced back over his shoulder. He gave them one last wave, trying not to feel miserable, and set off to find the pathway in the trees.

Initially, he had thought finding the pathway might be easy, but he had been wrong. Ten minutes passed and he hadn't seen anything that looked remotely like it.

"*Conner…*"

His mother called again, and this time her voice was clear enough that he was able to tell which direction it was coming from; there, just beyond a thick cluster of bushes, he saw it, the gate. "Yes!" he yelled in his excitement because he had become afraid that he truly might not be able to find the way back to his world. An owl took flight from a nearby tree — apparently disgruntled that someone had woken it up before nightfall. Conner watched it fly away, said an internal goodbye to Rohwen, and stepped through the gate.

* * *

In no time at all, he had made it back past the large fallen tree, past the circle of rocks that he had assumed was an old fire-pit near the stream, and was now able to catch occasional glimpses of his house through the trees. He started to feel thoroughly nervous about how he was going to explain his prolonged absence — there just wasn't any reasonable explanation. He knew he should keep his discovery of Rohwen to himself. Namely for the fact that his parents would probably think he had gone crazy if he told them he had discovered another world.

He looked down at his tunic. Holes with singed edges covered the front of it. There was no way he could show up at home wearing this. He would just have to lie, tell his parents that his shirt had ripped on a tree branch or something.

"Conner."

A deep, resounding voice echoed from somewhere close behind him. He turned to look as he pulled the tunic over his head and tossed it under a nearby bush. A dog that stood nearly three feet tall and had thick fluffy fur, which varied in color, was running toward him. The dog's underside, legs, and snout were a tawny color, as opposed to his body, which was predominantly gray, with browns, darker grays, and white speckled in. There was a black streak running along his spine, and the dark fur that decorated his face looked almost like a mask, accenting his golden yellow eyes.

Conner's heart leapt as Zelimir walked up to him. "Zelimir, you're alive!"

"Yes, I defeated Rais."

"Come on. Come up to my house with me. Oh, and act like a dog. Don't talk or anything. My parents will freak." Zelimir nodded as Conner started toward his house, the wolf on his heels. As he turned the corner to the front of the house, he saw his mom heading inside. She was walking with distinct aggravation.

"Mom!" Conner yelled to get her attention.

Mrs. Mathews rounded on her son, looking furious. "Gone all day!" she shrieked.

'All day,' Conner thought. What did she mean "all day?" He'd been gone for weeks.

"You know the rules, Conner!" she continued, dragging him from his curious thoughts. "Just because we moved does *not* excuse you from coming home this late! Dinner was five hours ago and — what the!" Her eyes grew with shock as she noticed that her son was shirtless and there was a large dog just behind him. "Is that a wolf?"

"What's going on?" Mr. Mathews asked as he arrived at the doorway next to his wife. He pulled his face into a similar expression as Breanne's when he saw the dog standing there. "Conner that's a —"

It's okay," Conner said quickly. "He's nice! He's my friend!" Zelimir licked his hand affectionately, fortifying the truth in his words.

"Where did he come from?" Mr. Mathews queried, sounding as though he wasn't quite sure what to make of the situation.

"I — er — well — uh" — the truth was just not going to work here, so Conner invented a story he hoped would work — "he came up to me while I was out in the woods, and we — we became friends." The dog licked his hand again and went on to sit very properly at his side.

Scott looked impressed. "That is a really good looking dog, Conner," he said, tapping a finger against his chin.

"Can I keep him?" Conner begged. He knew all too well that look of approval on his father's face and wasted no time in seizing his chance to act.

"Are you sure he's friendly?" Mrs. Mathews asked, voicing the obvious concern that comes with keeping a wolf as a pet.

"He's definitely friendly," Conner responded enthusiastically. "He's been with me all day, and he hasn't shown a single sign of aggression."

"Well..." his mom contemplated.

"Oh, let him have the dog, Breanne," urged Mr. Mathews. "A boy needs a dog. Especially with all this property to run around on."

"Okay, Conner... You can keep him."

"*Yes!*" Conner exclaimed triumphantly.

"What will you name him?" Mr. Mathews asked with interest.

"Zelimir," Conner answered without hesitation.

"Zelimir... Huh, that's an interesting name," Mr. Mathews replied, rubbing his chin. "Well, Zelimir — welcome to the family," he laughed, clearly amused by his son's name choice.

The dog barked in acknowledgment of its being accepted.

"Come on, Zelimir," Conner said, full of excitement. "I'll show you our room." And with those words, they ran into the house, leaving Mr. and Mrs. Mathews in the doorway, smiling.